HOOKED ON YOU

PATRICE WILTON

ISBN: 0-9912770-9-0
ISBN-13: 978-0-9912770-9-4

Other books by Patrice Wilton

REPLACING BARNIE
—book one in the Candy Bar series

WHERE WISHES COME TRUE
—book two in the Candy Bar series

NIGHT MUSIC
—book three in the Candy Bar series

REVENGE IS SWEET
—single title Women's Fiction

CHAMPAGNE FOR TWO
—single title Contemporary Romance

ALL OF ME
—single title Women's Fiction

CATERED AFFAIR
—single title Women's Fiction

A HERO LIES WITHIN
—Contemporary Romance

HANDLE WITH CARE
—Contemporary Romance

AT FIRST SIGHT
—Contemporary Romance

SERENDIPITY FALLS
—book one in the Serendipity Falls series

WEDDING FEVER
—book two in the Serendipity Falls series

LOVE STRUCK
—book three in the Serendipity Falls series

TROUBLE IN VEGAS
—Romantic-comedy, first book in Vegas series

HOT NIGHT IN VEGAS
— Romantic-comedy, second book in Vegas series

PARADISE COVE
—book one in a new series

DEDICATION

A huge thank-you to the amazing Tammie Gurgiola for her research help with this book. Not only did this terrific lady invite myself and Traci Hall, my wonderful editor, fellow writer, and great friend, to Islamorada for a sail fishing tournament but also arranged for us to go out on a 53 foot boat. Thank you so much Captain Scott Feltman and his charming crew—Angler, Jamie Roberts, and the two mates, Cody and Colby. We had a great day on The Floridian. I highly recommend you look up Captain Scott if you're ever down in the Keys and want a great day game fishing.

CHAPTER ONE

"Opening day and not one customer has come in!" Taylor Holmes said by way of greeting as Juanita Hernandez entered the kitchen through the back door of the cafe.

"No problem." Juanita's round face broke into a big smile. Her dark brown hair was pulled back into a bun and she wore a cheery yellow sundress. "It's early yet. You've been open what? Half an hour?"

Taylor rotated her neck, trying to ease the tension in her shoulders. She had a quiche warming in the oven, and two blends of coffee made. What if nobody showed? "I'm a worry wart. And impatient too."

"What's that?" Juanita reached for Taylor's hand, inspecting her palm. "You have warts?"

"No!" Taylor pulled her hand free and laughed with affection for this kind woman who had come to them in the most unusual way. "Just worries."

Juanita and her husband Miguel had fled Cuba last year with their son Raul. Her English was remarkably better than when their bedraggled bodies had shown up in Paradise Cove, but they'd never understand all of the quirky American expressions.

"*Si. Si.* Plenty of worries. Me?" Juanita shook her head. "No more since we are here with you." She tied an apron around her ample waist. "What can I do to help?"

"Drum up some customers," Taylor answered, then seeing Juanita's puzzled expression, she smiled and patted a chair. The compact kitchen only had room for a round bistro table, two chairs and a stool by the bar counter. "Never mind. You can sit down and enjoy a good cup of coffee. Dark roast, or hazelnut?"

"Hazelnut."

Taylor poured them each a fragrant mug, her third cup of the day, and perched on the stool so she could see the front door while talking. "How's Merica this morning? Did she fuss when you left her?"

"No. She loves your mom. Anna was bouncing Merica on her knee, singing 'itsy-bitsy spider' to her." Juanita's face glowed. "My sweet baby was trying to catch your mother's fingers." She touched her heart, her dark brown eyes misty. "*Precioso.*"

Taylor could easily imagine the scene. "Mom's never been happier than in the past few months--since you all returned to us. She's been dying for grandchildren, and loves Raul and Merica like her own."

"They love her too." She stirred cream into her cup with a plastic teaspoon instead of using the fine new cutlery. "Anna is a big-hearted woman, taking us all in like *familia.*"

"You are part of *our* family now." Taylor sipped her coffee, remembering the morning that they'd been rescued at sea by her sister Kayla's fiancé. Luckily he'd been out on his boat and had spotted them clinging to a few planks of wood. Their home-made raft had broken apart a half-mile before safely reaching the Florida Keys. Juanita had been seven months pregnant, and so the women had offered them a cottage until the baby was born. After that the Cuban Refugee center stepped in—reuniting them with Miguel's cousin in Miami, who had grudgingly made room for the Hernandez family.

They'd stayed in touch through her youngest sister Brittany, who now lived in Miami and worked with a dance company. When Taylor heard that Miguel got laid off from his construction job, she'd convinced the whole family to come back to Paradise Cove and work at the resort.

Within three months, Miguel had built Taylor her dream cafe and accepted a full-time position as Paradise Cove's gardener and handyman. Juanita split her time between the resort and the café, and Raul was already registered for sixth grade at Marathon's middle school.

Juanita sniffed and pointed her mug toward the industrial oven. "Smells good. What did you make?"

"Cheese and mushroom quiche and orange pecan French toast." Taylor pushed aside her coffee mug, eyes watching the door. She could feel a worried frown pinching between her brows and stroked it lightly. *What if she'd made a huge mistake?* She had a lot riding on this side venture, and had no idea how she'd repay the bank loan if things didn't work out.

"Soon people will come." Juanita stood up and rested her hands on Taylor's tensed shoulders. "You wait and see."

Taylor slipped off the bar stool and wiped her damp palms on her flowered cotton print skirt. She sighed, and shot another quick glance out the window. "Maybe I was optimistic, but I'd hoped people would be eager to try out my new place." She'd spent the past week putting flyers up everywhere and had paid for advertising in the Reporter, a local newspaper in Tavernier.

The three sisters and their mother had inherited the small guest resort, Paradise Cove Cottages, just over a year ago, and they'd already taken out a hefty loan to update the grounds and cabins. With the addition of her cafe, they were walking a tightrope. She couldn't allow her dream to destroy her family's business.

"Did you see the sign when you came in?" Taylor walked out of the kitchen. "It didn't get blown away in last night's wind, did it?"

Juanita's dark brown eyes lit up with humor. "No. *It's plain as day.*" She giggled as if proud of her American slang.

"Good one, Juanita." Opening the front door that led out to a dirt parking strip, she saw the large neon sign hanging overhead glaringly clear. Taylor's Cafe at Paradise Cove. And on the door a smaller sign. *Now Open.* At night the pink and green sign with a flamingo on the side flickered on and off. Not too tacky, but eye catching enough for travelers from the north to spot from the road while visiting the Keys.

The cafe was nestled among some raggedy old pines next to the street. Long and narrow, it fronted the Overseas Highway, the only road to and from Key West. People had to drive right past her door if they wanted to go farther south than Islamorada--although she couldn't figure out why anyone would. It really was paradise, right here.

Taylor shut the door and faced the kitchen, pride warring with fear as she surveyed her domain.

Inside along the window were rows of wooden tables that sat four, and across an aisle were matching tables for two. The interior was painted ocean blue, and she'd kept to a nautical theme with fishnet hanging from the ceiling, and ceramic crabs climbing the walls. A giant tin rendition of a Sailfish hung behind the counter where her customers would order their meals.

It seated twenty-four people, but in the back was an additional outdoor area with a thatched roof and picnic tables covered in red and white plastic cloths. Little jars of fresh flowers anchored the cheap tablecloths down. The purpose for this extra seating was to entice travelers looking for free internet service along with a cup of coffee and a slice of pie.

Her stomach gurgled. She'd been up at five to bake her goodies for the morning crowd and had skipped breakfast with too much caffeine. Her nervous stomach was dancing around like a cricket on speed.

The front door opened with a clang of a bell and Taylor whirled around to see a friendly familiar face. She couldn't be happier to see anybody in her life.

"Colt!" Colt Travis ran a small charter business in Islamorada, one of the fishing capitals of the world. However, charters were extremely competitive especially during the hot summers in the tropical Keys. Things picked up during tourist season—late October through

April. "Please tell me you're here for my fabulous breakfast? Being the very first customer, yours is free."

"Naw. I just came for a cup of java." He hugged Juanita. "How's my favorite girl?"

Juanita slapped his hand with a dishtowel and giggled. "Taylor's your favorite girl."

He turned his wicked smile on her. "No. She won't have me, so I'm hanging around, hoping to lure you away from Miguel."

"You are a bad boy," Juanita told him. "So, you're here for breakfast? No?"

"*Si*." He winked at Taylor. "Of course I am. I just dropped Jamie and Raul off at baseball camp, and I came to see how you're making out." He faced the counter and glanced at the chalkboard menu hanging on the wall. "So, what's good?"

"You are," Juanita answered. "Very good to Raul. He loves baseball and practices very hard."

"He's a natural. And Jamie likes to have him around." His eyes swept over to Taylor, who waited with her hand on her hip, anxious for him to order. "What do you recommend?"

"Everything." She couldn't stop smiling. He'd just brightened her day. But then, he usually did. Easy-going, Colt had long shaggy blond hair, the bluest eyes she'd ever seen, a body that was shamefully hunky, and dimples to drool over. On the negative side, he was a babe magnet. Recently divorced, she'd watched him strut around town with a bevy of pretty women. Several months ago, he'd tried sniffing around her back door, but when she wouldn't go out with him, he'd quickly moved on.

Her stomach rumbled again and she laughed, putting her palm to her belly.

"Sounds like you should eat too," he said with a wink. "So what are *we* having?"

Suddenly she was starving. "I made fresh croissants this morning--good with sausage and eggs, or I have orange pecan French toast, or a cheese and mushroom quiche. Any of those appeal to you?"

"My mouth is watering already. How about the French toast? But only if you two ladies will join me."

He'd gone for the sweet dish instead of the healthier choice, Taylor noticed. But then he and his son probably ate lean at home. "I guess we could--unless someone else shows up."

He gave her his double-dimpled grin and raised a brow. "We could eat in the kitchen--if you'd have me."

Her jumpy stomach did a triple-barrel somersault. *Have him*? Why did that sound so enticing? Must be the fact she was hungry, because no way was she going to add her name to the ever-growing list of Colt's girls. *Uh-uh*. One day, when she had time for dating and romance, she wanted to be special. Singled out. Maybe it was that middle child hang-up, but she was fed up with leftovers.

Having heard the conversation, Juanita busied herself slicing the orange pecan French toast, warm from the oven. Taylor knew Juanita hoped for a romance between her and Colt, but it was *not* going to happen. They were friends, and both liked it that way.

"It's comfy in the kitchen, come around." She waved him toward the swinging door. "I don't have a table for three in here though. You could take a seat out back if you like."

"No, thanks. The view is better right here." He put his elbow along the bar and looked at her with a grin.

Her pulse raced. "You are such a big flirt, Colt Travis. Stop it and behave."

"Yes, Mother," he teased. Dressed in a white tee, with CT Charters circled on his left upper chest, sunglasses tucked into the front of his shirt, and baggy cargo shorts that rode low on his slim hips, he shouldn't be so cute.

Taking a casual stance, he leaned against the doorframe, crossed his ankles and watched her pour his coffee. "Nobody showed up?" He gave her a solicitous look. "You upset?"

Hearing the sympathy in his voice made Taylor's eyes water. She blinked rapidly before handing him his steaming cup of dark roast coffee. "Doesn't matter. You're here now, and soon there'll be plenty of others."

Juanita gave Colt a gentle push. "Go on now. There's no room in the kitchen for everybody. Take a table. I will bring the food."

Taylor knew better than to argue. She followed Colt and sat down across from him at the four-person square table she'd painted a glossy yellow. "She's so bossy," she whispered jokingly. "I feel like I have a second mother."

"You're lucky." He slid into the chair, his shoulder to the wall. "I barely have one."

Juanita carried cutlery and two plates loaded with Taylor's orange pecan French toast to their table.

"Now this is looking mighty fine," Colt said, unwrapping his silverware from the napkin. "I make French toast at home with Jamie. Great way to use up stale bread." He cut into it, studying the fluffy layers of bread and nuts. "Got a feeling that yours is a little more special. Not straight out of a frying pan."

Juanita brought out another plate for herself and set it on the table next to Taylor. "Who wants confectioner's sugar or whipped cream?"

"Whipped cream for me," Colt answered quickly.

Taylor sat back in her chair, relaxing for the first time. "This recipe is pretty simple but loaded with yummy stuff," she told him. "It takes about an hour to make from scratch so the prep has to be done early, even the night before. Then it needs thirty minutes in the oven. I have another one partially made that will reheat in ten." If they got more customers—no—*when* they got more customers.

Juanita arrived with the whipped cream and sat down. She smiled broadly, waiting for Colt to take a bite. "You like?" she asked, and cut a piece with her fork.

Taylor held her breath in anticipation.

"Incredible," Colt mumbled around a mouthful.

"Okay, tell us the secret." Juanita speared a piece and swirled it in the zesty sweet sauce.

"Well, first you pour a mixture of brown sugar, butter and corn syrup into the baking dish, then sprinkle pecans over it all. After that I used thick slices of French bread, baked yesterday, and laid it on top. The topping has to be made first and put over the bread to absorb. I did that part early this morning. Eggs, cinnamon, vanilla, orange juice and zest from the orange. Comes out a nice golden brown and then you can eat it plain or topped with anything you want."

Even if nobody else came in, watching Juanita and Colt enjoy her food made her incredibly happy—so happy, she hadn't had a bite for herself yet.

The door opened again and her older sister raced in.

Taylor lifted her hand. "Hey, Kayla! Come join us. Nobody's here but Colt. My first and only customer."

"Oh, no. Sorry to hear that. I rushed like crazy to get here, but the florist called this morning and I had to go see her about the satin ribbon. They ran out of the kind I ordered, and can't get more in. So, I just picked one that was close enough." She made a face. "One thing after another."

Kayla and Sean were getting married in a month. They'd had to postpone their wedding twice. Now, come hell or high water, the marriage would take place. Especially now that Kayla might be pregnant. Again. Hopefully this time she could carry to full term.

"No problem. As you can see, nobody showed up." Taylor patted her hand. "How's the house coming along?"

The past year had brought many changes to her sister's life. Dr. Sean Flannigan had left Boston for good and taken a job at Mount Sinai, and then Kayla moved out of the cottages to live with him in a rented apartment. A few months later, Kayla had been over the moon excited to find out she was pregnant. At eight weeks, she lost the baby. To take her mind off her loss, Sean bought an older home on the Intracoastal Waterway near Key Largo. One that had good bones but needed a complete remodel. It was a two-story place with four bedrooms--room for the children they hoped to have one day.

"Don't get me going on the house," Kayla murmured. "It's a disaster." She smiled. "But it will be very beautiful. Eventually. We had the kitchen torn out and a wall removed to create a great room, instead of the smaller family room that had been there before. We have a huge deck out back now, and well, one thing leads to another."

"I know it's a lot of work. I'm surprised you're here as much as you are." Taylor was happy that Kayla had the house as a distraction after losing her baby. It had all but broken her heart.

"Yes, I love the cottages as much as you all do." She sighed and pushed her hair off her shoulders. "After the wedding, hopefully our home will be ready for us to show it off."

She bent to kiss Taylor's and Juanita's cheeks, and pat Colt on the shoulder. "Enough about me and my problems. How's it going? Where's Jamie?" she asked Colt.

"Baseball camp with Raul. Just until noon. Then maybe I'll take the boys fishing."

"Sounds like the perfect summer plan. When does school start?"

"Few more weeks. He's excited about it, but learning comes easy for him." Colt gave Kayla a self-deprecating grin and swallowed some coffee. "Smart like his mom."

"And he gets his good looks from you," Kayla answered back. "Jamie's a lucky kid." She was the oldest of the three girls, thirty-two, and tall like they all were, with the same olive skin, dark hair and hazel eyes. "What are you guys eating? Sure looks good."

Juanita stood up. "I'll get you a plate. There's plenty more warming in the oven."

"Sit and finish. I can help myself." Kayla headed toward the kitchen and returned a minute later, digging eagerly into the French toast.

Suddenly Taylor's disappointing morning didn't seem so bad. She had her family and friends and what could possibly be better than that?

She felt Colt's eyes on her, and met his steady gaze. She smiled and his dimples flashed. A warm flush spread from the tips of her toes to the roots of her dark hair, and she wondered if he affected every female this way. Considering how many girls had come and gone in the past six months? Probably. *Definitely.*

Taylor congratulated herself on giving Colt a pass. Lusting after a guy like him would not only be a waste of good time, it would never be enough. Not for her. When—and if—she was ready for a relationship, she'd not only want to be special, but she'd be looking for someone with the same hopes and dreams. Money didn't drive her, but being successful did. She wanted the resort and her cafe to do well enough to support them all. Colt was sweet, but he was the most laid-back man she knew. Fishing and his son were all he cared about. *And a cute gal in his bed.*

Kayla kept up a lively conversation with Colt and Juanita, and Taylor sat back to enjoy the moment and drink it all in. It had only been six months ago that Kayla had to face the disappointment of a miscarriage and cancel her wedding plans. Now she was optimistic that she might be pregnant once again. Although it was too soon to tell everyone the good news, her sisters and her mother were in on the secret.

Colt pushed his empty plate away and wiped some of the whipped cream from his upper lip. His sky-blue eyes looked directly into hers. "You outdid yourself."

She looked at his mouth and had a ridiculous urge to lick away the whipped cream. Would he taste sweet, soft, or hot and sexy? Did his kiss drive all the young women wild? Her ex-boyfriends' kisses had been nice, but hadn't set off any explosions. She could barely remember them.

"Taylor?" Colt tapped the table between them with his tanned forefinger.

"Hmm?" She blinked and looked away. What had made her mind go there? With Colt? He was a buddy. She liked him. He liked her. They were *not* into each other. He gave her fresh fish if he had extra from a charter. She gave him free food during Paradise Cove's happy hour. Not exactly a recipe for romance.

"You were looking at me strange." He tilted his head.

"No, I wasn't." No way. Not her. Of course her gaze dropped to his mouth.

"You have whipped cream on your lip," Kayla told him, glancing at Taylor's flushed cheeks. "That probably distracted Taylor." She gave her a sly wink.

"Why should it?" she answered hotly.

"Ask yourself," Kayla said. "How should I know why you're staring at Colt's mouth?"

Taylor shrugged and scooted back in her chair. "This is ridiculous. Where is everybody? Why won't they come in?

I made some super breakfast selections and the only one enjoying it is us. Pathetic."

Juanita got up to remove the plates, and Kayla followed. "Why don't you two go outside and round up some more people?" Her lilting voice matched the teasing light in her eye.

Colt stood and offered his hand. "Come on, Tay. Let's do it. One look at you and the cars will come to a sliding stop."

She laughed, looking down at her sleeveless coral blouse and floral print skirt. Wash and wear, with a slight nod to fashion. "You are such an idiot."

"And you should take a good look at yourself once in awhile." He nodded at her matching Sketchers. "Some guy's going to be a lucky man."

Her heart pounded at his intense perusal but she stayed with the jokes. "He better not show up today. I'm too busy!"

The two-lane highway had a steady stream of traffic, and she held her breath as Colt valiantly jumped onto the road. He put one hand out to stop traffic, and with his other arm outstretched he pointed at her standing next to the sign that read Taylor's Cafe.

She lifted her hand and waved at people who honked their horns and then carefully made their way around the mad man standing in the middle of the road—to continue toward their destination.

After a few minutes, he loped back to her with a silly grin. "Well, you can't say I didn't try."

"You are something else. I'll give you that." Sweet, gorgeous and so not for her. She put a hand on her hip.

"Why don't you bring Jamie around for happy hour? I'll make him his favorite personal pepperoni pizza."

"He'll love it and so will I. Later, babe." He went around the café to the back area that connected to Paradise Cove.

She watched him go and gritted her teeth, hating when he called her that. Taylor could guarantee that she'd never be one of his “babes”.

CHAPTER TWO

Colt walked through the Paradise Cove cottages on his way to the marina. He could have gone around on the main road, but he liked to say hello to Anna and knew she'd have the chubby-faced Merica with her. The baby was in love with him, and he had a soft spot for her as well. He'd put a few fresh strawberries from the breakfast plates into a napkin, knowing she couldn't resist the sweet treat.

The office was set well back from the highway, down a dusty dirt road overgrown with bushes and shrubs, and straggly pines. The twelve guest cottages--all freshly painted--were built around the pool area and nearer the beach, but separated by environmentally protected mangroves. Unfortunately the mangroves were directly blocking the beach and so judicious trimming was a necessary evil.

"Good morning, Anna!" He called, poking his head into the open office door. "You got any company?"

A tiny hand gripped his knee. He glanced down at the wobbling one-year-old, dressed in denim rompers. "Me!" She pulled at the hem of his shorts.

Merica Hernandez had dark curly hair, sparkling eyes, and a pink binkie in her rosy mouth. He reached down and swept her up into his arms, giving her plump cheeks a big smack. "Hey, Meri. How's my baby this morning? I brought you some strawberries."

She pulled the binkie out of her mouth and smiled. "Sawberry." She reached for his hand. He opened the napkin and she popped one in her mouth. Making a grab for the others, two fell to the floor. She let out a cry, flailing madly in his arms.

Anna gave him a bright smile as she came around the front desk and scooped up the strawberries. "Morning, Colt. I'll just give these a quick rinse." She cleaned the fresh berries in the small bathroom adjoining the office and then returned to hand feed Merica's eager mouth. "She's been watching the door, waiting for you. Were you at the cafe?"

Anna was a petite version of her daughters. Not more than five feet two or three, but full of vitality and verve. A good-looking woman with personality and a big heart. He wished his own mother was like that, but she and his sister, Chrissy, were two peas in a pod. Both of them driven by money instead of love. They owned a real estate office in Miami and lived in a penthouse apartment overlooking Biscayne Bay. They both drove new modeled Mercedes, kept their bodies and faces primed by Botox and expensive gyms, but their hearts were cold and empty.

"Yeah. I checked in on her." He shook his head. "She hasn't had any customers yet. Not a one. Poor kid." He knew Taylor was only a few years younger than himself, but out of necessity he'd had to grow up fast. Taylor seemed incredibly innocent, untouched by the tawdry side of life. He'd like to see her stay that way.

Anna made a sympathetic clicking noise. "Oh, dear. That is awful. But it's early yet. Half past eight, and in the summer people don't rush around like crazy. They will get there when they're good and ready."

"That's true." The Keys had its own rhythm, with tranquil days and breezy nights. "Still, quite a few cars went by—but nobody stopped. Even after I tried to wave them down."

He jostled the baby in his arms as she played patty-cake with his face. "It'll work out, but I know how disappointed she was. She's been talking about this opening for weeks."

"And dreaming about it for years," Anna added with a concerned frown. Then she shook the sad look off and asked, "So, what time do the boys get done with baseball camp?"

"Noon, then I figured we'd all go fishing." He'd taken Raul under his wing this summer while his daddy built Taylor's Cafe. Juanita had been busy with the baby and working as a housekeeper for the cottages. Raul was a good kid and Jamie liked him fine. Which was surprising as hell. His son had been getting into fights with a few of his former friends at school. Last spring, Colt had been called in a few times to the principal's office. The separation, and all the ugliness it entailed, had been hard. The divorce was worse. He understood Jamie acting out, but couldn't condone bad behavior.

"Good idea, but before that you could take them to the cafe, couldn't you? For lunch?" Anna wiped a strawberry seed from Merica's cheek.

"Of course. They'll be starving after practice and Raul will want to check in with his mom." He put the baby in a mobile swing and lined up another two strawberries for her to eat. Merica immediately banged her binkie down on the tray. "I can hang here for an hour or so, if you want to run down and see the girls."

"You are too sweet, but that's not necessary. I've got to run the new ads for the resort. If I get bored I can close up for fifteen minutes and take Merica for a quick stroll." The cafe was within sight of the office, just a few hundred feet down the dirt road.

"Okay." He bent over to give the toddler a kiss and got a sloppy one back. "Bye, baby." Her little face puckered and he could see she was getting ready to let one loose. He backed away quickly. "I'm outta here."

"Chicken," Anna called as he rushed out the door.

The sound of the girl's cries followed him down the road. Merica was a cutie, but he was glad that Jamie was too old for tantrums.

Colt checked his watch. He still had a couple of hours left before getting the boys and he wanted to catch some yellowtail snapper for the local market. Although being a licensed fisherman didn't make the kind of money that charters did, it helped put food on the table in off-peak season.

A half-day's charter brought in four hundred, plus tips. Out of that he'd pay one or two mates, depending on how many anglers were fishing. The mates were local boys who worked for him and other bigger boats. It was a decent enough living, and took care of his creature comforts.

That was one of the things he and his ex-wife had fought about. He'd had an opportunity to take a private job for a guy who owned his own company. The pay was lucrative, with plenty of perks, but it would have meant spending months away from home. From Jamie. He wasn't willing to do that.

Like his mom and sister, Sharon had wanted the good life, and she'd hoped a doctor that she was seeing on the side might give her just that. So far, no proposal on the table. But she'd given him the house to keep so she could move into an apartment closer to the hospital where she worked as an ER nurse. Made it easier for her to spend time with her resident doctor, too. He and Sharon split custody: Colt had his son Monday to Thursday night, and Sharon had him for a three day weekend. It suited them both fine. Jamie, well, Jamie was adjusting.

He skirted the pool, and walked toward the wharf. It was a small marina, and his 43 foot Hatteras, "Bait Me" was the largest boat there--at a fraction of the price he'd pay to moor it at one of the other marinas with more foot traffic. He'd bought his ten-year-old Fisherman Sport after his wife left. Cost him a pretty penny, but he figured it was better than giving it all to her. Besides, he needed the bigger boat to attract the bigger clients.

Once he had his boat readied, he headed out near a reef where the fish were plentiful. Several other boats were already there, and he called them up on the radio to see what was biting. They were a tight community, and no secrets were sacred. Someone acted out on a Saturday night, by Sunday everyone knew. On the other hand, you ever had trouble? A friend was a radio call away.

Within minutes he'd caught enough baitfish to last him the day and tossed the little ballyhoos and pilchards into a tank full of water. He used chum to get the snapper to follow as he trolled the reef. Once he had their attention, he cut up some fresh bait, allowing it to drift back to the yellowtails. They were pretty smart, known to be line-shy, so Colt released a long length of lightweight line attached to a saltwater reel and set the fiberglass rod aside.

It was only nine in the morning, but the sun was brilliant, glistening off the turquoise sea. Colt adjusted his dark sunglasses against the blinding glare, tugging his white cap down over his forehead.

The breeze kept it from being too damn hot. As he sat back in his fixed chair at the back of the boat to wait, he figured mornings like this were close to perfect. After fifteen minutes or so, he felt a little tug on the line and gave it a snap. There! Adrenalin pumped and he went from relaxed to ready in less than a second. The hooked fish shook its head, putting up a good fight as Colt quickly reeled it in. Within an hour he had half a dozen decent-sized fish, and decided to head back. There was plenty of time to clean the fish and himself before picking up the boys. As he made his way to the marina, he found himself anxious to see how Taylor was making out.

* * *

"Juanita, we need two quiches, and someone has asked for eggs Benedict at table four. I'll get that going right away." Her face was flushed with excitement and nerves. "Why did everyone come in at once! How can we handle this? Eggs Benedict is messy and it wasn't even on the menu!"

"Breathe," Kayla said. "I'll pour the mimosas, and offer a basket of your fresh muffins. That will keep the customers happy until you have time to prepare the meals. Oh, and I need two cups of lobster bisque and two conch chowder for table twelve."

"Thanks, Kayla. Keep the champagne flowing. Juanita, can you get the soup and the quiche while I get busy with the hollandaise sauce?"

"*Si*." She wiped her hands on her apron and took down four soup bowls. "So exciting. We have nine customers at once."

Taylor was melting butter into a saucepan, adding four egg yolks, and whisking quickly to keep it from clumping. She popped an English muffin in the toaster and grabbed a small poaching pan for the two eggs. As the water boiled, she squeezed fresh lemon into the hollandaise sauce and started another pan with the Canadian bacon.

The door opened and two men entered, taking table number two. She glanced at Kayla. "Please?"

"No problem. I'll take their orders, and give them drinks." Her big sis grinned. "This is fun."

"Fun for you. I'm freakin' out. I want everything to be perfect."

"And it is. Take a second and look at your customers. Not one grumpy expression or single complaint."

She nodded, seeing it was true. A table of four women enjoyed their hearty bowls of soup, munching away on the free muffins, and sipping on three-dollar mimosas. They were taking selfies and pictures of the decor.

"Yikes! My sauce is bubbling." She grabbed a mitt and rescued it from the stove. She cracked two eggs and added them to the poacher, then buttered the English muffin, adding sliced mango and fresh strawberries to the plate.

When she served the dish and the bacon and mushroom quiche to the threesome, they were already on their second mimosas. "This place is awesome," the twenty-something woman said. She wore shorts and a halter top, boldly displaying the ink on her arms. She sat across from two guys in biker clothes, with bald heads, droopy mustaches, and more ink.

"You Taylor?" One of the bikers asked. He was big and beefy, perhaps two fifty. She hoped he didn't have a complaint.

"That's me." She looked at their faces, never having seen them before. "You guys from around here?"

"No. Homestead. Just heading down to Key West for a day's ride." He sucked back his mimosa. "You got any beer?"

"Sure. What's your pleasure?"

"Something light."

Taylor nearly laughed, relieved to see he wasn't planning on getting drunk. "Coming right up. Anyone else?"

"More mimosa," his female companion said.

"Nice place you've got here. When we get back tonight, maybe you and I could take a little ride?" the third guy said.

"Uh--sounds like a real nice offer, but I'm gonna be busy." She grinned and hurried away, happy to retreat to the kitchen and away from the too-happy customers.

The door opened again, and in walked a guy who'd stand out in any crowd. Kayla nudged her. "Look at Mr. GQ."

The kitchen had an open window so she could see her customers and take their orders when the place was busy. The guy her sister referred to was around their age, and had a thick head of dark hair that was professionally layered and fell just right. Broad shoulders, a slim build, and must have stood six feet four or five. Definitely taller than her five-foot-eleven stature. His face was tanned and exquisite--a strong chin, a straight nose, dark brown eyes that seemed to take in everything at once. He looked like someone....someone she'd once known long ago.

His gaze met hers and stopped.

She breathed in deeply, and felt her cheeks flame. Her heart began to hammer, and she sighed. "Oh, my." Turning aside, she whispered to Kayla. "He reminds me of a guy I dated my first year in college. But it couldn't be, right? I mean, no way. This guy looks like he just waltzed out of a movie premiere."

"Pretty fancy for around here, that's for sure. Give me a moment, and I'll find out."

Kayla poured a glass of iced water and took it over to his table. He flashed his pearly whites. "Not just one, but two beautiful women. Is the food nearly as good?"

"See for yourself." She showed him the menu on the wall. "Taylor's my sister and she cooks like an angel. What would you like?"

"Looks like one too." He glanced back at Taylor and winked. "I'll let her surprise me."

"She's darn good at that." Kayla smiled. "So, you want to stick with water, or try one of our famous mimosas? Only three bucks. Best deal in town."

"How can they be famous? Sign out front says this is opening day. Free coffee."

"So you want coffee?"

"Nope. You sold me on the mimosa." He eyed her up and down. "You don't look like an island girl. Been here long?"

"A year, and I'm staying. We own Paradise Cove Cottages, and my future husband works at Mount Sinai." She waved her diamond ring in his face, setting that fact straight, just in case he'd been hitting on her. "You need a place to rent? Our cottages are efficiency units, and cater to lengthy visits."

"Naw. I'm just here for a summer swordfish tournament down in Key West. Joining a buddy of mine who's into this kind of thing. Had some business in Miami, and figured why not? Never fished for swordfish. So what can I lose? "

"Nothing but a little time and money, I suppose. The bets get heavy in these kinds of events."

"I've been known to take a bet or two." He glanced again at Taylor, his eyebrows pinched together. "So that sister of yours...got a feeling I might know her. Where you girls from?"

"The New York/New Jersey area." She waved at Taylor, indicating she should come out and talk to the guy herself. Taylor shook her head, clearly not in agreement. "What about you? Where did you attend college?"

"Penn State. But that was a long time ago."

"So did she!"

"Taylor...." Again his eyes turned in her direction. "It can't be. Not Taylor Holmes?" He grinned and his eyes lit up. "Is that your sister?"

Kayla nodded and he stood up, spreading his arms wide. Taylor blushed and gave him a tentative wave, then rushed out of the kitchen. He enfolded her in a big hug. "Jack Warner. How the hell are you?" She stepped back from his embrace. "You look....pretty good, I guess."

She knew she was blushing and stammering, but it wasn't everyday that the guy who popped your cork and stamped on your heart stood before you, even more beautiful now than he was ten years ago.

"I guess?" Kayla laughed.

Taylor ducked her head. There had never been a more handsome man, or one as charming, as Jack Warner. He'd been born with that silver spoon in his mouth, and reaped the rewards.

She'd been an innocent nineteen-year-old when she'd first met him. They had dated for three whole months and he'd taught her a lot--mostly in the bedroom. He'd been a gentle and patient lover. But along came cheerleader number two. Then three. More notches in his belt.

She should hate him, but she didn't. He'd been her first lover--and the best. Taylor had never loved him, but when she'd been his girl it was like being with a rock star. An exciting, wonderful time when she'd felt privileged to be his chosen one. He was a prince among men. Star basketball player. On the Dean's list. A great debater and a better dancer--with plenty of moves. She'd never expected their romance to last, so wasn't surprised that it didn't. It was a fling, and she'd been totally into it too.

When it was over she'd carried the afterglow for weeks--knowing that a man like Jack Warner had picked her as a bedmate.

Since him, she'd only slept with two other men and neither one of them had lit any fires. She'd lived with her last boyfriend for two years, and never came close to a big "o". Jack had been the one and only man.

"Look at you! More beautiful than ever." He gave her a dazzling smile and put his warm hand on her shoulder. "What brought you down to the Keys?"

"My step-dad passed away eighteen months ago, and he'd bought the Paradise Resort cottages as his retirement plan. He left it to my sisters and I. Mom's here too."

"You like living on this little island?" He glanced from Kayla back to her. "I'm sure I'd get bored to tears."

"Couldn't be happier." Taylor tilted her head to glance up at him, taking in his sultry good looks. Damn if he didn't look like a Hollywood heartthrob. "So what about you? Married? Divorced? Here for the Film Festival? Gay Pride?"

He chuckled. "None of the above. Sailfish tournament. Remember Joey Hammond? He's a big sports fisherman and invited me down. Since I had some business in Miami, I decided to combine the two."

"Great. Say "hi" for me." She shivered as his hand slid down her bare arm, stopping at her wrist. "So what are you doing now?" She squeaked. "Did you join your dad's law firm?"

"I did. Made partner two years ago."

"Wow." She nodded and looked at Kayla, wanting to get back to the kitchen. "Cool." She stepped back.

"So can you get away for a night?" He tugged her forward. "Come down to the Keys with me."

"No way. I'm a working girl. Got two businesses to run." Taylor was glad for an excuse, as she knew he could be persuasive and didn't have any inclination to go there again. It was nice to see him and show him how well she'd done for herself, but spending a night admiring his good looks? *No thanks.* She freed her wrist from his seductive grasp.

Taylor turned when she heard the front door open, relieved to see Colt with Jamie and Raul. "Hey," she smiled brightly at the three of them. "Take a table. I'll be with you in a minute."

"I know you're busy," Jack said as she began to move away. "But can I get your number? I might come back for a few nights before heading home."

She hesitated for the briefest of seconds, but the warmth in his eyes turned her stomach to mush. What could dinner hurt? "Sure." She scribbled it down on her notepad and handed it to him. "Good luck in the tournament. It's been great seeing you again."

"And you." Jack leaned down to whisper in her ear. "You've turned into a stunning woman, but I remember plenty about you as a young girl."

She laughed and tossed her hair, almost light-headed by his attention. And the fact that Colt was watching. "Right," she whispered in an aside. "I was just one in the long parade."

"Quantity, not quality." He gave her an apologetic look. "I've learned a few things over the years. I wouldn't go back and change them, but I sure wouldn't repeat them either."

"Stop with the charm." She folded her arms under her breasts and saw his eyes drop to her cleavage. "Take a table, Jack, and tell me what you'd like for lunch. I can't stand around all day flirting with you. I have customers." Finally, she added silently. It would have been terribly embarrassing if he'd shown up earlier.

"I'll take a crab cake sandwich. Fries on the side." He pulled his iPhone out of his pocket. "Hang on a sec." He sighed and shook his head. "Dammit. Just got a business text. I'll have to forget the lunch, I'm afraid. This is going to take more than a few minutes."

"Oh, that's too bad." Over Jack's shoulder, she could see Colt. His damp hair was curling around his nape, as if he'd just gotten out of the shower.

"Let's set something up. How about dinner on Sunday? You've got to eat, right? I'll pick you up at seven."

On Sunday? She couldn't think of a reason to refuse, try as she might. "Yeah. Okay." She shot a glance toward Colt and the boys. "Maybe. Call me."

"I'll do that, but I'm not taking no for an answer." Jack gave Kayla a jaunty wave and then let himself out.

Kayla raised a questioning brow. Taylor shrugged, non-committal, then sauntered over to the table with her favorite three boys. "Hey, guys. Glad you came for lunch. How was camp today?"

"Good." Raul removed his cap and grinned. "I had a home run."

Juanita had left the kitchen in time to hear her son's news. She ruffled his hair with pride. "Good boy," she said. "Your daddy will be proud."

"And I pitched three people out," Jamie said, glancing at his father.

"Well done, son," Colt responded, then his eyes met hers. "Who was that?"

"You mean the guy that just left?" She watched Juanita mumble something to Raul and give him a nudge. The boy stood and headed toward the bathroom in the back, probably to wash up.

"Who else would I mean?"

She shifted her gaze back to Colt and ran her damp palms over the soft material of her skirt. She rarely saw him angry or heard him raise his voice, but by the set of his jaw, his flashing blue eyes, she knew he was pissed.

"Why?"

Colt picked up the salt shaker and moved it around the table. He wouldn't look at her, and she wondered what crawled up his ass. "It's just a question. You don't want to answer it, fine."

She didn't like his tone of voice or the look on his face. Wasn't like she'd done anything wrong. She hadn't been flirting, nor had she accepted a date--and even if she had, why should he care?

"He's not important," she finally answered. "Just someone I knew a lifetime ago." She shrugged her shoulders. "It was quite a surprise seeing him here."

"You gave him your number?" He stopped playing with the salt shaker, and leaned back in the chair. His eyes were a deep turbulent blue, like an angry ocean.

"I did." She shifted her feet, and felt a blush creep up her cheeks. "So what?"

"I thought you didn't have time to date."

Juanita brought Raul back to the table then left. The boy took the seat next to Jamie--his big eyes were on her, as if he could sense the friction in the air.

She smiled at Raul, and bit back an angry retort to Colt's stinging comment. This conversation was going in a bad direction, and she didn't want to say anything she'd later regret, or to push any buttons.

"I don't," Taylor said pleasantly, eager to make light of it. "It's not exactly a date. We're just going to catch up on old times." She crossed her arms around her middle, wondering why she felt so damn defensive. It was none of his business who she went out with. Did she ask him about his dates?

"Right." His eyes glittered. "Where?"

"I have no idea." Angry now, she asked, "Does it matter?" Seeing Jack had given her spirit a much needed jolt--like a double shot of good tequila.

Colt was doing everything he could to ruin her happy mood. Why was he being such a prick? What was it to him if she spent a few hours with an old friend? Did she question every moment *he* spent with all the girls in town? Hardly. She wouldn't even want to know.

"It does to me." Colt drummed his thumb along the table.

"What's the matter, Dad?" Jamie glanced from one angry face to another. "I'm hungry. Can't we just eat?"

"Yeah. We can eat," he snapped. "Brought the boys in here because I was afraid you might not have any business. Looks to me like you're doing just fine."

"I am. You don't need to worry about me." She turned her attention to the boys. "How about fish and chips, or a chili dog?" Taylor had made up a limited menu for children, but she could improvise when necessary.

"Fish and chips," Jamie said, and Raul quickly agreed.

"And for you?" she asked Colt, seething underneath her too-polite tone. He had some nerve! Guy was getting laid every day of the week, and he resented her seeing someone for one night. One night! Well, she just might make damn sure that one night was a good one. After all, didn't she deserve a little fun under the covers, as much as the next guy? Or girl. Hell, yeah!

His steely blue eyes slid up and down the length of her--almost as if he were seeing her for the very first time. His jaw worked, and his hands were clasped tightly on the table. "I'll have the same, and a beer. Boys, you want a soda?"

"Sure. Coke, please, Taylor." Jamie shot his father a funny look. "What are you so grumpy about? You were in a good mood when we came in."

"Just adult stuff. Nothing to worry about." His eyes flickered to hers and she felt her toes curl, and a ton of feelings flooded her senses. What was going on? This was Colton Travis. Buddy. A man she adored, like she would an older brother.

There was an awareness in Colt's eyes that she hadn't seen before. He was looking at her like he wanted...wanted...to do things with her that he did to every other damn girl in town. And something else. There was a possessiveness that didn't belong on his sweet face. Not for her. Not for them.

CHAPTER THREE

Colt had watched the fancy dude with his gold Rolex, Italian loafers and elegantly styled slicked-back hair as he flirted with Taylor, and had wanted to rearrange a few features on his arrogant face.

The Taylor he knew would never be interested in a guy like that. He shouted money, privilege, and trust fund, like it was stamped with a pedigree seal on his forehead. Colt knew plenty of women who'd be all over that, including his ex-wife, mother, and sister--but Taylor and her family were different. They didn't care about material things. Sure, they worked hard and wanted their resort to succeed, but they drove an old SUV, shared a two bedroom cottage, didn't wear fancy clothes or visit places where they needed designer logos or diamonds. All their money and efforts were poured into making their step-dad's dream and legacy a sustaining and profitable venture. It was not material greed that drove them, only a love for each other, and for Paradise Cove.

He didn't want to believe otherwise, but he'd seen the way Taylor had flirted with the rich dude. She didn't date the local guys, yet she had handed Mr. Wall Street her number. God damn it! How dare she do that--in front of him, no less. He'd seen the way Taylor's skin flushed when the dude whispered something in her ear. That unconscious bodily betrayal had all but killed him. He--Colt Travis--was the man who made her blush and stammer.

Not often enough, it seemed. If she was ready for a good time, why the hell hadn't she let him know? What were friends for? She could trust him with that. If she needed to get laid, if she needed a kiss, a cuddle, someone to hold her at night. Hell, he was the man for the job. Not some jackass with a big expense account and a sleek Jaguar that probably compensated for his small dick.

The more he thought about it, the more his stomach churned. Acid indigestion rose in his throat, and he damn near choked on it. He tossed his napkin on the table, and stood up. "Finish up boys. I just need to have a word with Taylor, then off we go."

He went through the door with the hanging beads that led directly to the kitchen. Juanita looked up from the bowl of soup she was plating. "Colt? Anything wrong?"

Kayla's gaze fell on him. She shook her head. "Sheesh, Colt. What's got you all hot and bothered?"

He gave her a sharp look but didn't answer. He took Taylor by the elbow and steered her out the back door toward the picnic table under the thatched roof. "Sit."

"I don't want to sit. What the hell is going on with you?" She put her hands on her hips akimbo style. Her chest was heaving, and the rise and fall of her breasts got his attention.

"I have work to do. No time to sit around and stroke your ego." Her eyes narrowed. "Are you pissed because some guy took an interest in me? Is it that strange that someone might actually find me attractive? Interesting?"

"No, not at all. You're a beautiful woman. All three of you. Four, including your mother. That's not it, and you darn well know it." He ran a frustrated hand through his hair and heaved a weary sigh. "Just not with the likes of him. You want to date someone, why not one of the local guys? That fellow's got heartache written all over him. He'd use you, and leave you flat, no questions asked."

"Don't be ridiculous. Jack's not a stranger. I went out with him in college. We're old friends. That's all."

Colt had hitched his butt on the table, now he shot forward, grabbing her by the hips. "You slept with him? You want to again?"

"How dare you ask me that!" Her chin jutted. "What's it to you?"

He pulled her forward until his face was inches from hers. Her breasts crushed against his chest and he sensed her fear. Why would she be frightened of him? She had to know that he would never, ever hurt her. He only wanted to make sure she was happy, satisfied and well taken care of.

She trembled.

Colt breathed in her scent and his engines fired up. Did she think for one minute that she could date Mr. Rich Guy and not pay a price? Guys like him took what they wanted and didn't look back. He should know. He was one of them.

But not with her. Never with her.

Tugging her close, he moved his hips suggestively against hers. "If this is what you want, then I'm the one to give it to you. Not that guy. Me." He looked down at her mouth, wanting to taste it so fiercely, he got hard. "I care about you, Tay."

"Get off me!" She shoved at his chest, and he let her go. "How dare you?" Her hazel eyes sparked with anger.

"I only want to save you from making a big mistake." He patted his chest. "I wouldn't hurt you. But that guy? He'll strip away your resistance one stroke at a time." He made his tone sensual, wanting her to feel what he felt.

His plan back-fired. "And what makes you think I might not like that?" She tossed him an icy glare. "Besides, why should I be any different than you? How many women did you sleep with this week?" With that she turned and raced back inside.

* * *

It was closing time and most of the customers had left. One table of four women lingered over their coffees while sharing a chocolate cheesecake dessert. Taylor's emotions went from high to low, but kept coming back to the way Colt had bumped his hips to hers as if she'd just fall backward and let him in.

"What was that all about? You and Colt?" Kayla asked, pouring three iced teas. She handed an icy glass to her, and another to Juanita, then stood back and sipped on her own.

"He's an idiot. That's what!" Taylor tossed back her lemony tea, and ice splashed down her sleeveless coral blouse. She swiped at it with a hand towel, which just made the splotch bigger. "He's mad at me for giving my number to Jack. Why should he care who I date?"

"He's jealous. You know he's got a crush on you." Kayla took the towel from Taylor and folded it on the counter.

"No, he doesn't. That's ridiculous." It had to be a joke. "He's got tons of girlfriends, and is definitely not lying around pining for me." She turned her eyes on Juanita. "Isn't that right?"

Juanita made a clucking sound. "Not so, Taylor. Why do you think he hangs around? You think it's your fancy cooking? No! He's waiting for the go ahead." She took the leftovers out of the fridge and began dividing them up into stacks so they could each take some home. Having grown up in a country that never had enough, she didn't want anything to go to waste. "That boy is crazy about you."

"You are both crazy." Panic was building inside, making it impossible to swallow. "We're buddies, nothing more."

Anna entered from the back entrance, wheeling a stroller. "What? Having a tea break?" She glanced at the three faces. "What happened?" Her eyes met Taylor's with concern. "Bad day, hon?"

Taylor was spared from answering as Merica caught sight of her mother. Crying, "Mama, Mama!" her chubby fingers clawed the air, and her tiny body fought to be free from the stroller. Juanita unhooked the restraining belt and swung her up and into her arms, giving her a big smack on both cheeks.

They all made a fuss over the baby, who wiggled and giggled, loving every minute of the attention. She was the sweetest, happiest baby, and that one sweet child made all the women happy. Taylor took her little hand and pretended to nibble on it.

"Yum, yum, yum, I could eat you up."

Merica shoved her other hand toward Taylor's mouth, enjoying the game.

Taylor was glad for the distraction--eager to turn the conversation away from Colt and her love-life. Or lack of.

Taylor gave the fingers a last kiss and then held up her hand. "Let me give the ladies their check and put the closed sign on the door. Have some iced tea and something to eat, Mom. Knowing you, you probably skipped lunch."

"We had apples, and cheese and crackers. I've been putting weight on since I moved here, and I've got to stop. A woman my age doesn't need love handles."

Taylor and Kayla exchanged smiles, and it was still on her face as she reached the table of women. They had their credit cards ready, and within a few minutes the transaction was completed and they were ready to leave. They praised the restaurant and the food, saying they'd help spread the word.

As Taylor locked the door behind them, a flush of happiness rippled inside her. The episode with Colton was forgotten, and she proudly marched back into the kitchen and gazed at all their faces. Here was her family. These wonderful women who would support anything she did. Whether it be men, or business or babies, they would rally around her, and she for them.

Tears blurred her vision as emotions threatened to overwhelm her. Then blinking rapidly, she wiped away her tears and laughed with delight. "Woo-hoo! Great day, everyone! We did it! Yeah us!"

Kayla hugged her. "Congratulations, Taylor. Your opening was a huge success. I only heard positive things about the food, the decor. Not one complaint."

Her mother had a slice of quiche that she shared with the baby. She gave her a spoonful, then beamed at her daughters. "It is wonderful, isn't it, Meri?" The pet name Colt used for the baby suited her, and was easier on the tongue.

Juanita bent down to wipe some crumbs from her baby's rosy little mouth. "Hey, little one, let's go home and take a nap. I'm tired, and you must be too."

"I enjoyed having her today," Anna said. "She's so easy to please."

"*Si.* She is full of love."

The women waited until the two of them were gone, then Anna walked to the fridge and pulled out a bottle of champagne. "It's time for a toast."

She uncorked the bottle, laughing as the cork flew across the kitchen. Kayla captured the spurt of champagne in a fluted glass. When all three flutes were poured, she raised a toast. "To Taylor's Cafe at Paradise Cove. And to the women I love most in the world. You too, Brittany, wherever you are!"

"To Brittany," they all said, and sipped as one.

"Let's call her," Taylor suggested and punched the number on her phone.

Brit answered on the third ring. "Hey, Taylor girl, what's up?"

"What do you mean, what's up? We just opened today. Taylor's Cafe. I sent you an email invite. Remember?"

"So how did it go?"

"Awesome. Slow at the beginning, but by ten, ten thirty, we had a steady stream of customers." Taylor glanced at her mom and Kayla, and got teary-eyed again. "We closed a few minutes ago, and we're having champagne to celebrate. We miss you."

"I miss you too. Why don't you look out the front window?"

"What?" Taylor waved her hand at Kayla. "Look out the window. Hurry."

The three women ran to the window in time to see Brittany pull up in a little red convertible. She waved at them and hopped out of the car. "Now pour me a glass, will ya?"

When Brittany waltzed in, all glammed up in a pair of pink spandex pants, an off the shoulder white top, and slinky heels, Kayla let out a whistle. She was a knockout by anyone's standards. Standing nearly six feet tall, with dark wavy hair down to her butt, flashing brown eyes, and dancer's legs, she turned heads everywhere she went.

"Whoa, baby. You look hot, hot, hot." Kayla blew out a breath.

Brit grinned. "That's because I take after my three sisters, and the prettiest mom I ever did see."

"I can't believe you came for my opening," Taylor said, giving her a huge hug. She'd missed the work part but showed up for the champagne. So Brittany. Taylor gave her a hug. "I'm so glad you're here."

"Of course I came. I'm just sorry I'm late."

Everyone crowded in to give her a hug. She laughed with delight, loving being the center of attention. "I planned to be here early, but then Jose dropped in as I was leaving. He's my manager and a great dancer. *Momma mia*, that guy has some moves."

Kayla laughed. "Now that's the best excuse I've heard of for you missing work."

Brittany licked her red lips and rolled her eyes. "I was dressed and ready to go, then he used some of those moves to get me back into bed. That put me behind an hour. Or two." She sighed. "But it was worth every heavenly minute."

"Now, now, dear." Anna put a hand to her heart. "You know I want to hear all about it, but this is going to call for more champagne. Let's replenish our drinks, then we can all sit down while you tell us about your dreamy man."

Kayla poured Brittany a flute then topped the other glasses off, but not her own. They took a square table by the front window and Brittany chugalugged half her drink. She wiped her mouth and grinned.

“Share,” Taylor said. “You’ve been so busy this summer!”

"Okay. As you know, we've been touring for the past few months--all over the east coast. Rhode Island, New Hampshire, Boston. It's been a blast, and with all that travel and close proximity Jose and I have gotten to know each other pretty well. He's forty and gorgeous, as well as loaded." She flipped her long hair over her shoulder, looking pretty pleased with herself. "He runs the dance company. Been married three times, but he says he's in love with me. I don't know... I mean I like him a lot, but he doesn't have a very good track record, now does he?"

"Be careful." Taylor envied her baby sister's zest for life, but had always been more cautious with her heart. Of the three sisters, Brit was more like their mother in temperament.

"Some men are just for fun," Anna said primly. "Good time Charlies."

Kayla and Taylor exchanged a look before all of them started laughing.

Brit raised her flute in Taylor's direction. "Enough about me. Taylor, I'm so proud of you." She gave her a warm, genuine smile and squeezed her fingers in the palm of her hand. "Congratulations! This place is awesome." She rose from her seat to wander around, checking everything out. "It's so darn cute. Adorable. Did you do the decor?"

"Mostly. But Kayla and Juanita helped. We went to flea markets, and some local shops for the more interesting artwork."

"Miguel and Colt found the fishnet and hung it from the rafters," Anna told her. "Colt Travis was Taylor's first customer."

"Super cute Colt?" Brittany clarified. "With the fishing charter?"

"Yes," Anna confirmed as Taylor finished her champagne. "He's always there in a pinch. Yet, Taylor refuses to give him the time of day."

Kayla shot Taylor a look--part sympathy, part warning. "Colt's hanging in the wings, biding his time. But today a guy Taylor dated back in college showed up, out of the blue. He's on his way to Key West, and wants to take her out when he returns. And he's gorgeous." Kayla tilted her head. "So? Are you going?"

"I haven't decided, but after the way Colt reacted, I darn well think I should." Taylor straightened her shoulders, recalling his hip to hers, her breasts against his hard chest.

"Tell me," Brittany said. "What happened?"

"Colt came back for lunch with Jamie and Raul just as I was giving Jack my number." Taylor looked at her sisters, hoping for some support. "Then acted like a big jerk about it." It wasn't like she and Colt were dating. She'd been very careful to keep things friendly.

"Oh my!" Anna's eyes twinkled. "How exciting. What did he do?"

Taylor's cheeks heated. "He was angry for starters. Told me if I wanted a man that he was the guy for the job." She tossed her head. "Really? I mean, *really*? What an ego!"

Anna laughed and clapped her hands. "Bravo! He's staking his claim," she said. "Good for him."

"He has no right." Taylor leaned against the table. "He dates half the women in Paradise Cove. Or at least sleeps with them. So he damn well can't have me too!" What made everything worse was that her body had responded to Colt's "claim"—wasn't she stronger than that? She glanced at all three faces, with their mischievous smiles. "Matter of fact, if Jack calls, I will go out with him. He's intelligent, interesting, and definitely eye candy." He could also satisfy her in ways no man had been able to before. Maybe that was what she needed. A hot night under the covers.

Anna covered Taylor's hand and squeezed. "But what about poor Colt? He's such a dear man." She glanced at her older, more sensible daughter. "Kayla! Help me out here. Taylor will listen to you, more than she will me."

"I'm right here, Mother," Taylor said crisply, pulling her hand free.

Anna ignored her and spoke again to Kayla, who had more common sense than any of them. "You know your sister as well as I do, and she's a homebody by nature. So what do you advise her to do? Get some action with a guy who's not from around here and won't be staying, or open her eyes to what's standing right in front of her?"

"Don't discuss me like I'm not in the room." Taylor scooted back from the table. "I know what I'm doing. I know Jack. He's a great guy. Partner in his father's law firm. Successful. Killer good looks. And he came on to me! I'd have to be completely nuts to turn him down. After all, there aren't a whole lot of quality guys to date around here. Even if they outnumber the women three to one, there isn't a big selection. Take Colt as an example. He's a good daddy, a nice man, but he's in debt up to his eyeballs, and has no intentions of getting into any type of relationship with anyone. He just wants a body to cuddle in bed."

Taylor reached for her champagne glass, realized it was empty, and put it back down. "Guy should get a freakin' dog."

Brittany put a hand on one slim hip and tapped her heeled toe. "Taylor, Taylor, how did you ever get to be my sister? Where did your genes go wrong? Mom has more gumption than you do. Married twice, and looking for number three. You, on the other hand run scared."

“Hey!” Anna said, pretending her feelings were hurt.

“Brittany,” Kayla warned. "Tread lightly. Everyone is different--there is no right or wrong."

"I do not run scared! I lived with my last boyfriend for two whole years." The only running she did, was running two full-time businesses. Any fear on her part had everything to do with failing. Not falling in love.

"Yes, and what did he used to call you? Ice. Ice, ice, baby."

Kayla smoothed Taylor’s hair in silent comfort.

"That was my fault." Taylor jumped to his defense, wishing she’d never shared that story with her sister. "I know it sounds awful, but I started that whole thing. After we'd been together for a year or more, he wanted to know if I was happy in bed. I told him I was, then made a lame comment about how I could have played the part of Elsa in Frozen. You know....in bed. I have a hard time reaching a climax."

"So he was a lousy lover. You shouldn't have taken the blame.” Brittany sat across from her. “A good guy could turn you around in an instant," she told her, putting a hand over hers. "Now, here's the plan. You go out with your hot guy from the city, screw his brains out. Use a condom, and don't worry. Or give Colt the thrill of his lifetime and do him instead. But you are not a nun. Not even Catholic. And you are certainly not frozen. You're a warm, affectionate, joyful person. All you need is to start living before it's too late."

Brittany took a sip of her champagne as she glanced around the table. "We of all people know that life doesn't come with a guarantee. We have to live for the moment, or it may never come."

She spoke a harsh truth, a lesson they'd all learned the hard way.

Taylor shook her head sadly. She wasn't built like her sister. Her beliefs were different, and she had to be true to them. Yes, she could go out more often, but that didn't mean she'd "enjoy" her life more.

"I know what you're saying, Brit. But I'm not like you, and I don't want to be."

"Okay, enough about your love life," Brittany said, turning to face Kayla. "How's the bride-to-be feeling? I see you're not drinking. Hopefully that's good news."

"Maybe, but I'm afraid to get too excited or optimistic. I had another false alarm a few months back." Kayla put her hand over her flat stomach.

"Oh, no!" Anna's eyes grew wide. "I didn't know, honey. You never said anything."

"Well, there was nothing to say. My period was late, that's all."

"I'm sure that Sean has you seeing the best doctors in the field and is keeping an eye on you," Anna said in comfort. "But you shouldn't be working so hard. Why don't you sit home and watch all those cute workmen banging around your new home?"

The girls laughed.

Anna sniffed. "Well, that's precisely what I would do."

Brittany rose and kissed her mother's cheek. "As would I. But I think my siblings have our father's genes."

"When I see genes," Anna said with a twinkle in her eye, "I want a hot guy wearing them."

CHAPTER FOUR

Colt sat back in his Captain's chair on the upper deck as the boys trolled for fish. He kept one eye on them, and steered with his hands behind him. He was good at multi-tasking. He was good at a lot of things, but one thing he wasn't good at was keeping his emotions locked down.

You'd think being newly divorced, he'd have no problems with that. The fighting and anger and hurt when he discovered his wife had cheated on him. Coming to terms with that. Deciding it was for the best. He wasn't the man she wanted, and he didn't want to be. The past year had seen plenty of emotional upheaval. It had been hard on all of them, but they were getting to a solid place now. He felt more at peace than he had in a long time.

His life was uncomplicated and he aimed to keep it that way. One thing for sure--he didn't do emotions with the girls he dated. They came. They went. So what the hell had happened today with Taylor?

He took a long slug of water and then replaced the bottle in the holder. His eyes were trained on the lines, but instead of seeing the wake behind him, all he saw was the look of shock and distaste on Taylor's face. He raised his cap off his head, mopped up some sweat, then shoved it back down.

He didn't blame her. He'd been a complete idiot back at the cafe. Coming on to her the way he did. Showing her in graphic style exactly how she'd affected him. What had he been thinking? She'd be running scared now for damn sure.

Besides that, she was right. He had no say in who she dated. She'd made it loud and clear that she certainly did *not* want him--but that didn't stop him from wanting her. At least physically. Of all the women he knew, she was the one he'd give his left nut to have in his bed. Problem was, he wasn't looking for a wife and having buddy-sex with Taylor wouldn't sit right. Not with him. Or her. And sure in hell not with the rest of her family. The women were close and protective of each other, and he respected them all too much to mess around with Taylor just for fun.

Even if she wanted it—which she didn't. He was between a rock and a hard place. The hard place was the fact he couldn't stop thinking about her, and laid awake many nights wondering how she'd feel under him. Sometimes he thought of her when he was with another woman. She was beginning to feel like a disease.

"How's it going, boys?" Colt called down over the rail. He could see for himself they were having a good time, joking around, talking fish and baseball, too young to have girl problems.

They each waved up at him, then went back to scanning the clear blue water for fish. Colt popped another Tums in his mouth. The third in the past hour.

Acid roiled around his stomach. Had heartburn too. Everything hurt inside and it was her damn fault. He'd been fine all morning. This sickness hadn't started until she'd given her number to that asshole who looked like a daytime soap star. Handsome to the point of ridiculous. That thick black hair, blinding white teeth. What did she see in that guy?

She'd dated him years ago. Colt knew she'd slept with him—her eyes had danced with excitement when he'd whispered something in her ear. That prick had had her first, and that burned a hole in his gut.

But it wasn't just about sex. It was more the fact that she'd be attracted to a man like that in the first place. Maybe she wasn't all that different--could be he had believed it, because he'd wanted to. It was easy enough to be blinded by extreme wealth--the big house, the fancy cars, trips to anywhere in the world, first class resorts and high-end restaurants. His father had provided all that. They'd had a home in the Hamptons with a half-acre lot. Tennis court, huge pool, ocean at their doorstep. His father had kept a loft apartment in the City, on Madison Avenue, not far from the art gallery he owned.

His mother, Marjorie, had a full-time chef, a personal trainer, and never had to lift a finger except to call for one of their hired help. He and his sister Chrissy had gone to private schools. They'd had huge parties a few times a year, and Colton had been allowed sips of the best champagne from the time he was twelve. He was a connoisseur: the best caviar, the world's finest smoked salmon, a good shot of scotch or a vintage cognac--all by the time he was sixteen. His father had wanted his son to have refined taste and be a true gentleman. What a load of crap that was.

"Dad!" Jamie shouted. "We've got one."

Broken out of his reverie, Colt watched Jamie wrestle with a fish. He'd caught a mackerel on his line and it looked to be a pretty decent size. "Need any help down there?" he called down.

"Nope. I've got this." Jamie had been around boats all his life, and could fish almost as well as his dad, or liked to think so anyway. Jamie began to reel it in and Raul had a netted scoop in his hand.

Colt watched as the less experienced boy reached down with the long hooked net and nearly topple over. Jamie grabbed hold of Raul by his pants and together they got the flopping silver-coated fish on deck.

"You want this, Dad?" Jamie knew it wasn't a good eating fish, so he was ready to toss it back.

"Up to you. We could smoke it, or let it live another day."

"I don't like smoked fish. And we got grouper at home," he said and tossed the fish back into the sea.

Colt liked his decision. He'd taught his son to only keep what they wanted to eat--or for him to sell, and let the rest swim free. He guided “Bait Me” closer to the reefs, and his mind drifted off again.

Back to his dad, and how his world had come crashing down around them in an instant. Right after his sixteenth birthday, Colt woke up to learn that his father was dead, and that everything he believed was a lie. He had loved and worshipped his handsome, elegant, and brilliant father. Yet he hadn't known him at all. The man his father portrayed was a fictional character. What lay beneath the expensive clothes and sophisticated exterior was a clever, gifted sociopath who made his living duping other people. His dad had been an extremely talented artist, but his real gift was copying famous artist's styles and selling new work under their names. He displayed them from his well respected art gallery and had them on loan to museums. Over two decades, he'd managed to deceive the art critics of the world, and the most discerning collectors too. How he did it was anyone's guess, but he thrived for years until the night he was found dead in his Jacuzzi tub. Vials of coke and an empty bottle of champagne--two glasses, one with bright red lipstick, scattered near his naked body.

When the police found him, the Travis family learned that his paintings had been under investigation for some time. The law suits following his death totally bankrupted the family. By the time they settled, they were officially broke.

Gone went the servants. No more private schools and parties. No mansion in the Hamptons, no fancy cars, or invitations, or friends. They were outcasts now, and had to get out of town as quickly as they could. His mom sold a great many pieces of jewelry and dozens of silver plates to buy their airline tickets to Miami, and with nothing but their clothes they left to start a new life.

Colt didn't want any stinking money. He'd had it, but what did it mean? It hadn't brought happiness or any real, lasting pleasure. It was all a lark, a night of frivolity, and a day of fun. Nothing of substance. Nothing real.

He didn't want that for himself. He understood his mother and his sister and their needs. They craved what was taken away from them. They worked their asses off to try to get a glimmer of it back. But Colt... he had what he wanted. A peaceful existence. Lazy days of fishing. Camaraderie in like-minded people. Friendships developed over the pride of their catch, not the size of their boat. Lulled by the gentle waves of the ocean and the hull of his boat, he had found real happiness in Paradise Cove. It was a good life for him and his son.

"What are you doing, Dad?"

Colt blinked. "Daydreaming. What's up?"

"I'm bored."

"You're bored? How about you, Raul? You bored too?"

"No, Mr. C. I like it out here. And your boat is way bigger and better than ours." He grinned, his teeth flashing white in his brown little face. "Shitty little raft."

"Don't swear," Colt said automatically.

Colt was one of the few people who knew how Juanita, Miguel and Raul ended up here. Rescued at sea, and Juanita seven month's pregnant, Dr. Sean Flannigan had taken them to his rented cottage at Paradise Cove. If the coastguard had found them they'd have been sent back to Cuba.

"Sorry," Raul said. "My uncle called it that. Said dad was stupid for coming across in a 'shitty little raft'." He shaded his big brown eyes and looked up to the bridge, trying to see Colt's face. "What's shitty?"

Jamie laughed. "It's poop, dude." He slapped his friend's back. "A poopy raft that almost killed you all."

Raul took the teasing good-naturedly. "It was. But my dad was brave. Not stupid. Look at us now. Americans," he said proudly.

"That's right, Raul." Colt spoke loudly, knowing from his perch it was difficult for the boys to hear. "You should be proud of your family."

"*Si*," he bobbed his head. "I am."

Colt leaned over the railing. "Want to head back?"

"I do." Jamie put his rod back into the holder, and turned to his bud. "Want a Coke?" he asked Raul.

"Sure." Raul carefully put his rod away and followed Jamie inside the cabin.

Colt turned the boat around and headed back. It took them nearly forty minutes to reach the marina. He was walking up the path with the boys when Miguel came toward them.

"There you are," he called to his son. "You out fishing again?" Miguel doffed his head to Colt. "Thanks for taking my boy all day. You don't need to do that. He can stay with me."

Colt knew Miguel was a proud man who understood the value of hard work, and that you don't get things for nothing. He wanted his son to learn this valuable lesson, but Colt didn't think it had to be done quite yet. Raul was only eleven.

Although both men respected each other, they'd never see eye-to-eye on those issues. "Jamie likes having him around. I do too." He ruffled the boy's dark hair, long enough now that it fell to his shoulders. "Tell your dad how you did today."

"I hit a home run," Raul said proudly.

"That's good." Miguel gave a single nod. "But you can't just play all summer long. Baseball and fishing." His tone scolded. "Thought you were going to do some weeding for Miss Kayla."

"I did some yesterday," Raul was quick to answer. "Miss Kayla says it only needs to be done every few days."

"Fine. See that it is." Miguel put a hand on his son's shoulder. "Time to go home. Your mother needs help with Merica. She worked all day too."

Raul hung his head. "I can give her a bath," he said.

Colt hated the boy's hang-dog expression. "See you tomorrow, Raul. Pick you up at seven, right?"

Raul looked at his dad, who shook his head. "No, not tomorrow. I have to work."

"That's fine. The next day then." They reached the parking lot and he waved to the boy and his dad as they climbed into their pickup truck. Though older than his son, the blue Chevy was clean and cared for.

"I wish Raul could play ball tomorrow," Jamie grumbled. "It's not fair that he has to work all the time."

"I know, but his father isn't being cruel. He thinks what he's doing is right." Colt might not agree with Miguel, but the man was teaching his son the way he'd been taught.

Not how to drink fine cognac and decipher the difference between caviar from the Caspian Sea, or a good domestic brand.

Jamie was quiet on the drive, and Colt knew the day's activities had worn him out. When they pulled up in front of the three-bedroom cabin that they called home, he told

Jamie to take a shower, then stepped into his own. He wouldn't be taking Jamie to happy hour at the Paradise Cove cottages tonight. The offer from Taylor to make pizza for Jamie would have to wait. Not only would he have a hard time facing her, but he'd likely be thrown out if he did.

He'd let the dust settle, then somehow find a way to make things right.

CHAPTER FIVE

Taylor was still out of sorts, although she hid it from her mom and sisters. It was near five o'clock and Colt and Jamie hadn't shown up. Just as well, as she had a whole lot of things she wanted to say to him and none of them were pretty. But she couldn't refrain from checking the walkway every ten minutes or so. And she was keeping an eye on her watch too.

He disturbed her. There was no getting around it. When he'd pulled her close, she'd felt a zing from the tips of her toes to her center core, and she couldn't remember anyone...not even Jack, affecting her so. Colton Travis should think about harnessing that sexual energy. It could get a girl interested in a real hurry.

He didn't want a relationship any more than she did. Matter of fact that's what she wanted to talk to him about. It might be a good idea if he didn't hang around quite so much. She'd made up her mind--with gentle persuasion from Brittany--to start living a little. Not a whole lot, but going out once in awhile with the male species had to be more entertaining than spending every night here with her mother.

It was different when there was the four of them, but with Brittany living in Miami and Kayla with her fiancé, she was starting to feel like an old maid. Sitting around playing cards with her mom and their guests, going to bed early so she could get up early. Listening to the lively chorus of crickets while lying in bed was the highlight of her evening.

Dammit! Colt had shown her what she'd been missing, and that sexual spark had felt good. There had to be someone within a twenty mile radius who could make her feel like that again.

"Hey, Tay, come sit with us!" Brittany waved her over to the only table of men. They were rugged guys, outdoorsy types from the Panhandle here for some fishing. Dressed in baggy tees and cargo shorts, their feet in sandals, the men were not looking for women--but had found one nonetheless. Taylor guessed their ages to be mid-forties, all were married, but no one could remain oblivious to Brittany's many charms.

"Later. Got to make my rounds," she called back. Her rounds would take her all of a minute or two.

They only had two cabins booked this week, and their guests included the three men chatting with her sister, and a friend of Anna's with her recently divorced daughter. Anna had worked at the same school with Joan in Princeton, New Jersey for ten years. They had shared plenty of stories about their children over the years, and it came as no surprise to Anna when Joan booked the cabin for a two-week stay, saying Carole had left her husband.

Taylor knew Carole was going through a hard time. Her ex was a verbally abusive man and still making her life miserable. Since Anna and Joan were gossiping about people they knew, Taylor took a moment to sit down beside Carole and ask about her day.

"It was wonderful," Carole told her. “I walked for miles, and snorkeled down by the pier. I've never seen such beautiful fish in my life, and the water is so clear. You are very lucky."

"Yes, we are." Taylor gave her a measuring glance. "Do you like living up north? Maybe you need a change of scene. We sure could use some help around here."

"Oh, I couldn't possibly do that!" Carole darted a quick look at her mother. "Dad passed away four years ago, and my brother is no help to Mom at all. She needs me."

"I'm sure she'd like you to be happy too."

Taylor liked Carole--who was close to her own age, but looked haggard and thin as if she'd given up taking care of herself. Her long brown hair was pulled straight off her face into a ponytail, and when she attempted a smile it never quite reached her eyes. They were a light blue and might have been pretty once; now they looked dull and gray. Yet, by her bone structure, it was obvious that with a little weight gain and a good hair salon she would be a very attractive woman.

"I'll be happy once I get Hank off my back. He keeps driving by at night and calling me at all hours."

"Aren't you scared? I mean if you're divorced, then he should let you get on with your life."

"He's never been physical. I'm not afraid of him. But he doesn't want to let me go. I know what he's doing--but I'm not going back." She lifted her chin and there was more fire in her eyes than Taylor had seen in the past few days. "I'm living with Mom now," she said firmly. "She needs me, and it's good company."

Taylor nodded. She lived with her mother too, although the circumstance was entirely different. Anna and her sisters had come to Paradise Cove to build something together. They were protective of each other, but the door was open. Heck, Anna couldn't wait to get her girls married and out of the house--or cabin, as it were.

The resort cottages all had exotic names. Rhapsody, Serenity, Tranquility, and Harmony were the larger, two-bedroom units. The smaller ones facing the pool had simpler names--Bliss, Happy Days, Smooth Sailing, and Hooked and Baited. The ones closer to the office were Hibiscus, Bougainvillea, The Palms and theirs--attached to the Office, had been misnamed Passions. After the cottages had been painted, they'd changed it to Birds Of Paradise. So far two birds had flown off. Taylor was the only one left.

Before long all the cabins would be rented and they'd need more hired help. She was sincere in her offer, and would love Carole to reconsider. "Well, if you ever change your mind, just call us, okay?"

"Sure, but I don't think so. I work at the library, and I've been there for twelve years." That sounded about as exciting to Taylor as a pan of uncooked dough.

"Sounds like pleasant work," she managed, then took a long sip from her mango daiquiri. She'd love to help her, but how? There were some things in life that you just had to figure out yourself. Like she did with Colt, and Jack, and life in general. She and her sisters had lost their father in the Twin Towers on 9/11, and like all Americans they'd been devastated by this inexplicable, monstrous attack. For them it had been deeply personal. Her mom and the three girls, all teenagers at the time, had no game plan. They simply put one step forward each morning and somehow survived. Carole would learn to do that too.

The women continued to sit and chat while the men stuck to their local beers and kept to themselves. They were eating a big plate of nachos that Taylor had whipped up, and some toasted flat bread with chicken and spinach.

After a few minutes, Taylor excused herself so she could help Kayla serve. She picked up the tray of food, and Kayla a pitcher, and they floated between the two tables, making sure the drinks were full and their plates not empty. Brittany, being a natural born flirt, and having a penchant for escaping work, remained seated with the guys. And by the laughter at that table, she seemed to be entertaining them well.

By six o'clock the party broke up, and the men headed back to their cabin. Kayla returned to her home in Key Largo to wait for Sean to get off work. He was a cardiac surgeon and often worked very long hours. This was agreeable to them all, as it gave Kayla plenty of hours in her day to work the resort--and now with the opening of Taylor's Cafe her time with them was even more important.

Taylor left her mother, Brittany, Joan and Carole to play gin rummy, and headed back home. She had worked a very long day, and with the excitement and nerves thrown in, she was bone-tired. She filled the tub with hibiscus-scented bubble bath, lit a candle and sunk in for a long, quiet soak.

It might have been ten or fifteen minutes later when she heard a scratching at her door. What the hell? Then she heard a soft knock.

"Who is it?"

"It's me." Her sister, Brittany. "Why did you lock the door?"

"We always do now."

"Well open it. I've got to go to the bathroom."

They only had one and she was using it. "Go in the office. I'm in the tub."

"The office is locked too. What's going on around here? We never locked up before."

"Brit. Go pee somewhere else. I'm enjoying my bath. Or was!"

"You can go back in a minute. Hurry and open up. It's urgent!"

Taylor climbed out of the tub, wanting to kill her sister. She wrapped a big towel around herself and went to the door.

"At last," Brittany said, swaying as she headed for the bathroom.

How many drinks had she had? Fuming, Taylor stood outside the bathroom, tapping her toe.

The toilet flushed and Brittany pranced out. "Well. That was close. So tell me why you're locking up. That seems just weird. Here in the boondocks, with nothing but critters around."

"After you left for Miami with the Hernandez family, and Sean left too, it was just us three women by ourselves. We heard some noises one night, like someone was trying to get in. We yelled out, and then there was silence, but we never really felt totally safe again."

"It was probably a raccoon or something."

"I agree. I'm sure it was, but still. With only Mom and I here, and cabins full of strangers, it just seems smart to lock our doors. Right?"

"I guess." Brittany kicked off her shoes. "So? You going back to your bath?"

"I was planning on it."

"Oh, don't! We haven't seen each other in four months. Stay up and let's make some popcorn and talk half the night."

"Right. I need to be up by five."

"Good. That gives us nine hours to catch up!"

Taylor rolled her eyes. "You're one crazy gal."

"And I'm just getting started."

* * *

It was half past ten before Taylor made it to bed, and she was up and out before her sister blinked an eye. Despite the lack of sleep, Taylor was glad she'd stayed up to spend the extra time with her, not knowing when she'd see her again.

The second morning at Taylor's Café went better than the first, as a steady stream of customers filtered in, with only short lolls in between. Kayla had arrived early, and she had Juanita there too, so when Brittany showed up around nine, Taylor was able to take a short break.

Together, they sat at the small bistro table in the kitchen and enjoyed an egg white, mushroom and spinach omelet with fresh fruit on the side. Brittany regaled them all through breakfast with exciting stories about her new life and the people she'd met and places she'd been.

Their sister was living her dream and the happiness it brought her was undeniable. Going to Miami and joining a traveling dance troupe had been the best thing she could have done for herself.

Taylor was happy for her, but felt something tugging at her inside. It wasn't jealousy as she would never want to live that vagabond life, but with Kayla living down the road at Key Largo now, things just weren't the same. She missed the long talks with her sisters, the walks and worries they'd shared. Soon Kayla would be married, a wife and hopefully a mother herself. And Brittany was off and flying. In a super exciting, but dangerous new world.

Taylor's life dimmed in comparison, yet she wouldn't trade one minute of it for either of her sisters. But she felt a strange longing inside, as though something might be missing. What could it be? Her life was so full. She had never been more content.

"Great omelet, Taylor," Brittany said, using her napkin to dab at her mouth. "You've always been such a little Suzy Homemaker. And this cafe suits you."

"Thanks, Brit." For some reason her words stung. "I do love it."

"You should. It's wonderful, and I'm so proud of you." Brittany glanced at her watch, stood up and stretched.

"This has been so much fun. I'll have to try to get down here more often." She hugged Juanita, then kissed Kayla's and Taylor's cheek. "Good luck with everything, Kayla." She glanced down at her tummy, and smiled. "I'll see you all next month. What's more fun than a wedding?"

Kayla laughed. "Being the bride?"

"Not for me," Brittany said, tossing her hair off her shoulders. "I'm going to wait until I'm in my thirties like you two. That gives me at least another four years to have fun, fun, fun."

"Don't have too much," Taylor warned, suddenly feeling a rush of concern. Her sister was so beautiful, so carefree and careless. "It's a big, bad world out there, and I worry about you."

"Don't. I'm in good hands. Jose is different than my other boyfriends. Older, more sophisticated. He looks after me."

"I'm glad to hear it." Taylor held her sister's hand and looked her in the eye. "You know we are always here for you if you ever need us."

Miami's dance scene was a very different world--young pretty girls were prey for danger and drugs, and men who would use them up.

"Not to worry. I always know where home is." Brittany gave them a last hug then strode to the door. "Love you!" She tossed them a kiss then swept out of the cafe. Gone. Rushing off to Miami and her exciting new life.

More customers showed up and kept Taylor busy for the rest of the afternoon. So busy that she didn't have time to worry about Brittany. Or Colt. Although when he didn't show up for happy hour that night, her stomach knotted. She'd had water instead of a cocktail, but that hadn't helped.

She wasn't overly concerned, but she did find it odd as another two whole days and nights went by without a Colt Travis sighting. Taylor hadn't seen him down at the marina. Not out fishing or hanging around with Jamie and Raul. He hadn't been to see her mother or Merica either.

Had she ticked him off for good? The idea that she might have pushed him away burned a hole in her gut. He was her best friend. Probably her only friend in Paradise Cove, outside of Juanita and their family. Maybe that was what was lacking in her life, keeping her from being one hundred percent content. She didn't have any real friends. Or time for them if she did.

Taylor had never been a girly-girl who chummed around with a lot of girlfriends. Not even when she'd been young and in school. She'd never felt the need for someone to confide in because she'd always had her sisters. She didn't lack for female companionship and never would.

But Colt, she missed, and she didn't like it a bit. Knowing him, he wouldn't be moping around for her. No sirree! He'd be out finding his pleasure elsewhere. Heartless and uncaring, and darn right stupid. Getting all upset because she'd given her number out to some guy.

Really? The idea was so infuriating that she refused to breathe his name. He could take his friendship elsewhere, and she hoped he caught crabs!

She went to sleep that night--angry, frustrated--at herself more than at him.

She woke up with a headache that was slightly relieved by extra strength pain medication. Business was good, with plenty of customers who kept her occupied. Then Jack called around ten and her spirits lifted. A date with Jack was just what she needed!

Juanita and Kayla eyed her with curiosity as she hitched her fanny on the stool and grinned like a fool. “Hey, Jack," she greeted him with warm enthusiasm. "How was the tournament? Did you win?”

“I'll tell you all about it later, if you agree to dinner."

"I can do dinner," she said simply. "So was it fun?"

"We had a hellova good time." He chuckled, and she could picture his dimple flashing. She might even kiss that dimple later--if he'd let her.

"I’m leaving Key West around noon. I’d love to stay the night, if you’ve got a cabin free?”

"Of course!" She didn't even try to hide her excitement. Why bother? She wanted a good time. He wanted a good time. So why the hell not? They were consenting adults with a history together. Maybe they could make some present day memories to take into the future. The ones she had now were sadly stale.

"Our cabins are virtually empty," she told him. "We have only two occupied, so we can give you one with a water view." She had promised herself to start living a little, and tonight was as good a time to start as any.

“That's great. Last time we talked you were a little standoffish."

"Oh, that's because it was opening day and I had a lot on my mind. I wanted everything to be perfect, and then there you were. It threw me off my game a little."

"Well, I didn't notice. Glad you're up to a night out. Seems to me like you're working too hard."

"That's true. I have been. We only took this place over eighteen months ago, and it's been a little crazy. So yes. I'm looking forward to a night off."

"Will you be at the cafe for the next few hours? Should I meet you there?"

"Yes, do that. I close at two, but I've got prep work to do for tomorrow, so I can hang around if you're late. Then we have a happy hour here at four."

"I'll see you around two, two thirty and you can get me checked in."

"Looking forward to it." She hung up, and swung around to see two sets of eyes staring at her. Neither woman was smiling.

"You're going out with him?" Kayla asked.

"Sure. Why not?" Taylor swept her hair up from off her shoulders and twisted it in a knot. "He's going to stay the night. We could use the money."

"And what's the other reason?" she asked with a teasing glint in her eye.

"No other reason."

Juanita put her hands on her plump hips. "Where is Colt these days? We haven't seen him since that fight you two had. He hasn't called Raul either. Not for two whole days."

"I don't know." She shrugged as if she didn't care. "I'm not his keeper." She got up and grabbed a cold water bottle from the fridge and uncapped it, taking a long swallow. "I'm sure he's busy with Jamie. School starts up in a few weeks. Maybe they're catching up on a few things."

"Miguel told Colt that Raul had to work. He said no baseball, but he didn't mean no baseball anymore. Just not every day."

"Well you can tell him that when you see him. He should be stopping in soon. Can't imagine him disappearing for good. Probably misses his free meals.."

Kayla nodded, her eyes searching Taylor's face. "He might feel bad for the things he said to you, and doesn't know how to apologize." Her brow creased with concern. "When he hears about this date of yours, it'll send him over the edge."

"Well, I hope not. I miss having him around as a friend." She swallowed a lump in her throat. "He's the only friend I have here, except for the two of you."

"You will always have us, no matter what," Kayla said giving her a hug.

Their conversation came to an abrupt stop as the door opened and four fishermen came in. They sat down at a table, took off their caps, and shot a glance at the blackboard menu.

Kayla marched over to them. "Hi boys. We have some great conch chowder, or beef and barley soup, and half a sandwich to go with that. It's a luncheon special for the bargain price of $5.99." She gave them a plastic menu which stated the daily specials. "Here's the list of sandwiches. And we have local beer at $3.99."

The men glanced at her, and grinned. "You know how to make a sale. What sandwich should I have?"

"You look like a pastrami and rye type of guy."

He laughed. "You ever been married? You'd make a hellova wife."

"That's on my agenda, sir." She took the rest of their orders and returned to the kitchen with a big smile. "Specials and beers all around."

By two that afternoon, Taylor was glancing out the window, feeling on pins and needles. She wasn't all that sure if this date was a good idea, but now that she had agreed, she'd have to go through with it.

Kayla left early, and Taylor told Juanita that she could leave too. She cleaned up in the bathroom the best she could. Brushed her teeth, refreshed her lipstick, used deodorant and a spray of cologne. Too nervous to make dough or do anything constructive she sat down at one of the tables to wait for this prince among men to drive up in his Jag. Even the fact she thought of him in such glowing terms, made her feel ill at ease. Inferior.

The wait didn't take long, but by the time he arrived, her stomach was in knots and she was doing breathing exercises. She'd locked the door so customers wouldn't barge in, but she heard his car pull up, and went to open the door.

She watched him get out of his sleek and shiny car, and catching sight of her, he grinned and waved. He was wearing a collared white shirt, sleeves rolled up, and knee length dark blue shorts, with expensive loafers, no socks. His dark, wavy hair was just long enough to caress his perfect ears.

There was not one darn thing about him that a girl couldn't admire. Jack was long and lean, with a handsome face and a great smile. If he had one flaw, the only one Taylor could see, was that he was *too* perfect.

Taylor turned on the “closed” sign and pulled the door shut behind her, locking it up. She faced him with a smile. "Right on time, I see."

"Didn't want to keep you waiting." Jack reached her side and pulled her in for a quick kiss.

She allowed the kiss, but then pulled back a little. "So did you win?"

"Of course we did. You wouldn't expect us to lose, would you?" He laughed. "It was only a thousand dollar prize, but the side bets made it worthwhile."

"Do you ever lose at anything?" she asked, wondering why it bothered her. He was the golden boy, and life had picked him.

"Not often," he admitted, his eyes wore a devilish twinkle. "And not for lack of trying."

She didn't know if he included her in that, and was not eager to find out. Taylor flipped her hair back, changing the subject. "Mom dropped off a key to one of our best cottages. We should take your car, as it's easier to park outside the cabin."

"Great. How's your mother doing? Is she happy down here?"

"Sure is. Loves to entertain the guests at our happy hours." Taylor followed him to his Jag and he opened the passenger door. She slid into the creamy soft leather seat, and glanced at the fancy dashboard. He stepped around to the driver’s side and climbed in—her gaze settled on his long, tanned legs and then traveled upward to his perfect profile. Was that a cleft in his chin? She didn't remember one, but it added to his charisma.

"What are you smiling about?" he asked with a grin.

"You." She sat back in her seat and gestured to the car, his hair, to that sexy cleft. "How do you handle it? All this?"

"What?" He tilted his head as if he didn't have a clue what she was talking about. And he probably didn't. Jack was confident without being arrogant.

"Your life. You. Everything you have, and are." They were worlds apart and yet for some strange reason, they kept colliding.

"I can't change it." He gave her a funny look. "I don't have to make excuses either. I have a damn good life, and I'm not complaining."

Taylor nodded, and her smile disappeared. "Nor should you. And you wear it well—I wasn't criticizing, Jack." She leaned against the door and drew in a breath. "I just feel a little overwhelmed when I'm with you."

"Well, don't." He backed out of the lot and headed down the dirt road. She directed him to Rhapsody, the cabin where Sean had stayed for the first few months. The proximity to the beach and marina made it one of their most desirable units. Although it was a two-bedroom she only charged him the minimal fee.

"So this is your Paradise resort," he said, parking the car behind the cabin. He grabbed his bag out of the rear, and she led him down the path toward the front entrance. All the pathways had recently been redone. They were lined now with white rocks which Miguel had taken the time to do.

"Yup. What do you think?"

He took her hand in his and lifted it, giving it a kiss. "I see why you love it so much. Paradise Cove. It really is, isn't it? You have the place very well maintained, and I can hear the sound of the ocean, and smell the salt air from right here." His eyes were warm on her face. "I'm happy for you, Taylor. I really am."

She squeezed his hand, warmed by his praise. If he was feeding her bullshit just to get into her pants, he was halfway there.

CHAPTER SIX

Colt, cutting through Paradise Cove from the marina with Jamie on his heels, stopped abruptly on the dirt path. Jamie bumped into his back.

"What?" Jamie glanced at the path in front of them, then back up to his dad. "A snake?"

Sort of. "No." Colt adjusted his sunglasses. "It's nothing." It better be nothing, but he had a feeling, as he stared at Rhapsody, that he was too late. *That man* and Taylor were at the door of the cabin, and then he saw him kiss Taylor's hand.

It felt like a kick in his gut. His jaw clenched tight as he witnessed Taylor gazing into the bastard's eyes before going inside with him, hand in hand.

Waves crashed in his ears and his heart thundered.

"Dad?" Jamie nudged him in the side.

"It's nothing, Jamie." He put a hand on his son's shoulder and continued walking up the path. He shot a glance toward the cabin, hoping to catch a glimpse of Taylor through the window. What the hell was going on? Were they sneaking off for a little afternoon aerobics?

His stomach churned like butter. He wanted to pound on the door and tear this asshole off of her. That was his girl and nobody but him could have her! If Jamie hadn't been with him, he might have done just that.

And yet, he knew if he did anything that stupid she'd never speak to him again. He almost didn't care. It would be worth it. The thought of what she might be doing with that man right this very minute tore a hole in his gut.

He knew she wasn't his girl. Not officially. But he'd staked a claim on her a year ago when she'd caught his eye strutting down the beach with that sister of hers. They'd stopped and chatted with him as he fished off the pier. Taylor had flirted with him, throwing him teasing glances as they'd walked away. She'd come by herself several times after that. Things heated up between them, but never went all the way. He'd given her fresh fish, she'd paid him with casseroles and happy hour snacks for him and his son.

They were an item. Sort of. Sure, he dated lots of chicks. Not that it was dating exactly. He'd take them for a few drinks, then back to his boat for a quickie now and then. That wasn't dating. He didn't do relationships. Hell, he'd just gotten a divorce, and Jamie wouldn't like him hanging around with one woman all the time. His son liked Taylor because she fed him and fussed over him. And because she didn't sleep with his dad.

"Who was that with Taylor?" Jamie asked. He squinted his eyes to look up at him. "Was that the guy she was talking to the other day at the cafe?"

"I guess so." So, his son had noticed, too. "She knows him from her college days."

"You think she likes him?"

"I dunno." He jammed his hands in his pockets. "Want to go to happy hour today?"

"Uh. Sure. But maybe she won't be there. Maybe she'll be with this other guy."

Colt's mood darkened. "Why do you think that?"

"Well, Taylor's real pretty, and she's always working or hanging with her mom. Just doesn't seem right." He shrugged. "She's old enough to be married. Have kids even."

Kids? Babies? The thought blew his mind. "Maybe she doesn't want them. She's busy with the cafe."

"Yeah." Jamie snorted. "She cooks all the time. I mean *all the time*. What kind of life is that?" He glanced back at Rhapsody. "I hope she doesn't marry him and move away."

"She won't," he snapped. "No way. She has the resort and her cafe. And her sisters are here." A hard knot was settling in his throat and he pushed to speak around it. "She wouldn't go away and leave everything behind."

"Maybe not. But who knows? That's a hot looking car he drives. Maybe he's got tons of money and can give her everything she wants."

"Why do you say that?" Colt asked the question with anger stemming from a place his son didn't know about. "She's not like that. Money doesn't buy happiness. She's created a good life here. The work she does is not like work at all. When you love doing something, it's enjoyable and satisfying. Like my charter business. And fishing. There's nothing I'd rather be doing."

"Hmm." Jamie pondered that. "I'd think a guy like that could show her more enjoyable things to do than cook all day."

The boy's words stung. He sure in hell hoped not. But what if it were true? Maybe he should have done more than stake a claim—he should have moved in on the property.

"Dad, you could ask her out," Jamie said, shooting him a bright smile. "Take her fishing. Cook dinner *for her* on the boat. She might like that."

"You know, that's not a bad idea." He eyed his kid. "Maybe later if I can catch her alone."

"Yeah." Jamie's tone lowered. "If the other guy hasn't asked her first."

"Let's you and I go get cleaned up, then we can come back and swoop her away before she makes a big mistake with the wrong guy."

His son grinned. "Race you."

They hopped into his decade old Chevy truck and headed south a few miles, then turned onto a dirt road. They bumped along for about two blocks until arriving at their small boating community. He'd chosen the location as it had easy access to the Bay and was a short walk to the seawall. Jamie was happy here--he got a kick out of throwing stale bread to the seagulls and watching them squabble over the pieces. Another favorite past-time was to toss chum to the fish and make them jump.

Colt didn't bother to lock up his truck since it wasn't worth stealing. Their cottage wasn't grand, but it was affordable and took care of their needs. It had a bright, refurbished kitchen, open floor plan, and three small bedrooms. His ex-wife had put up some curtains on the large picture window, and painted the living area in soft yellow. They had throw rugs on the tiled floors, some local art work on the walls, a comfortable couch for his son and friends, and an easy chair that he claimed as his. A wooden bookshelf took up space on one wall and a fifty-inch flat screen adorned the other. All the comforts of home. Minus the ex-pain in the ass.

"Take your shower first, Jamie, and don't forget to wash behind your ears."

"My ears don't get dirty," he complained. "Why do you always tell me that?"

"I have no idea," Colt answered, popping the lid to a Corona light. He sucked on his beer and sat in his favorite chair, trying not to imagine what had taken place in Rhapsody this afternoon. The sound of the shower couldn't drown out the screaming in his head.

Had she or hadn't she? Was that the agenda when they'd slipped into the vacant cabin? He found it hard to believe she'd do such a thing, but hell, what woman wouldn't? Her ex-boyfriend was a class A stud, and she hadn't had any in awhile. Sure she'd be tempted. And she knew him, which made it all the easier to do. Taylor wasn't a tramp. She had principals, even if they were slightly lacking this afternoon.

Not that he was condemning her or anything. After all, he wasn't above having a stranger-danger meeting once in awhile. But he was a man. He knew how to protect himself. And a man had certain needs that most women found easy to ignore.

Did he really think that? Was he that archaic? Crap--he needed to get with the times. Women liked sex...well, that much he knew... it was just *Taylor*. She hadn't shown any interest before. And he didn't want her to now. Unless it was with him. And why not? He was trustworthy. He had an invested interest. And he had a way with women. Enough experience to make her feel pleasure like she'd never known before.

"Dad?"

"Yeah?"

"Your turn to shower. But there isn't much hot water left."

"Just as well." He took over the bathroom and stripped out of his clothes. The cold shower was exactly what he needed to wake him up and settle down his manhood. Showing up at happy hour with a hard-on for her would not win any brownie points. He could be charming. Maybe even bring out some of his old, almost forgotten habits like wearing a collared shirt tucked into his shorts. Which would require a belt. Did he even own one? What else had he forgotten over the years? Holding a chair out for a woman, folding one leg over another instead of sitting with his knees spread apart. Little things that just might get her notice.

He had tricks. He'd just forgotten how to use them.

* * *

Taylor saw Colt and Jamie the moment they stepped into the pool area. The two of them greeted her mother, said hello to their guests, then stepped up to the table with the drinks and appetizers and helped themselves.

Her skin burned. How dare he just show up uninvited and help himself as if he were a paying guest? And tonight of all nights! Why hadn't he come yesterday or the day before? This was so awkward, and so unfair!

"I have a problem," she whispered to Jack, who was on his second tumbler of single malt scotch.

"What is it?" He leaned back in his chair, his arm slung over hers. She felt his fingers caressing the back of her neck and twisted away. "Anything I can help you with?" he asked.

Taylor could tell that he wasn't enjoying their happy hour. He'd agreed to come for her sake, and then they were going for dinner at her favorite restaurant--Lazy Days where they could dine right on the beach, feet in the sand, with tiki torches to add to the romantic ambiance. She wanted tonight to be perfect--and romantic, as she planned to make this a night to remember.

"It's the guy over there," she told Jack, tilting her head in Colt's direction. "I didn't invite him but here he is anyway."

"Then tell him to get lost. If he's not a guest, he was no right to be freeloading. Looks like that's what he's doing." Jack had one knee hiked up on the other and tapped his toe. "Does he do this kind of thing often?"

"Yes. Usually a few times a week. He's a local fisherman and gives me fresh fish, and does charters for our guests too."

"Oh. Then I guess he feels welcome." His eyes searched her face. "So what's the problem?"

"We had a falling out the other day. Just words. It wasn't nice, and I'm angry with him." She folded her arms around her middle. "He upset me."

"Then tell him so."

"I can't. It would seem weird, and I don't want to embarrass his son. Jamie's really sweet." She smiled at the boy and wiggled her fingers.

He waved back, then said something to his dad.

Colt gave her a look that could have turned her to stone.

Asshole! Taylor stiffened, and then decided to do something that might really get his goat. She put a hand on Jack's knee, and leaned against his shoulder. She rubbed her cheek against the soft fabric of his expensive shirt.

Jack put his arm around her and dropped a kiss on the top of her head. "That's right. Forget about him. In another hour we can cut loose from here and go have that romantic dinner you were telling me about. They have the best grouper around?"

"Yes, but it is lobster season, and they'll definitely tempt you with that. Can't go wrong with either one." She grinned. "I've been going a little crazy on the stuff. Last week, Colt brought us about a dozen." She looked away, feeling a pang of regret. "Guess I won't be getting anymore."

"Have it tonight," Jack suggested. "We'll order two of the biggest and the best."

"Sounds good. We should start with a dozen raw oysters, and have either lobster or the Grouper Lorenzo.

It's rich though. Has a crab cake stacked on top and béarnaise sauce. To die for."

"We better have both and share plates. I know what I want for dessert."

She smiled and twisted around to look at him. "You do? You haven't even seen the selections yet."

"I've already selected mine." He waggled his brows and his eyes teased hers.

She gulped. "We better eat light in that case."

Just as the words left her mouth, she felt a presence behind her. She didn't have to turn her head to know it was Colt. She could feel his heat right through the back of her chair.

"Taylor. May I have a word with you?" he asked politely, not sounding like the Colt she knew so well.

"No, you may not. I'm busy right now, and you're lucky I'm not throwing you out."

"You want me to leave?" his voice was cold, angry and for some reason it sent a thrill down her spine. She wanted him mad. It made her happy, and she didn't have a clue why.

"Yes. No," she quickly corrected herself. "Stay and give Jamie something to eat." She turned around. "You haven't met Jack. Jack this is Colt Travis. Colt, this is Jack Warner. He's visiting from New York."

"Nice to meet you," Jack said offering his hand.

"Likewise," Colt replied, giving the hand a firm shake.

Very firm by the look that passed over Jack's face. He shook his hand after and laughed. "That's quite a shake you got there."

"My father always told me that it's a measure of a man."

"Your father was right," Jack answered. "So, where did you grow up?"

"Hamptons." Colt straightened his shoulders. "Can't seem to get away from the ocean."

"Nice place to grow up." Jack narrowed his gaze. "What did your dad do? Was he a fisherman too?"

Taylor knew Jack intended the remark as a putdown, yet Colt laughed. "Hardly. He owned an art gallery in the city."

"I didn't know you came from New York," Taylor said, her eyes widening in surprise. She gave him a long look, noting his attire for the first time. He was wearing a light blue shirt tucked into white shorts. He was attractive even in his ratty clothes, but this was a better look on him. Nice. "Is that a belt you're wearing?"

"Came with the shorts," he answered, his eyes still on Jack. "So when are you headed home?"

"That depends on Taylor," Jack answered. "We're catching up on old times. I can take a few more days. I haven't had a real holiday in the past couple of years."

"He works for his father's law firm," Taylor added, for no particular reason except to piss Colt off.

"I could have worked for my dad's art gallery, but this suits me better," Colt offered in response.

"How come you never told me about this stuff? You've never mentioned your dad." Taylor gazed at him, wanting to know more.

"He's dead. Nothing to tell."

Jamie came up and joined them. "Hi, Taylor." He put out a hand to Jack. "My name's Jamie."

"Jack Warner." He smiled at the boy. "Your mom didn't come with you tonight?"

"No. They're divorced." Jamie shrugged. "She's a nurse in the ER. Dates a doctor, but I don't like him much."

Taylor winced at the boy's statement. Though she'd lost her dad through death and not divorce, she remembered her mom dating, not always successfully, before Anna had found their step-dad. She reached out for his hand. "Jamie, did you get some of those deep fried fish bites? They're delicious with the cilantro lime sauce."

"No. They musta been all gone."

Taylor stood up. "I'll just run back to the house and bring out another platter," she said, ignoring Jack's head-shake. "Gotta take care of our guests," she said, looking at the two tables who were chatting together. Carole seemed more animated tonight, sitting with the men from the tournament.

"I'll help," Colt said, taking her elbow and leading her away.

When they were out of hearing distance he turned to her. "Alone at last."

She tore her elbow from his grip. "Why did you come tonight? When you didn't show last night I figured you'd got the message."

"What message is that?" His eyes were steady on hers.

He looked impossibly handsome all of a sudden. Clean-shaven, enticing cologne. A cocky smile on his face. New clothes that made him look different--like a man who wanted the same things she did. Someone who wasn't content to just drift along without a care in the world.

"You know." Her head snapped up. "You stepped out of line. I'm entitled to a life. Matter-of-fact, Jack and I are going to Lazy's tonight. It should be fun."

"Did you sleep with him today? I saw you go into Rhapsody together." His jaw clenched. "In the middle of the afternoon." He grabbed her arm and pulled her to a stop. "Tell me you didn't."

"It's none of your business. I won't answer your question because it's ridiculous. I was showing him to his cabin. He's staying tonight and possibly tomorrow."

"So you didn't?" His face relaxed and he let out a long breath. His eyes grew soft as they looked at her. "I could kiss you right now."

"You better not."

He did anyway. She stood rigid in his arms, not moving and not offering anything back. He didn't seem to notice, or if he did, he was determined to see how far he could go.

His hands ran up and down her bare arms. His mouth fit over hers, slanting one way then another, soft one moment, increasing the pressure the next. His lips were warm, moist, tasting sweet as honey. She willed herself not to feel anything. He was not the right man for her. She loved him like a brother. She wouldn't kiss her brother.

I'm not enjoying this, she told herself. Then before she could guard against it, his tongue slid her lips apart and he was in. The jolt of electricity shot right through her. It was like a lightning strike and yet the skies were clear.

She gasped in shock and frantically pushed him away.

"I've got to go. The fish bites." Then she dashed off, afraid that if she'd stayed another minute she would want to stay longer.

CHAPTER SEVEN

During dinner Jack had been his amusing self. She had listened to him talk about people they both once knew, and telling her antics about the fishing trip with Joey had cracked her up. He was the perfect companion, charming, knowledgeable, self-assured. They sucked back a dozen Oysters Moscow with horseradish sauce, topped with caviar. Two shots of iced Russian vodka had helped the oysters go down. Then came the fresh lobster dipped in lemon butter, and the grouper as well.

Stuffed to the gills, she leaned back in her chair and just looked at Jack and listened to him speak. He was a natural leader, a king among men. He was very adept at keeping a one-way conversation going as she attempted to do her part. Laughed at the right moment, asked the right questions, and stayed present.

Whatever was the matter with her, she wanted it to go away. She tried. She really did.

They sipped on their wine and watched the sunset in all its glory. The vivid hues had colored the sky like an artist's brush, then faded to pink and mauve swirls as the red-tinted sun settled over the ocean. A soft warm breeze stirred the air. It couldn't have been a more perfect setting. A more perfect night.

Yet, she couldn't shake the feeling that something was wrong. She was having the most wonderful dinner with this really great guy, but she had to force her laughter and work up a smile.

"Everything okay?"

"Yes." She sighed, misty-eyed. The sunset had moved her as it always did. It made her emotional, feeling vulnerable, a little out of control. It talked to her senses, and overruled her head. "It's the sunset. Gets me every time."

Jack nodded and reached across their chairs to squeeze her hand. "It's incredible. So beautiful."

She wasn't sure if he meant the sunset or her. Her emotions were all over the place, wanting this, wanting that. Right now she wanted him to kiss her--to know how his kiss would taste and feel.

Would it stir her like Colt's? Would it be as deliciously sweet, as enticing and exciting? She hadn't expected to like Colt's kisses quite so much. Oh, she knew they would be good, after all he'd had plenty of practice, but they were better than good. They were yummy, like a sweet, ripe peach. Decadent, and left you wanting more.

She'd done the right thing by running off like that. Imagine if she'd stayed? Why, anything could have happened, and then what would she have done with poor Jack?

Oh, why was she thinking of Colt right now? Jack had shown her a wonderful time. They'd had a lovely dinner, and he was looking at her like he'd enjoy kissing her too.

Guilt made her voice sweeter than ever. "It really is so good to be here with you tonight. Maybe we should get the tab, then go for a stroll down the beach. Or have a nightcap in your room. What do you think?"

He looked at her, his eyes lingering on her mouth. He stroked the stem of his wineglass, and she wondered how those hands would feel stroking her. "We could, but I have a feeling your mind might be elsewhere."

"Where else? I want to be with you." She bobbed her head up and down. "I really do." If she said it often enough, perhaps she could make it true.

"You sure about that?"

"Yes, I'm sure." She glanced away, and fiddled with the napkin in her lap. "I think."

He laughed. "You are delightful, you really are." He put his hand over hers. "Relax. Enjoy your glass of wine. What happens later will unfold the way it should. Don't try to plan it or think too much. Go with the flow."

Go with the flow. Easy for him to say. She was trying to embark on a journey she'd never taken before. A one-nighter with a guy she doubted she'd ever see again. Sex for the sake of sex. How unlike her!

She took a sip from her Chardonnay and put the glass down. "You're right. I always have to micromanage everything. That's just my style. I'm not exactly what one would call spontaneous. But I do know that I want you to kiss me."

"Lean over."

"Right here?"

"Sure. Why not?" He leaned across the table, and feeling kind of stupid she did the same. His lips brushed hers, but it wasn't a real kiss. Not the kind she was looking for.

"Thanks." She licked her lips, feeling a little deflated.

"You're welcome." His eyes lit up. "You finished with your dinner? You didn't eat much."

"I know. The oysters filled me up."

"No one can get full on oysters. No matter how they dress them up."

She tossed her long hair off her shoulders. "Too many fish bites then. I ate almost three."

"You shared them with me."

"So I did." She peeked at him. "They were good, weren't they?"

"Very good."

"Colt gave me the fish. It was yellowtail snapper."

"He's a good friend to have. How long has he been divorced?"

"I'm not sure. Not long. Less than a year, I think."

"You two date?"

"No!" She laughed. "He's got a slew of girlfriends, but no one special. Not looking either."

"That's too bad."

"Why? It's okay. He was married and it didn't work out. He's got his son, doesn't need a wife."

"I guess." His eyes never left her face, and she knew he could read her like a book. Everyone could. "What about you? No interest in tying the knot? Having a bunch of kids to cook for?"

"Eventually." Just the thought of it made her insides squeeze. She did want children. She loved Meri, and that little girl had shown her what she was missing. "No time for that right now. In a few years, perhaps."

"Don't wait too long or the time may never be right."

"Isn't that the church preaching to the choir?"

His lips curled. "Touché. But a man can have a child at any age. I could be fifty, sixty. Makes no difference."

"That sucks."

"Not for me."

She laughed. "And there is something so immeasurably wrong with that!"

They finished the rest of the wine, paid the bill and headed back to the cottages. It was such a beautiful night, and she didn't want to end it just yet.

When they reached her cabin, she glanced at Jack. "I really would love a walk on the beach. Will you join me?"

"Of course." They parked the car outside Rhapsody, kicked off their shoes, and headed for the shore. It was just half past eight, and the night sky was etched like a painting. Swirls of pink and mauve created a backdrop for the navy blue sea. A few stars had popped out in the sky, and there was still enough light to pick their way through the mangroves. The sand was soft and warm on their feet.

She took his hand and they walked along the water's edge. She could easily have walked for miles, but the silence grew between them. It was odd. Had it been Colt on this moonlight stroll, the banter would be easy. Yet, she wasn't sure what to say to Jack. Or he to her. Earlier today she'd made a decision to sleep with him, but now she found that difficult to believe.

"You okay?" he asked, sliding a hand around her waist and leading her back. "You got all quiet suddenly."

"Just thinking."

"You shouldn't do that." His hand dropped down to the curve of her ass. "It was a nice night. I want to make it even more special."

"Jack." She moved slightly away. "I don't think so."

He put his hands on her shoulder and pulled her toward him. She felt his chest against her own. His heart was beating fast. He was going to kiss her. And suddenly she didn't want it anymore.

"Kiss me, Taylor. Like you used to. It was good between us and can be again," he whispered, his mouth on her neck.

She squirmed, but he held her tighter. "Don't fight it. Just enjoy it."

"I'm not into this. I'm sorry," she whispered and tried to break free.

He didn't release her. "Come on, Taylor. Don't play hard to get. You knew where this evening was going to lead. We're not children anymore."

Before she could get her wits about her, his mouth claimed hers. She wrestled to get free, but he pulled her in closer.

“Trust me,” Jack said, his hand rough at her breast. “You want this.” His mouth hardened across hers, demanding compliance.

“No.” She became frantic, knowing now that she didn't want it at all.

He put his fingers in her hair at the back of her head, forcing her to accept his kiss. Jack was the kind of man who took what he wanted. But not this time.

She wrenched her mouth free and stomped on his foot, pushing him away. Then she took off down the beach. She heard his amused laughter, but she kept running. Her scalp tingled from where he'd pulled her hair and her stomach rolled. Scrubbing her lips with the back of her hand, Taylor reviewed her dinner with Jack as she ran. How had she missed such a character flaw? Or maybe she hadn't seen it because he rarely was told no.

Her footsteps slowed, so she could catch her breath. Taylor glanced back down the beach, seeing Jack moving toward her in the fading light. How far would he go to get his own way?

She wasn't sticking around to find out. Her breath hitched and she took off again. Suddenly, someone stepped out from the mangroves by the path leading to Paradise Cove, blocking her way. Tears blurred her vision, and she used her fists to beat against a masculine chest.

"It's all right, Taylor. It's me."

She stopped flailing and looked up, blowing hair from her eyes. "Colt! What are you doing here?"

"I dropped Jamie off with his mom and came back to see you." He gripped her loosely by the upper arms. "We have unfinished business."

"Oh, Colt! I'm so glad you're here."

She hugged him tight and turned as Jack joined them on the sand. Eyes mocking, he asked, "You okay, Taylor?"

"I am now." She clung to Colt. "I hope you'll be leaving first thing in the morning." Just looking at him made her sick. "Leave the key in the room."

"Whatever." Jack seemed as if he wanted to say more, but seeing the possessive way Colt held her, he backed off. "Your loss." With that he sauntered off.

"Did he do anything to you?" Colt asked in angry, low tones. "You want me to go after him?"

"No. He doesn't matter. Stay with me."

“Always." Colt folded her into his arms, and she wrapped herself around him, feeling safe and cared for. He kissed the top of her head. "Guess I don't have to ask how your evening went."

She laughed. Then tears spilled out. "He thought buying me dinner meant he could do anything he wanted. And I didn't want."

"I'm glad that you didn’t want to be with him." He caressed her cheek with the back of his hand, wiping away the tears. "I'm not going to say I told you so."

She smacked his arm, then smiled up at him. "You're such an ass."

"And that's all the appreciation I get?"

"You can get one more thing." She wrapped her arms around his back and lifted her face.

His eyes danced. "And what's that?"

"One more kiss. Just one. I want to enjoy it this time."

And, oh, she did. His mouth took hers sweetly, and he kissed her with gentle tenderness. Her emotions were close to the surface and she feared she might fall apart. Her ribs felt tight, as if her heart had swelled.

Colt rubbed her back, and stroked her as he would a child. It was a calming movement, not fraught with passion. She wasn't sure which one she wanted more. She knew which one was better for her, in the long run.

"I'm okay now. Walk me home?"

"If you're sure. Or we could sit here for awhile. The moon's just come out. I want to be with you. Hold you. Make sure you're all right."

"I am. Thanks to you." Oh, she was so tempted, but tonight had too many highs and lows and she didn't trust herself. Besides, she knew that with Colt she wouldn't be able to hold back, and that fragile heart of hers might just crack.

“You made the right choice. You should be with me instead.”

She understood his meaning and set him straight. "As much as we want to, we can't." Her voice hitched. "If we made love it would change things between us, and neither of us want that. We're such good friends, Colt. I think we should stay that way. Don't you?"

He glanced out to sea, his face equally as handsome to her as Jack’s, and didn't answer right away. "It's probably best. But is that what I want?” Colt looked at her, his blue eyes dark and shadowed in the moonlight. “No. I want the same thing Jack does. To do you everyway there is. I could get lost in you."

She swallowed hard, her body thrilling at the idea while her mind forced her to be realistic. "Then what?" Taylor removed her hand from his. "Like all the other girls, you'd leave me too?"

He had no answer to that, and with her heart aching, she slowly walked away. She’d had such high hopes for a night of passion only to end up alone.

CHAPTER EIGHT

The next morning Jack's car was gone and Taylor felt a sense of relief as she went into the cafe. She certainly did not want a guy like that, who thought he could buy anything or anyone he wanted. Heck, he probably thought he was doing her a favor. Relieving her boredom in this small island town. A dinner out, a hot night of sex. Lucky her.

Yes, well, lucky her that Colt had come along. What if he hadn't come back to check on her? Would Jack have forced the issue? She didn't think so, but she couldn't deny the fear in her body when he wouldn't let her go and forced his kiss.

Taylor found herself looking for Colt as she baked her muffins and croissants. With his admission that he wanted her physically, it was like Pandora's box had been opened. The things they said to each other couldn't be taken back. The thought of actually having sex with Colt had her insides doing cartwheels. She'd laid awake half the night thinking about it. She woke thinking of him with her pulse racing, her libido all worked up. She wanted him. She wanted to make a baby with him.

Oh, dear God in Heaven. Where had that thought come from?

Kayla called back an order, her engagement ring catching the light. “Two bacon quiche.”

Her sister, with her own bun in her oven, emanated happiness. Every day she grew more positive that this time she would carry the baby to full term. It had to happen. She was healthy and the doctors said there was no reason why she might lose this baby. She didn't need bed rest, just not to over do it.

Taylor would make sure that Kayla's work schedule was light. She could always hire a local woman to help wait tables in the busy months. Having this baby was crucial to her sister’s happiness. Kayla might not rebound from another disappointment. Taylor couldn't wait to be an aunt. If she was destined to be a spinster, at least she could spoil other people's children.

She plated the quiche and put everything on a tray for Kayla. The café had two of the four-person tables filled, and one of the two seaters. Two loners sat in the back outside area with their laptops. Where was Colt?

"Juanita. When did you first fall in love with Miguel? Did you know all at once, or did it build slowly?"

"Right away. We knew each other in school and he was my first real boyfriend."

"So, how long did you date?"

"We married as soon as we finished school." Juanita rinsed a mixing bowl and put it in the dishwasher. "He's a good man, and good to me."

"Yes. You both are very lucky." Taylor took the pan of chocolate almond croissants from the oven and left them on the counter to cool. She then added a tray of caramel apple breakfast pudding, which smelled so divine, nobody would be able to resist.

Juanita was no help in matters of *her* heart. Brittany might be a better confident for this sort of thing. Taylor knew that her sister would advise her to do exactly what she was thinking. To enjoy what Colt offered and take it a day at a time. It was the encouragement she needed--and the permission she wanted.

No guarantees, remember! That was Brittany to a T. She lived for the moment and with no regrets. It wasn't a bad view on life. It just wasn't her own.

She was living her dream right now too. Taylor's Cafe. The resort. Getting them both on financially solid ground. She had a three year plan. By then she'd only be thirty-three, and then she'd get serious about finding a husband and start having a houseful of kids.

Three years before she got serious, which meant doing Colt might not be a bad idea. She could have all the sex she wanted while they remained friends. Perfect.

"What are you smiling about?" Kayla asked as she and Juanita switched places. "Did your date with Jack go well?" Her hazel eyes glittered with excitement. "Will you be seeing him again? He's really something, isn't he?"

"Yeah, he's something all right." Taylor checked the timer. Five more minutes. "A real jerk!"

"What?" Kayla's mouth fell open. "Taylor, honey, what happened?"

"He came on kind of strong, and wasn't taking no for an answer. We were walking the beach, and I ended up stomping on his foot to get him to release me." She shivered at the memory.

"Oh, hon, that's awful. You poor thing. He is a jerk."

"I know. We had had a nice evening, and I thought I might sleep with him, but during the stroll I realized that I couldn't go through with it." She'd thought about each move they'd made over and over. "I didn't lead him on."

"I'm sure you didn't." Kayla rubbed Taylor's back. "He had no right to be forceful. You stepped on his foot?"

"It frightened me, and I just reacted. Anyway, I dashed off and when I got back to Paradise Cove, Colt was on the beach looking for me."

"I think I need a cup of coffee."

Taylor poured them both a cup as she surveyed the tables. Juanita was clearing two that had just emptied, which left two folks finishing their quiche and the people out back. How much of this story did she want to share?

"So tell me about Colt," Kayla encouraged, sitting at the small bistro table. "I knew he was jealous the other day. Did he say anything?"

Taylor took a sip of her coffee before answering. Kayla was the voice of reason, and as her older sister Taylor had always confided in her. Keeping her emotions a secret was not much of an option. Kayla knew when she was troubled and wouldn't stop digging until she could help.

"Colt admitted that he has a thing for me. Physically, at least. I'm attracted to him as well." She lowered her eyes, looking for answers in her dark roast. "But he doesn't do relationships. It's too soon after his divorce, and he's not ready for a second Mrs. Travis. Besides, I don't have time to get romantically involved with anyone, let alone get married." Taylor swept her gaze over the restaurant, avoiding her sister's sympathy. "So basically, I told him we should remain friends."

"Uh-huh. What did he say to that?"

"Said it was probably best, but I could tell he didn't mean it." Her throat closed.

"And what about you?" Kayla tugged at Taylor's shirt sleeve, demanding her attention. "Do you want to sleep with him?"

Taylor, seeing that Juanita had everything under control, sank into the chair opposite her sister. "Yes, and no. I'm afraid, Kayla." She looked into her sister's eyes, hoping the answer would be there. "Do you think I could handle a casual affair, or would I wind up with a broken, bleeding heart?"

Her sister wrapped both hands around her mug, maintaining eye contact. "That's a difficult question that only you can answer."

"Oh, Kayla, I just don't know. I'm very tempted. Couldn't sleep last night thinking about it. I haven't been with anyone since I moved here." She blew out a frustrated breath. "It's been over eighteen months. I really want to be with him. And he with me. It's more than just physical attraction. We really like each other."

Kayla sighed. "I know you do, and that's half the problem." She reached out a hand and squeezed Taylor's. "I like Colt a lot too. But unless he's ready to commit to you, I'd stay away. You aren't built that way. You're a very passionate woman, the kind that will probably only truly love one man in her life. Don't rush anything. Your time will come. Just wait."

Taylor looked down at their joined hands. She knew Kayla was probably right. She was the most sensible woman she knew. But still she wished just for once, that she could be wrong. It was why she'd wanted to talk with Juanita and Brittany instead—she and Kayla were the most alike.

"So I can't have Colt? Not even a little bit?"

Juanita pushed her way through the beaded door. "Why don't we all have a chocolate almond croissant instead?"

"Juanita? Have you been listening?"

"I couldn't help but hear." She put her hands on Taylor's shoulders, and kneaded them to soothe her stress. "Colt is a good man. Like my Miguel. Do what your heart tells you."

Tears blurred Taylor's vision but she swiped them away. "My heart is not speaking, and my stomach is churning."

"Everything will turn out as it should. Warm chocolate croissants will help you feel better. Just wait and see." She put a tray in the center of the small table. "Eat up now. You drink too much coffee."

"I like coffee," Taylor retorted, but too tired to argue she picked up the croissant. Sinking her teeth into the rich chocolate center, Taylor had to agree. There was nothing like a little chocolate to make a woman feel better.

Before she had a chance to finish the delicious pastry two couples entered and she returned to work. For the next few hours the three women were kept busy, and Taylor was happy for the distraction.

There was a lull between the breakfast hours and lunch, but it quickly picked up again. Taylor had made crab quiche with Gruyere cheese which was selling well, and flatbreads with various toppings. She had an assortment of wraps and salads, and a large pot of clam chowder. Plus her best-selling luncheon special offered quiche and a side salad, or a cup of soup and half a sandwich.

The afternoon flew by—with no sign of Colt—and then Anna came in with Meri. They all took turns giving her hugs and kisses, and the little girl's bright smile and happy giggles warmed the cafe.

After Juanita and Meri left, Taylor saw the longing on Kayla's face, hoping she didn't wear that same look. "She's a sweetheart, isn't she?"

"Too precious for words. I love her to death," Kayla said, putting a hand to her heart.

"Me too." Taylor nodded with understanding. "I want a dozen just like her."

"Oh, Tay, I so hope I can too," Kayla said with a catch in her voice.

"You will. The one you are carrying will be just as precious, I'm sure."

"To God's ears," she replied.

Anna had heard the brief exchange, and sent her a sympathetic glance. They didn't say anything more on the subject, not wanting to jinx their luck.

"What time is Sean getting home tonight?" Taylor asked. "You need to take half the leftovers home for him. Save you from cooking. You've been working all day."

"It's not hard work. Not like the weeding I used to do before Miguel took over." Kayla made a face. "Or prepping the cabins for the paint job. Now that was hard work. Waiting on tables? A piece of cake."

"Still, we need to divide this up every night. Mom and I can't eat it all, and Juanita takes all the food her fridge can handle. I would hate to throw it out."

"I know, but I have a wedding dress that I need to fit into one month from now. So I'll take home lean leftovers. And the soup for Sean. He loves clam chowder." She yawned. "Sean might like one of the quiches too. I am feeling a little tired."

"I'm just about finished packing up your food," Taylor said, working quickly, "then you can go home and rest. You want to be lively when your fiancé returns from saving lives all day."

She laughed. "I am so proud of him. How did I ever get so lucky?"

"He's lucky too. You saved him, Kayla. You really did."

"Oh, Taylor, I think I gave you bad advice earlier today." Kayla put her arm around Taylor's waist. "Remember when Sean first came to stay? I knew he was hurting and that he didn't want me, or anyone, bothering him. He just wanted to be alone to grieve. But I couldn't let him hurt like that. I refused to leave him alone. I was afraid for him. His heart was broken beyond repair, but there was a spark between us, and slowly he responded to my nurturing. He opened up a little more each day."

"I know." Taylor found a quart size plastic container and filled it with the chunky clam chowder soup. "But if you're relating this to Colt, it's completely different. He didn't suffer a tragedy. I mean, I know his wife had an affair but I don't think it destroyed him or anything."

"Maybe there is something else in his past. Some hurt that holds him captive. I could be wrong but I do feel as if the endless parade of girls is a telltale sign. He doesn't want to let anyone in. He's afraid to love."

Anna sighed. "I agree with Kayla. Something's holding him back."

"That doesn't help me much." Taylor grabbed her water bottle and gulped half of it down. She knew her mom and sister wanted to help, but really, they were way off base here. Colt didn't love her the way Sean did Kayla. He might not even be capable of that much love.

"That something is the fact he's enjoying his freedom. For now. Maybe one day he'll remarry, but Jamie is still hurting over the divorce. It wouldn't be fair to him."

Kayla considered this, then she shook her head. "I agree about Jamie, but I still believe that Colt is holding back emotionally. You just have to break through his guard one day at a time. Show him that loving you is worth it."

"How do I do that?"

"By just being you. Open your heart to him and see what happens. I took the plunge, and I couldn't be happier."

"You and Sean are completely compatible. Perfect for each other. Colt and I are very different. I'm driven. He's not."

"Then find out why," Kayla suggested. "He's hard working and is always helping us out here, without being asked."

"He's certainly not lazy," her mom put in, helping Taylor sort the remainder of the food. "And I must say he cleaned up very nice last night for happy hour."

"If it bothers you, make a point to find out why he doesn't push his charter business more." Kayla started stacking the containers to take home, and put them next to the door. "He doesn't even have a website. He's moored here instead of one of the bigger marinas. I thought it was because of you."

"He was here before he even met me," Taylor answered.

"Well then, dig a little under the surface and see what's holding him back."

"Not sure if he'll talk to me. You know Colt. Likes to keep things light."

"So do you, Taylor." Anna found a large brown bag to put Kayla's food in, then left to put it in her car.

"I know you're both trying to help," Taylor said, "but really, it's okay how things stand. I don't want to be digging around, pulling out old family secrets." Still she did wonder what he was hiding. She'd had no idea he was from New York, or that his family had an art gallery. Why would he keep that information secret?

"Depends how much you want it, I suppose."

Taylor thought of the way he'd kissed her last night, and how much she wanted that again. She did want him, but how much was she willing to fight for it?

"If I keep after Colt the way you did Sean, well, he'd probably never speak to me again."

"Well, then you have your answer. You'll know he's not worthy of you." Kayla smiled with reassurance. "But you have a lot more to gain by taking a chance."

CHAPTER NINE

Colt was up early, the crack of dawn. He was taking the three men from the Panhandle out fishing at seven, but he got to the marina early, while it was still dark. Had a lousy night anyway. Couldn't sleep. He kept thinking about Jack and Taylor and how things might have shaped up if he hadn't gone down to the beach on a hunch. The idea of them together had plagued him all evening, and he knew they were out for dinner. He'd walked by Rhapsody several times. No lights were on, and no sounds were coming from the bedroom. He knew because he had shamelessly listened. If that was to be their love nest, he damn well had to intervene somehow.

Instinct had taken him to the beach. He knew Taylor was a Pisces and how the moon and the water could influence her moods. If she was conflicted at all about whether or not she should go to bed with Jack, she'd head for the beach to search her soul. He'd seen her wandering the beach at night many times, always when she was troubled.

Luckily she did last night too--she'd been so fragile when he'd held her in his arms. What had that asshole done or said to her to shake her up so bad? A part of him was glad that Jack had shown his true colors. Might make her think twice about going out with someone else. On the other hand, he felt sorry for her.

Taylor worked hard, day in and day out, and didn't have any stress release. No one to hold her in his arms, to kiss her and make her feel better. She didn't go out drinking or dancing or dining. She spent every night with her mother and entertaining their guests, before retiring alone to bed. He knew. He'd kept tabs on her over the past year.

Had she been dating, he'd have played his cards. Swept right in, and taken her away from any asshole who tried. He'd have been successful too. She had a soft spot for him, and if he was truly a heartless jerk, he'd milk it for all it was worth. But where would that get him?

In deep shit. He couldn't do it to her, or himself.

There was something about Taylor that made her different from every other girl. She was special. Incredibly beautiful inside and out. He'd never known such a pure, good-hearted person.

Perhaps it was his fault. Ever since he'd discovered the truth about his father, he had a hard time trusting anyone. He listened to people's words, their actions, and didn't take any of it at face value. How did he know if they were being honest, or feeding him a line of bullshit? Every girl he met, every guy he could have become friends with, he kept at bay. At the age of sixteen, he'd become skeptical, cautious, a cynic. If his own father could have fooled him and his own family for all those years, how could he possibly trust a stranger?

The scandal after his father's death had shaped his life. He didn't regret it. Matter-of-fact, he was grateful that his eyes had been opened, and his youthful innocence stripped away. He'd be nobody's fool.

And yet when it came to Taylor, he was a fool. He wanted her, but couldn't have her. What kind of man was satisfied with friendship from a woman like that? If he was gay, sure, they could hang out and have some laughs together, but every day it was getting harder to be around her without touching her.

He let her push him away last night, because she was right. He didn't want a relationship or another wife. He'd made an error in judgment once, trusting Sharon, thinking that she was different too. Only to find out years later that she'd wanted a better life, a material world, more than she wanted him.

Taylor might not be like that, but how could he be sure? She worked hard, too hard, and something drove her. If it wasn't money, then what was it?

Colt had the engines on the Hatteras running when his crew showed up. He'd asked them to stop and buy the food for the charter this morning. There was a market that catered to the charters and stayed open all night. Colby and Cody, his regular mates, picked up sandwiches for everyone and a bucket of fried chicken.

He took the packages of food out of their hands as they jumped on board.

"Hey, boss," Cody said. "What time did you get here this morning?"

"'Bout an hour ago." He nodded hello. They were in their mid-twenties and had lived in the Keys their whole lives. Fishing was all they knew, and besides girls, all they wanted to know.

"You guys get any sleep?" The two young men had a way with the women, and got more action than he did.

"Not much," one answered. "New girl in town. Didn't want to miss my turn."

Colt laughed. As men outnumbered the women by far, the saying in town was that you didn't lose a girl, you just lost your turn dating her.

"Want some coffee?" He gestured to the inside of the cabin where a percolator brewed.

Colby rubbed his trim abdomen. "Naw. I'll stick to my Red Bull."

"Did you see three men hanging around out there? They can't miss the boat. It's the only one this size here." Colt drank from his coffee mug.

Cody pointed to the far end of the dock. "I think I hear them now." Colby jumped off the boat to greet them.

If the marina hadn't bordered on Paradise Cove cottages he wouldn't have any business during the slow summer. But they always directed their guests to him, so he had that steady income--small as it may be.

"Good morning," he shouted out as the men neared. "We're ready for you. Come aboard." Colt offered his hand as they stepped off the pier and onto his boat. He knew their names, Ken, Martin, and Jerry, but wasn't sure who was who.

"Morning, Colt." They shook his hand and introduced themselves to the crew, and accepted the offer of coffee.

They were avid fishermen, and wanted to fish for dolphin—the fish, not the mammal. They'd leave the marina at seven sharp, and were booked for four hours.

Once they set out to sea Colby and Cody put on some music. The upbeat sound blared from the indoor speakers as they sprinted to the popular fishing spot near the reefs. The two young mates boogied to the music as the boat tore up the waves.

Martin was hanging on tight to the side of the boat, and Jerry and Ken were seated in the fly bridge with Colt.

"You been doing this awhile?" Jerry asked, making easy conversation.

"I've lived here fifteen years. Had my fishing license all that time, but got my own boat and a captain license about ten years back."

He cut the engine as they neared the reefs, and watched as Cody and Colby got the reels in place and captured the live bait from along the blue edge of water. As the muck from the bottom lifted, the water turned green, making it difficult to see the patches of bait fish.

The two men climbed down and took their reels, and within a short time Colby shouted, "line three," and the action started. Within the next two hours the men had caught their legal limit of ten apiece. They weighed about two to three pounds each, but were good eating fish. His clients were happy, knocking back a few iced cold beers as the two mates drank their Red Bulls and took selfies.

After Colt dropped the guys back at the dock, he saw Carole down at the beach. She was in her snorkeling gear and making her way into the water. He waved and called out to her. "Hey, Carole. Come on board. You want to snorkel, I know better spots than this."

"Really?" She splashed out of the water, and sat down in the sand to take off her flippers. Then dangling them at her side she ran up the pier. "Do I need anything? I could run back to the cabin. It wouldn't take long."

"You can if you want to, but I have lots of sunscreen and you can borrow a t-shirt and a hat of mine."

"Awesome. This is so kind of you, Colt."

Her light blue eyes gazed up at him and she wore a big smile. In the two weeks he'd known her, he'd rarely seen her happy and the smile transformed her from plain to pretty.

He took her face mask off the top of her head, careful not to get it tangled in her long brown hair. Then he directed her into the cabin. "My berth is in the front. Help yourself to a tee and a cap, while I turn this boat around."

"This is so cool. Can't believe you're doing this. I could pay you, of course," she added hastily as an afterthought.

"Of course not. I'm inviting you out for an hour or two. No big deal. And we have sandwiches left over from the guys this morning. So lunch is on them."

"Even better."

When she returned to the aft of the boat, he was on the bridge and called down to her. "Come on up."

When she did, he noticed the light blue t-shirt she'd chosen with the big sailfish in the middle. It was loose and fell down to the middle of her thighs. Under it she had a conservative black one piece, but the woman was much too thin, her hip bones protruded and her legs looked like twigs. Standing next to him, she barely came to his shoulder. She must have been about five two or three, and a hundred pounds, if that.

He couldn't help but think of Taylor who was close to his own height of five eleven. Her mouth reached his chin. He barely needed to dip his head to taste those luscious lips of hers. But he could forget about kissing her. Wasn't going to happen again. Not unless he totally lost his senses, anyhow.

"The top's a bit big, but it'll keep the wind and the sun off of you." He squinted behind his glasses. "There's some beer and cold drinks in the cooler. Help yourself."

"You want a beer?" she asked.

"No, thanks. Not yet. Toss me a Coke."

She pulled out two, and popped his lid. "Here." She toasted him with her diet soda. "Cheers."

"This snorkeling area is one of the best in the Keys," he told her. "Matecumbe has better reefs than either Key West or Key Largo. Their reefs might be better known but they're not nearly as spectacular. That's a fact. And ours can only be reached by boat. We have a lot of tours during prime season."

"Great. My own private boat tour." She flashed him a look. "How did I get so lucky?"

"You're an important guest of Anna's, and I can't let you spend your vacation snorkeling around the pier. The water's murky there. Wait until you see the spot I'm taking you. Crystal clear, with coral and fish."

"How can you tell where you are out here? Doesn't it all look the same?" She grabbed a bottle of sunscreen and started rubbing it on her arms and legs. The scent of the lotion always reminded him of summer days on the beach growing up. The salt air and the clean scent of the Hamptons.

He shook off the memory. "I know the area well, and we have navigational maps and systems on board. I don't usually refer to it, but it's there if I need it." He turned the wheel to the left. "We're heading for my favorite spot. There's several little patch reefs half-way between the key and the outer barrier reef edge but it can have a lot of algae and not be all that clear. So if you don't mind we'll head out further."

She nodded as if she understood, and let him just take the lead.

"It's called the Alligator Reef Lighthouse, and actually has a tall lighthouse structure. It's fairly shallow, but you're going to love it. There are purple sea fans, and sponges, but no coral. We'd see the coral at the other reefs but it's too murky today."

"How come it won't be murky where we're going?"

"The distance from shore. The water is blue instead of green. That means the visibility will be excellent, and we'll see a wider selection of fish. They seem to like the shade of the lighthouse."

"Where does the alligator come in?" she asked.

"It was the name of a ship that sunk here in the 1800's. You'll see a mound of stones which is all that's left from the ship. It's really something."

"Anything to be afraid of?"

"That depends. There's a deeper area on the left of the lighthouse and you'll see plenty of barracudas."

"No thank you." She shivered. "What about sharks?"

"Well, we are in the ocean, but they have other things to feed on besides you."

"Oh! Well, I sure hope they know that."

He laughed. "We'll hang a sign around your neck."

"No. Seriously." Her eyes widened. "I don't want to be shark bait. I don't even like sharks."

"Trust me. They prefer more meat on their bones."

"Ouch." She stuck out her pointed chin. "That hurt."

He touched her rib. "Not too much, I hope."

She moved a little closer, and he realized that his intentions might be misconstrued. He stepped away to release the anchor, and knew he'd better tone it down a notch. He was so used to flirting, he didn't even know when he was.

"I'll grab my snorkeling gear too and show you around. I won't let anything bad happen to you."

She donned her gear while waiting for him, and then he lowered the ladder, and they both jumped in. He waited to see how experienced she was, and when he could see that she knew what she was doing he indicated that they were going under to see the fish up close.

She followed him down, her eyes wide as saucers, then she shot up for air. She blew the water out of her snorkel and removed it from her mouth so she could speak. "My God, it is incredible. The colors are amazing. The pretty yellow striped fish, and some are so blue it takes my breath away. And pink, and oh my! I'm gushing, but there's so many different species of fish I feel like I'm in an aquarium." She grinned. "Thank you for this."

"You're very welcome. And I'm pleased to see that you're an accomplished swimmer and snorkeler. Want to go again?"

In answer, she led the dive. He loaned her an underwater camera and for the next half hour her fears were forgotten. Behind a wall of pinkish sea sponge, she snapped pictures as fish flashed before her eyes. A sunken boat was home to a school of parrot fish, and he pointed out a sea turtle the size of a round table swimming an arm's length away. A barracuda with snaggle-teeth came around a coral reef and her eyes widened behind the clear snorkel mask before she dropped the camera and swam for the surface.

Chuckling to himself, Colt retrieved the camera from the sandy ocean floor and then popped up beside her.

"Oh, my God! What was that thing? It was huge!"

"A barracuda. They can be pretty ugly." They swam back to the boat, and he helped her up.

"Are they dangerous?"

"Not usually. They prefer fish to humans."

She shivered. "Sorry I dropped the camera, but it just about gave me a heart attack."

He laughed and handed her a clean towel from the supply he kept on board. "You'll be a big hit at happy hour tonight. Wait 'til they see your pictures."

"Will you come?" She wrapped the towel around her thin body. "I haven't seen you in days."

So, Taylor hadn't been talking to anybody about why he wasn't welcome? He shook the water from his hair, letting the sun dry his skin. "No. I won't be able to make it tonight—I've got to pick up my son from his mother's."

"Oh. That's too bad." She glanced at him with speculative interest before patting at her damp swimsuit.

Was that disappointment? His flirtatious nature sometimes sent the wrong message, so he tried to set the record straight without offending her.

"I may have overstayed my welcome the other night." He referred to the last time he was there, when Taylor had not been happy to see him. He didn't mention the way he'd sneaked Taylor away from her guests for a stolen kiss, or how he'd had to save her from a jackass who thought his money could buy anything or anybody he wanted. Nor did he bring up the fact that she'd left him on the beach because he had nothing of substance to offer her. "Thought I'd give Taylor some space," he said in explanation.

Carole leaned over to dry her foot, showing off her long legs. "I doubt she'd want that."

"She knows my number if she doesn't." Colt put an end to the conversation by lifting the anchor and turning on the engine. "There are sandwiches in the fridge. Help yourself. Should take about a half hour to get back."

She nodded, understanding in her eyes. "Sounds good. Thanks."

The last thing he needed was another complication. Letting Carole know his interest was elsewhere was the kindest thing he could do, though he empathized with her. Going through a divorce wasn't easy.

He liked to think of himself as a nice guy, yet disappointing women seemed to be his fatal flaw.

She came to the end of the shots. "There's only fish on here." Taylor lifted the camera, relief warring with confusion. "Didn't Colt dive with you?"

"He did, but I accidentally deleted a couple of pictures."

Taylor swallowed a lump in her throat. What had she deleted? And why? Had he done something she didn't want to show?

Carole pointed to a picture of a giant fish with blue and yellow coloring. "Do you know what that is?"

"Haven't a clue." Had Carole erased an underwater picture of her with Colt? Her stomach clenched and throat felt tight. "I don't fish."

"It's a French angelfish. See that barracuda, behind it? Darn thing swished right by me, and scared me half to death. I dropped the camera and Colt dove back down for it. He's quite a guy, isn't he?" Her astute gaze took in Taylor's flushed face.

"Oh, he's something, all right!" Taylor heard the rising tones in her voice and breathed deep in order to calm down. He and Carole hadn't done anything wrong. Why didn't she believe that? "He's not planning on coming here tonight, is he?"

"No." Carole shook her head. "He said he had to pick up his son."

Good! Taylor knew she couldn't face him tonight. She might accuse him unjustly and say things that couldn't be undone. She had always trusted him before, what had changed that? Carole's obvious admiration? The way Jack behaved? Or the fact Colt had given up on her so easily?

Either way, he wasn't welcome here. Not tonight, and not for some time. And if it meant that she'd be sending him into some other woman's bed, so be it. Oh, but she didn't mean that. She couldn't bear the thought of Colt naked, loving another woman.

"Oh, here's one of us on the fly bridge," Carole said, showing a picture of herself with her arm around Colt's back, smiling into the camera.

"Nice." Taylor's nails bit into the palms of her hands. "Is that his shirt?" she asked. What was Carole wearing underneath that big, long tee? Anything?

"Hmm. It is. We had such a fun afternoon." Then she laughed and poked Taylor on the shoulder. "Oh, Taylor, you really should see your face. You wear your heart on your sleeve. In this case, on your face."

"My heart's got nothing to do with it," she snapped. "God, sorry." It wasn't Carole's fault that she was a mess over Colt. "You should be enjoying yourself while you're here."

"I am, and I should apologize to you. It's obvious you care about him, and he about you." She sighed and touched Taylor's arm. "When I asked if he was coming here tonight, he said he'd worn out his welcome. That he wanted to give you some space."

"He said that?" She looked into Carole's sincere blue eyes. "Will you be seeing him again?"

"Not unless I run into him in town. To be honest, I wanted to know if you cared." She gave Taylor a hug. "You do. Good luck. He's worth it."

In her heart she knew Carole was right, but she also knew that Colt had some issues to work out before he was ready to commit again. "He might be in the long run," she agreed. "As you know, divorce can do a head trip on anybody, and I think he's still figuring some things out." Taylor grinned at her. "Let me grab us a fresh drink then we can talk some more. Sorry if I sounded like a shrew."

"You didn't!"

Taylor returned with two full glasses of iced sangria and a plate of nachos. Sitting next to Carole, she said, "You know that job offer is still open. We will be hiring this winter so if you get back home and find your situation has changed, please give us a call."

"I will. I promise." Carole sipped on her tall glass of fruity wine. "I see why you love it. It's super hot this time of the year, but there's always a nice breeze by the shore. And your mom said that you learn to adapt. Stay inside with the air conditioning during the mid-day--if you can--and don't go anywhere without your 50 plus sunscreen. Right now it's perfect. I hear waves breaking on the shore, and palm trees swaying in the breeze. To watch the sun set each night over the ocean? It's tempting, I must admit."

"Stay as long as you like. The cottages aren't booked until next month, and that's only for a week. Kayla's wedding. All the out-of-towners will be staying with us, or at the Islander resort. Mostly Sean's guests will be there. The hotel is much bigger than we are, and the property is gorgeous. Have a great restaurant too."

"So do you." Carole took a nacho chip, balancing a sliced black olive. "And bigger doesn't always mean better. I love your cottages—they're sweet." She held up her sangria glass as if featuring the treats. "I bet they don't have happy hours like this. Free drinks and wonderful appetizers every night." She sipped. "I feel half-looped already."

"Eat more," Taylor answered with a nod at the loaded chip. "A day in the sun can make you light-headed."

Especially when spent with a fun, gorgeous guy named Colt. She kept that thought to herself, wishing she didn't think of him quite so often. She really did need a boyfriend--if only to get Colt out of her head.

* * *

Colt walked by Taylor's Cafe each day as he parked his truck next door. He avoided looking into the window, as one sight of Taylor might weaken his resolve. The dirt parking lot was usually full, a sure sign her business was doing well. She didn't need him. Taylor was living her dream--a steady stream of customers, a combination of locals and visitors to the area.

When he cut through her property to reach the marina he noticed that her outdoor deck was busy too. Miguel had included a long high-top table against the main wall where folks could plug in their devices and work while seated on wicker stools.

This morning he kept his head low, his hands in his pockets as he walked past the covered area. The sky was dark with thunder clouds, and Colt had no plans to be on the water. With Jamie and Raul at baseball practice, he'd use the free time to do a maintenance check on the Hatteras.

Colt didn't see Taylor until he heard her laugh, then he looked up, his gaze zeroing in on her chatting with someone he didn't recognize. Not a local—the dude was dressed too well for that. Nice shorts, a Tommy Bahamas short-sleeved shirt, with light brown hair trimmed around his ears. Not Jack. Another guy just passing through.

The stranger was on his laptop, drinking her coffee, and smiling at her like she was really something. Well, she was. They had that much in common. Difference was, Taylor had stopped smiling Colt's way.

Taylor handed the guy a plate of something that smelled delicious--eggs, sausage and onion—better than his own burned bagel he'd had for breakfast, that's for sure. He missed her breakfasts. And her lunches. Especially her happy hours. He missed her smiles, the sound of her laughter, the pretty crinkles around her eyes when she squinted up at him. He missed teasing her and seeing her blush.

Dammit, if she wasn't blushing right now! That meant only one thing. This city guy, whoever he was, must be flirting with her. Colt's ears fired up with jealous heat. The tightness in his chest had nothing to do with a clogged artery.

He unclenched his fingers, wanting to put a fist into the guys' face, even though they'd never met. What was wrong with him these days? He was not a violent man. He was a peace-loving, easy-going son-of-a-bitch who wanted the one girl he couldn't have.

His boat shoes scuffed the gravel as he stopped moving, staring at her. The bob of her ponytail down her back, the peep of calf below her sundress. She looked up.

Saw him standing there like an idiot. She froze too. Then she did something totally unexpected--Taylor walked over to him with a warm smile that got his heart pumping big time.

"Hi Colt. You haven't been around lately. I've missed you and Jamie. How's he doing?"

"Uh. Fine." Was this a trick? Was he dreaming? "He's got a sailfish tournament coming up in a couple of weeks. Pretty excited about that. And school starts the following Monday."

"Good for him. He's probably ready to get back. Summers around here can be a little long." She looked at him with dark brown eyes that could sparkle like diamonds one minute, or flash with warning the next. She was mellow and nice most of the time, but she could be fiery as hell too.

Today her eyes were welcoming, and brightened the gloomy day. She wore a pretty flowered sundress in a pale blue that left her lovely arms bare, and hugged her curves just right.

He wanted to hug her curves just right.

"So," she tilted her head as she looked at him. "What have you been up to? You know that Carole and her mother are leaving this Sunday?"

"No. I didn't know." He shifted his feet, wondering if she was mad at him for taking Carole snorkeling. Couldn't figure the woman out. Any woman for that matter.

"It might be nice for you to drop in before she leaves. She enjoyed the reef and got some great pictures."

Taylor's small white teeth flashed in her tanned face. "Thanks for taking her out."

"No problem." That was more like it. He'd done something nice for one of her guests and she wasn't going to give him shit for it.

"Why don't you come around tonight or tomorrow? Happy hour. Bring Jamie. We miss him too."

What did she mean by too? Did that include him in that too? Had to, right?

His hopes grew and he lifted his eyes to hers. "Sounds good. Want some fresh fish? You haven't had any from me lately."

"That would be nice. Not necessary. But if you have some, great." She looked up at the sky. "You're not going out today, I hope. Weather looks nasty."

"I wouldn't give you day-old fish."

"Then forget it today. Next time you go out, drop one off."

Ah. Next time. Things were definitely looking up. "Will do." He grinned, and ran a hand through his shaggy blond hair. Maybe it was time to get it cut. Around the ears like that other guy.

"How's your mom?" he asked for no reason except to prolong the conversation.

"Good. Getting excited about the wedding. It's in three weeks you know."

"Really? That soon."

"Yup. September 14th. You're coming, aren't you?"

"Wouldn't miss it for the world."

"Miguel has some special plans for staging the wedding. He wants to go over them with us this weekend."

"Now he's a wedding planner?" Colt joked. "A jack of all trades."

"Don't mention that name to me," she said with a pretend shudder. "Still haven't thanked you properly for being around that night."

"Sure you did. Unless you have a more special thank you in mind," he said with a teasing wink.

She laughed. "You wish."

"I do." And yet he'd been right on the beach the other night. He didn't have jack shit to offer her.

Her smile faded. "Yeah. We should talk about that sometime."

"Why bother?" he asked, ignoring the sheer misery he'd been suffering without her the past few days. "Just let me know if you change your mind."

"Sure." She tilted her head. "And you let me know if you ever get tired of one-night stands."

Touche! Strike one for Taylor. He stuck his hands in his front pockets. She was an amazing woman—a dynamite combination of wit and compassion. *What if I am pushing away the chance at something great, just because the timing isn't right?* "How about tonight?" he countered.

"Didn't Carole see you in Lorelei's the other night? Buxom blonde clinging to your arm. Ring any bells?"

God. She had spies everywhere. Explaining the blonde wouldn't help, so he shrugged. "That was the other night. In the past."

"And today is the future?" She tapped her sneakered toe.

"Future has to start sometime, doesn't it? Beginning precisely at 4 o'clock PM. Set your watch by it."

“I don’t know what you mean.” She gestured toward the back patio. "Got to get back to work. Enjoy the present Colt. It's all we've got."

He winked. "Will do." He strolled away with just one quick backward glance. She was talking to that guy again. But it didn't matter. The stranger would be leaving soon, and Colt had a new future that looked much brighter.

CHAPTER ELEVEN

Colt was particular about the maintenance on his Hatteras. He had a lot of money invested and wanted to get a good many years out of the boat. He'd just had a full vessel assessment at Islamorada Marine. All systems and components were checked and replaced when needed, but to keep the costs down, he preferred to do most of the work himself. Once every few months, he'd wash down the boat exterior, and inspect it for oxidation, cracks and blisters. He used Collinite's marine wax for a protective finish. The interior required weekly maintenance to keep it spotless for his paying guests. All surfaces had to be washed down and treated. That included the upholstery, the vinyl, aluminum and plastic throughout the entire boat.

A stormy day was perfect for interior work, and strangely he looked forward to such days. He'd plug in some good music and scrub, polish and wax every surface until it shined. Toilets and showers gleamed too. Best of all, between singing and scrubbing, thoughts of Taylor were at a minimum.

He didn't have to pick up Jamie and Raul until three. There had been an end of season picnic scheduled after their game today—because of the inclement weather, the kids would be at the Fish Bowl, which had an arcade to go with nine bowling lanes and pizza.

The party was just breaking up when he arrived, hot, dirty, smelling like lemon-foaming bathroom cleaner. He had hoped to finish in time to dash home and clean up, but the work had taken him longer than expected.

One mom spotted him the moment he found his group of little leaguers, and made a beeline for him. He still had one hour of present left in him so he gave her a smile, and a half-hearted hug.

Meghan Carter sniffed and wrinkled her tiny upturned nose. "Eeuhh! What did you do today? Don't tell me." She sniffed his neck. "You smell like body odor and Clorox. Rubbing down 'Bait me' again? I keep telling you there's something better you could rub down." Meghan gave him a sly smile. "You know how my man's always out of town." Batting her thickly lacquered eye lashes, she said, "Three months this time. And you haven't come around lately."

Jerry Carter was a private boat captain. Made a lot of bucks, had a big house and a wife who didn't sit around waiting. Guy was a cuckold, or just didn't give a damn, Colt figured. Perhaps he'd taken the job to get away from Meghan--hell if he knew what her husband was thinking.

Meghan was nice enough and probably deserved better. She was pretty in a too-bleached, overdone way. The kind of woman who tried too hard. Colt had serviced her a few times over the past year, but he didn't like dicking another captain's lady. And he liked his ladies with a little more class.

Or lady, in particular. Taylor. If he had any sense at all he'd take Meghan up on what she was offering, and have his own "happy hour" with her. But he'd told Taylor that he was going to reform. He didn't want to let her down, anymore than himself.

"Hey, Dad. Whatcha doing?" Jamie grabbed him by the hand and began to pull him away. He didn't like his dad talking to anyone other than Taylor. He was kind of sweet on her too.

He ruffled Jamie's curly blond hair. "I was looking for you—Meghan was pointing me in the right direction. How was your day?"

"Good. Great. Had fun. Got a strike too." Jamie grinned and dropped his head. "Three actually."

"That's my boy." He winked at him. "You're a natural born athlete. Proud of you, son. Where's Raul? Is he here with you?"

"No. His dad picked him up an hour ago." He sniffed. "How come you smell so bad?"

"Worked on the boat." He swung an arm around Jamie's shoulder and started walking him to the door. "You got anything you need to pick up before we leave?"

"Just some end of the year prizes. Coach Thomas has the stuff."

Colt looked toward the coach and waved. "Well, you go on over and tell Coach I'm taking you home—and thanks. I'll bring the car around. It's raining hard."

"Okay, Dad. We going home now?"

"Yup. Time to get cleaned up. Taylor invited us to happy hour. What do you say? Should we go or wait until tomorrow when the sky should be clear?"

"Dunno." Jamie looked up at him. "Did you tell her we'd come?"

"Pretty sure I did."

"Then we better go. Beside, it'll be at the cafe instead of the pool. I like the sound the tin roof makes when it's raining. It's cool."

"You're pretty cool too." He noticed Meghan had moved on, and was glad he didn't have to extend his courtesy any further. He didn't like to lie, or hurt anyone's feelings. Just some things had to be done. He didn't want to be her occasional bedmate any longer.

He was turning over a new leaf. There would be a new man about town. Might get himself one of those city haircuts too.

* * *

Showered, dressed in jeans and a Henley, Colt ruffled his hair the rest of the way dry then tried to keep the natural waves behind his ears. He felt like a kid again, wanting to impress the popular girl at school. He hoped Taylor wasn't regretting inviting him and Jamie to their happy hour. Not just because of the free drinks and good food either--he missed that hour or two when he could watch her mingle with her guests, casting him a smile when she'd catch his eyes on her. He missed so many things about being with her--the sound of her laugh, the way her eyes lit up when she looked at him, how her skin got hot when he touched her. And now that he knew how good her kisses tasted, he wanted a whole lot more of them.

Jamie came out of the shower, his short hair gelled up into a Mohawk of spikes. "What do you think? Will Taylor like it this way?"

Colt hid his smile. "Sure, she will. You're the best looking guy around."

He made a face. "Then why won't she date me?"

"Uh...because you're shorter than her?"

"No, I don't think it's that. It's an age thing. She thinks she's too old for me." He puffed out his thin little chest. "I like older women, and she's real pretty."

"Did she tell you she's too old?" He didn't know his son had had the courage to ask her out. He was aware the boy had a crush on her, but didn't honestly think he'd make it known. Poor Taylor had two Travis boys after her.

"She said if she was ten years younger, she'd take me up on it. Then suggested I should date Jessie from school. She wears braces!" he said with disgust. "What if I tried to kiss her? My lips might get stuck."

He chuckled. "That couldn't happen. And I think Taylor is right. You should look for a girl a little closer to your age. Taylor's way old. She's probably thirty at least." He grinned. "Maybe she's got false teeth and puts them in a glass of water when she goes to bed."

"I'm going to tell her you said that," Jamie retorted, and went into his bedroom to dress. He came back wearing jeans and a Miami Heat t-shirt. "This makes me look like I've got muscles," he said, flexing his thin arms.

"You're right. It does." Colt agreed, and opened the door. With a flourish, he waved his son through. "Your chariot awaits."

"You talk weird."

"That's 'cuz I am. Got a weird son too."

They parked on the side of Taylor's Cafe, and found the front door unlocked. The lights were dimmed so as not to attract drivers passing by. Colt and Jamie followed the sound of voices to the back. Lanterns and a row of fairy lights turned the outdoor terrace into a romantic setting. With the trees blowing and the rain pelting down outside, they were cocooned in a safe place to enjoy the roll of thunder.

Taylor looked up and waved them over. "You came! I didn't expect to see you tonight. Not in this storm." She hugged them. "You're both crazy."

"Dad is," Jamie said, eyes twinkling with fun. "He said you have false teeth and put them in a glass at night."

"He did?" Her eyes narrowed, and she put her hands on her hips. "My teeth happen to be my own," she said, baring them. "All the better to eat you with." She grabbed Jamie's hand and pretended to take a bite.

He giggled and pulled away. "I'm going to get a Coke," he said, hightailing away. He glanced back nervously to see if she was following him.

Colt snickered. "Think you scared him half to death."

"You know he asked me out?"

"So I heard. That's why I said you were old. Really old."

"Nice. You say the sweetest things."

"I don't mind old broads." He moved closer and bumped her shoulder, just so he could touch her. "It's after four."

"I noticed." She smiled and looked at her watch. "And you're here. Very responsible of you."

"I came to see Carole," he lied, his eyes never leaving her face. God, how he wanted to kiss her.

She gave him a knowing look. "Of course you did."

Joan and Carole sat with Anna, and there were two new couples at another table. He was surprised anyone had shown up on a wet night like this. But they had to eat somewhere, he supposed.

"Go talk to them," she said. "The two couples came together. They're from the Jersey shore." She lowered her voice. "They're worried about the storm that's supposed to hit in a couple of days. It's being called a category one."

He'd heard about the upcoming storm—when you made your living on the ocean, weather patterns mattered. "Yeah, but they usually dissipate out at sea," he said. And category one's tended to be wind events. Not a big deal if you prepared for it.

"I told them the same thing," she said into his ear, "but the latest news isn't good."

What could have changed in an hour? "What's up?"

Taylor nodded in their direction. "Go make friends. They'll tell you." She gave a brief smile. "I'll bring you a drink."

"What are you having?" he asked. His body craved being close to hers. They were close friends, but much more than that.

"A delicious red wine. Care to join me?"

"Thought you'd never ask."

He watched her walk away and then joined the three women eyeing him. "Hello, ladies. How did you manage to get here in this nasty weather without being blown to bits?"

"Rain gear," Anna told him.

He saw the heap of yellow jackets at an empty table. "I see." He put his windbreaker on the bench, and told Jamie to take off his jacket and have a seat. "I'll join you in a minute. After I meet the new guests." He'd become a regular at happy hour almost from the beginning, so it felt natural to greet the tourists.

He stepped over to the two couples who glanced up at him with worried expressions. He didn't blame them. The entire east coast had been hit hard the past few years, their seaboard washed away. Then after huge restoration had been made to the boardwalk and seaside neighborhood, they'd suffered another big hit.

Colt's living and everyone else in the Keys were dependent on Mother Nature and the sea, so he could readily identify with their fears and concern. For these four people this weather was an added insult, an upsetting start to their vacation.

"I'm Colt Travis. Charter boat captain. I have the Hatteras, "Bait Me" down at the marina. When the weather settles down, perhaps I can take the four of you out."

"John Fuller, and my wife Trish." They shook hands.

"Phil Marley, and Susan." After the exchange of names, Phil added, "We've been talking about this storm.

We've seen plenty lately, and none of us are keen to sit here and be part of another."

"I get that." Colt leaned against the picnic table behind him and crossed his arms. "We see a lot of activity this time of the year, but the storms usually dissipate before they reach land. The outer islands get blasted year after year. Haiti's had more than their share, but this one isn't supposed to amount to much last I heard."

"We watched the update just before coming over." John's brows drew together in a scowl. "It's still a tropical storm, but there is a risk that it could escalate. This morning they said a cat one, now it's been changed to category two status." John shot a worried look to his wife. "Supposed to hit Tuesday."

Colt nodded. Two days from now. He mentally ran through the check list of things to do to ensure his Hatteras was safe in the marina.

Taylor showed up with a bottle of wine and glasses. She heard the last remark. "We took over Paradise Cove eighteen months ago," she told them, "and we've been lucky so far. Not looking forward to a hurricane, believe me—we've prepared quite a few times, only to have the storms fizzle." She poured out the wine, refilling the couple's glasses first. "I have lasagna in the oven. Fresh warm bread, and a green salad. We can go inside, have some dinner, and ride out this thunderstorm."

"If the status doesn't improve tomorrow, we might drive up to Miami," Trish said. "We don't want to get stuck here if a hurricane hits."

"I don't blame you. It won't be any problem," Taylor hastened to assure them. "We will refund your money completely, or offer you a fifty percent discount if you rebook again anytime within a year."

"That's very kind of you." Phil sipped on his wine. "Excellent bottle by the way." He glanced at the label, and twirled the balloon glass, sniffing it with appreciation.

"Glad you like it. Let me check on the lasagna and turn on some lights. Come in when you're all ready." She put a hand on Trish's shoulder. "Let's try not to worry. In two days the sun could come out, and the storm might never happen."

Taylor went inside and Colt was about to ask Phil what kind of fishing he liked to do when they heard the rumble of thunder, and a moment later a lightning strike rattled their glasses. Jamie jumped and knocked over his soda, and Joan let out a loud shriek.

She clutched her heart, and whispered, "My pills..."

Carole quickly grabbed her mother's handbag and found the tablets, putting one under her tongue. "Mom? How's that?"

Her hand trembled as she reached for the water to swallow the pill. "I can't breathe." Joan blew out short breaths. "It hurts."

"Can someone call 911?" Carole asked in a rush of concern. "Mom's got a heart condition. She might be having an attack."

Joan was already on her feet, pacing as Anna made the call. The couples picked up their belongings and wine glasses, hurrying inside. "Go with them, Jamie," Colt said. "I'll help the ladies."

Jamie held open the door for the others, waiting for him. Colt had a hand under Joan's elbow to help her stand when they heard a loud crack. One of the pine trees outside toppled and nearly hit the thatched roof.

Colt and Carole supported Joan as they walked her to an inside table. She sank into a chair and Carole took the seat next to her, a protective set to her shoulders.

Taylor had lit candles for the tables, and only had the kitchen lights on bright. She rushed out of the kitchen. "I heard a terrible noise. Is everything okay outside?"

When no one answered, her face blanched. "What is it? What's wrong?"

"Joan is having chest pains. We called 911," Colt said softly.

"Oh no!" She sat opposite Joan and reached for her hand. "What can we do for you until the ambulance arrives?"

"I took a pill." Her voice was weak. "I have angina. It'll be fine."

“One of the trees almost hit the back patio,” Jamie said.

Taylor nodded with understanding, but kept her attention on Joan.

Colt went back to check but nothing had been damaged. The thatched roof and open walls would need anchoring before a hurricane hit.

After a few minutes the blessed sound of an ambulance was heard and a sigh of relief was shared when the flashing lights pulled up front. Minutes later, Joan was bundled inside with her daughter accompanying her. Colt put a comforting arm around Taylor, who was staring at the taillights of the ambulance. "It's been quite a night. But Joan is in good hands, and I think your guests deserve a good meal, don't you?"

"The lasagna!" she said.

Anna jumped up. "Yes. Let me help. I need to keep busy. Oh, poor Joan. I didn't know. She never said anything."

"They will take care of her, Mom. Carole said she'd keep in touch and let us know how she's doing." Taylor patted Phil and John on the back, and poured more wine. "Please everyone take a seat. Jamie, honey, would you mind helping me and Ms. Anna serve?"

Jamie jumped up, his face beaming. "I sure will. You need help, I'm your man."

Taylor glanced over at Colt. He winked, and even in all the chaos the vibes between them were sizzling hot. He had no friggin' idea where this temptation would all lead, and whether he could be the man she wanted him to be. Hell, he didn't even know what that was. All he knew was somehow, sometime, he would have her in his bed, and what he'd do after that, he didn't have a clue.

CHAPTER TWELVE

Joan was released from the hospital the following day, and the two ladies decided to catch the first flight home. Taylor's Cafe had a closed sign on the door, as they had lost their power. An emergency generator was keeping the refrigerator running so the food wouldn't spoil. Taylor stayed to man the office at the resort while Anna drove her friends to the local airport where they'd catch a connecting flight to Newark.

Her mom popped into the office on her return. "How's it going? Did we get any more cancellations? Did you call FPL to report our power outage?"

"Yes, I called FPL—they are working on it, no to the cancellations, but then again, our landline isn't working, so that's probably a good thing." Taylor smiled, trying to ease her mother's worries. "How was Joan?"

"Fine. She just had a bad scare. Apparently she's had this condition for several years. Carole is a big help to her." Anna took a bottle of tepid water from the fridge and drank. The cooler wasn't working either. "When we said our goodbyes, they both promised to come back again soon. I have a good feeling they will."

"So do I. Get away from the winter weather. Why not?"

Taylor glanced out the window. The sky was clear, but the wind had left branches from the trees across their dirt road, and the grounds were a mess. The predicted storm was churning in the Atlantic, so Taylor saw no sense in rushing to clean it up.

"Miguel's out working already," Anna said. "Got Raul with him."

"I know. I had thought we could wait until the storm blows through, but Miguel can't sit still," Taylor said with a sigh. "Mind if I run off and give them a hand? He's got the boy doing some heavy lifting."

"Sure. But don't be doing too much either. We can hire a crew for this."

"Mom. Best if we conserve our money for now. If this hurricane comes we might need it for repairs later." The light blue sky gave no hint of a storm, though the winds were strong.

"Oh, dear. Do you think it might hit us after all?"

"According to the Weather Channel, we are in the warning cone." You'd think they'd be able to pinpoint hurricane landings with all of the scientific gear, but Mother Nature had a mind of her own.

"What shall we do?" Anna looked around the office. "I suppose we should leave. Go to Miami. Brittany can put us up for a few days. Or Kayla might put us all up, if they are staying." Kayla's home was only twenty miles north of them, on the Intracoastal side, not the ocean.

"If it looks ominous tomorrow morning, we'll decide then." Taylor spoke firmly. "But I might stick around here and take care of things."

"No!" Anna took her glasses off and stared at Taylor. "That's not a good idea."

"Somebody should and I don't mind. Colt's staying too."

"Colt. That's a relief. He'll be better company than me at any rate."

Taylor laughed, more afraid of leaving her café and resort open to looters than she was afraid of the storm. "Well, I will feel safer having him around if things get a little crazy around here."

"If it comes to that Taylor, you both should leave too."

"We will see what happens." Her mind was already made up, but she didn't want to add to her mother's worries. "The couples have decided to stay today, and will make a decision whether to go in the morning. Colt's taking them snorkeling later, with a picnic lunch. Let's hope the weather holds up. At least let them have this one perfect day."

"Yes. Let's pray the storm stays away. We have enough going on with Kayla's wedding in three weeks. Last thing we need is a mess on our hands." Anna paced before the desk.

"Look, I need to go, but FPL thinks the power should kick back on in a couple of hours." She grabbed a white cap and put it on. "Meanwhile, try not to bake."

"If I do, I'll head over to the cafe." Anna wiped her brow. "At least you have that generator over there."

"Couldn't do without it. Suppose we should think about installing one here as well. But right now that's another expense we don't need."

"We'll get by. Maybe next spring."

"Later, Mom." She left the screen door open to allow the breeze to blow through. It was the best they could do in the ninety degree heat.

She found Raul and Miguel hauling tree limbs and stray branches into a pile that Miguel would dispose of later. "Hey, Raul. Could you run down and see Anna? She needs you for something." She winked at him and he took off before his father could stop him. "Any damage to the cabins?" she asked, dragging a limb over to the pile.

"Couldn't see anything, but we might want to rethink that thatched roof at the back of the cafe. It's pretty and I know you wanted it, but it won't stand up in a big storm."

She grabbed another branch the size of an eight-foot piling and dragged it along the dirt. "Mom mentioned that too. She suggested a wooden A-frame with open windows so the storm could blow through."

Miguel nodded, his forehead shiny with perspiration. "We'll talk about it after. Once this storm passes."

"You think it will pass?" she asked, wiping her dirty hands on her khaki shorts.

"No way to tell." He shook his head at her. "You don't need to do any hard labor, Miss Taylor. My boy and I can do this." He wiped the sweat off his brow with a hankie, and then stuffed it back into his jeans pocket.

"Since when do the women not work around here? And stop with the "Miss" would you? We're not running a southern plantation. It's a guest resort, last I heard."

He grinned. "No, you heard right. But I want to teach my boy some manners, and if he calls you that, well, I should too."

She picked up a branch from one of the palms and lightly swatted him with it. "You want to fight me over it?"

His brown eyes grew big and he looked worried until he realized that she was teasing. Then he started to laugh, deep belly laughs, and had to sit down to catch his breath. Raul came running up with two bottles of water. "What's the matter? You okay, Dad?"

"Yes. But I'll take one of those waters you're carrying."

He twisted the lid and drank almost half before he stopped. "Guess I was thirstier than I thought." He wiped his mouth. "Looks like we've got ourselves another pair of hands. Taylor, Miss Taylor to you, wants to get hers dirty."

She patted Miguel's shoulder, then offered a hand to help him to his feet. "Much better. Raul, drink some water and then let's get back to work. Are we going to light this baby up, Miguel?"

"No. Not with this heat and wind. Might not be able to contain a small fire. Don't worry, by tomorrow you won't even know it was here."

"What are you? A magician now?" She bent over to grab another branch, and had to tug and tug.

"Nope. Just know a thing or two. Saw a lot of storms in my lifetime."

Dropping the stubborn branch she bent over in an effort to snap it in two. "Whoa, let me help with that."

Before she could straighten up, a pair of hands were on her hips. Her head snapped around.

"Colt. Jamie. What are you two doing here?" She turned around to face him. "Thought you were taking our guests out?"

"I am, but Jamie and I decided to come a little early and see how much damage there was."

"We still don't have power , but otherwise no major problems. The generator is saving the food in the kitchen, which just leaves this mess to clean up."

"I see that." He stomped on the branch and it broke in two. "We're here to help."

"No need to do that. Taking our guests out snorkeling will give us a chance to get things cleared." She bent over to pick up the two pieces, and could feel his eyes on her backside.

"And miss this splendid sight?" Colt said in a low voice. "No thank you."

Her pulse sped up. "And what sight would that be?"

He stepped closer. "You have a very fine ass. First class." The words were a mere whisper but the thrill of them turned her skin a bright pink.

"Being an expert, you should know."

He chuckled and stepped away. "You've been busy this morning," he said to Miguel. "Got most of the road cleared."

"Probably before you had breakfast," Miguel muttered under his breath.

Taylor snickered and looked at Colt's face. Miguel was protective of her and her family. Unlike Juanita, Miguel was suspicious of Colt, not trusting the younger man's intentions.

Meanwhile, Raul was showing off to Jamie, dragging the biggest branches he could find. Jamie flexed his own muscles, darting glances at her to see if she was watching.

Taylor did her best to ignore all the testosterone floating around and returned to the job at hand. An hour later they had the road leading to the occupied cottages cleaned up, and the others could wait. Colt helped load the piles into a large sized wheelbarrow, and Miguel took it to the far edge of the property to remove it from sight. By eleven a.m. the resort looked halfway presentable, and the power was restored.

Colt and Jamie washed up inside the cafe, while she put together a picnic lunch. He sidled up beside her, pretending to look in the basket. "Looks good. Turkey and Swiss cheese sandwiches, tuna wraps, bags of chips, and fresh fruit. The only thing missing is a good bottle of wine and a woman to share it with." His eyes caught hers. "Since you don't have any other guests, why not come with us?"

Jamie heard the question and dragged her by the hand. "Please come. Oh, please?"

She laughed. "I couldn't. I'm a mess."

"No, you're not," Jamie said. "Come. I'll show you where the barracudas hang out."

"I think I can pass on that." She shifted her gaze to Colt. He was watching her and there was something about his expression that made her change her mind. When was the last time she did anything for fun? And didn't she deserve an afternoon off after the back-breaking work she'd just done?

"Why...if you don't mind waiting fifteen minutes for me, I will."

"We'll wait, don't you worry." Colt's eyes danced. "We'll be down at the dock, getting the boat ready."

"I'm on it!" She ran off, feeling light-hearted and almost carefree. A whole afternoon off. This storm had been an unpleasant surprise, but it had given her a reward. An afternoon with sunny skies, nice company, and Colt.

CHAPTER THIRTEEN

Taylor ran into the cabin, tossing her dirty clothes onto the floor. "I'm going out snorkeling, Mom. I should be back in a few hours."

"That's nice, dear. I'm so pleased you're getting out." Anna beamed. "When was the last time you went snorkeling? I remember how much you love it."

"I don't know. I can't remember," Taylor said, heading for the bathroom shower.

Her mother picked up her clothes, and smiled as she walked into her daughter's bedroom. While Taylor cleaned up, Anna rummaged through her daughter's dresser to find the bikini that she'd bought for her 30th birthday, and had yet to wear. She cut off the sales tag, and laid it out with a pair of hot pink shorts and a white lacy shirt that she could tie under her breasts.

When Taylor returned to her bedroom, she saw the clothes lying on the bed.

"You want me to wear this?" She dangled the polka dot bikini in her mother's face. "We have guests, for heaven's sake."

"And they haven't seen a bikini before?" Anna tossed her head and snorted. "Don't be silly. It's a two piece. Not risqué at all. Besides, you'll have a vest on, won't you?"

"No. That's only for scuba." Taylor quickly dressed in the bikini and shorts then tossed on her pink Paradise T-shirt instead of the see through white shirt. "Okay. This is better."

She put her hair in a ponytail tucked in a pink cap. She slipped into a pair of canvas sneakers, and grabbed her lip gloss. "Okay, Mom. Nobody's around. Close the damn office and take the day off too. We deserve it, don't we?"

"Why, what a lovely idea. I might take the car and go into town. Look around the shops. Treat myself to a pedicure before the storm hits tomorrow." She smiled. "You be sweet to Colt. He's a good man, Taylor."

"I know, Mom." She let out a sigh. "Thing is, he's not ready for anything serious and neither am I." Her chin lifted. Nothing was going to spoil this day. "So we will have some non-serious fun together. No harm in that."

"Now you're talking my language. Enjoy yourself while you can."

Taylor grabbed a towel and her snorkeling gear, and headed for the pier. She could see the other guests were already on the boat waiting for her.

Jamie waved when he spotted her hurrying down the wharf, and Colt jumped onto the pier to help her aboard. She was certainly getting the royal treatment today.

"Sorry to keep you waiting," she called out to the guests. "Colt, did you remember the picnic basket?"

"Sure did. I added some beers and wine too."

Phil nodded. "I also brought a six pack. You got a fridge down below?"

"Here. I'll take it." Taylor had to put her own gear away, so she took the foam cooler as well. He had a few sodas and half a dozen Corona Lights which she emptied into the fridge.

A half hour later they were at one of the popular spots in the inner reefs. The shallow water, beautiful coral reefs, and bountiful fish made this a great spot for all divers, regardless of their experience.

Colt dropped the anchor, and helped the two couples find goggles and fins to fit, then waited until they were in the water. "Jamie, you want to join them?"

"Are you coming?" he asked.

"Yes. In a minute. Got to get a few things organized first."

"How about you?" Jamie asked Taylor.

"I'll help your dad. Not sure if I want to dive or not."

Jamie lowered his goggles. "You guys suck."

"Jamie," Colt said in warning. "Don't use that language or you'll be sitting alone in the cabin for the afternoon."

In answer, Jamie jumped into the water, then turned a triumphant face in their direction.

"Kids," Colt mumbled. "I should go after him, but he can swim like a fish." He called down to his son, "Stick with the others. We'll be keeping an eye on you."

Jamie fitted his regulator in his mouth and swam toward the couples. He waved, then dived under.

Colt turned to Taylor. "You don't have to wait for me."

"I want to." She didn't want to take her shirt off and let anyone see her in the bikini. But if she wore the tee in the water, she'd be a sopping mess when she got out.

"You brought your gear. You know how to dive, right?"

"Of course. It's just that I..."

"Can't stand being away from me?" he said with a twinkle in his eye.

"No. I'm wearing a bikini. Mom bought it for me, and I've never worn it. It's kind of skimpy with guests around."

"They aren't around. It's just you and me, baby. And I like bikinis. Even better than beer."

"I bet you do."

He took her arms and lifted them high, then slowly he slid the shirt up inch by inch, and over her head. Her heart raced. It almost felt like a striptease.

When her head popped out from the shirt he kissed her, and his hands slid around her bare waist. "Your mother has good taste," he said, kissing her shoulder. "Remind me to thank her."

"Colt. We have guests."

"They're in the water. They can't see us, and wouldn't care if they did."

"Your son..."

"Is fine." His hands pulled her closer, and she could feel the warmth of his naked chest. When had he taken his shirt off? She dropped her eyes, admiring his tanned sculpted chest and ripped abs up close. They were pretty much perfect. Not overly done like some clowns. Lean, sexy, with a light smattering of fine blond hair.

She let her hand trail down his chest, her eyes on his. He swallowed hard and stepped back. "I think I better go for that swim after all."

Without bothering with his snorkel he dived in. When his head popped out of the water, he beckoned to her. "Come in if you dare."

For once in her life, she did. Shimmying out of her shorts, she jumped feet first into the pristine water.

When she reached his side, he pulled her to the far side of the boat, out of sight from his son and her guests and gave her a long, hot, wet kiss. His leg wrapped around her, and she could feel the bulge in his swimsuit.

Oh my! All her fantasies about him were true.

Then he swam away, joining his son and the others, giving them both a chance to cool off. She was the first one back onboard, and that gave her time to redress, towel dry her hair, and lay out the picnic basket. It also gave her time to reflect on the passionate kiss and the burning desire inside of her that had been lit.

Did she know what she was doing? And would her heart break when he walked away?

* * *

Colt stayed well clear of her once he was back on board. He cracked open a beer, grabbed a turkey sandwich, and sat on the side of the boat, chatting with the men. It was a much safer place to be.

Taylor avoided looking at him too. She listened to the women as they went on and on about how spectacular the diving was here, and how they didn't have water like this up in New Jersey.

No shit! That's why he chose to live in Paradise Cove. It really was paradise. He didn't need the city life, or a big home. The sea was his home. Not only was it free, but it never remained stagnant. Ever-changing, it might be full of drama one minute, and calm the next. Quite like a woman in fact...and yet a man could never tire of it, get impatient with the mood swings, or want a younger model.

As a charter captain he was married to the sea. His only responsibility was to his son, and to his paying customers. That's the way he liked it, and wanted it.

So what was he going to do about this burning sensation inside of him that wanted to claim Taylor and make her his own? He didn't want any men sniffing around her. He wanted her in his bed, and in his life.

Well, a small part of his life anyway. He wished he could compartmentalize her. She would be the only woman he made love to, and then she could go about her life as usual and he could too. Perfect. Why should a woman demand more than that?

Sex was good. Sex was great. Like food and water. It was necessary for survival. One didn't need a commitment or a relationship with food and water. They simply took what they needed and drank until full. Should be the same with sex. He wanted to take what he needed, and have her do the same. Good for the goose--good for the gander.

He glanced over at her. She was smiling and laughing, and looked all flushed from the sun. She caught his eyes on her and shyly looked back. She bobbed her head and blushed. She had to be the sweetest thing ever--and that was just one of the countless reasons why he couldn't do all the things he wanted. Not to her. She deserved better. She deserved to be treated like a Queen, and have a man crazy about her. She should be given a fine home, fine clothes, and a dozen fine children.

He was in trouble. He knew it. Squirming, he got up and offered the men another beer. Taylor and the ladies were sharing the bottle of chardonnay and whispering to each other. They kept looking over at him, and he wished he knew what they were saying.

Jamie was on the fly bridge, resting in the sun after his busy day.

The sea was calm, like the calm before the storm. Just because the skies were blue right now, didn't mean they would stay that way. A wind had picked up and the air smelled different. Colt got on his radio for the latest report on the weather--which confirmed his worries. Tropical Storm Erica had been a slow moving storm hanging around the Caribbean, but it's direction and history brought to mind Hurricane Wilma, and more recently Sandy. That had been the highest storm surge the northeast coastline had ever seen. Wilma in 2005 had come close to wiping out the Florida Keys.

Colt truly hoped his instincts were a thousand miles off base just this once.

"Pack up everyone. Checked the storm status and Erica's gathering strength as it heads toward Cuba. We are fine right now, but you all should go inside," he called to his passengers.

He exchanged a look with Taylor, who nodded, and escorted her guests inside. "Jamie," he called to his son. "Time to come down from there. We're heading back to the marina—full steam ahead."

The anchor came up, and he hit full throttle. The Hatteras crested the waves as he drove the boat home. If the storm was coming, "Bait Me" needed to be prepared.

CHAPTER FOURTEEN

When Colt got back to Paradise Cove, he helped everyone off the boat then told Taylor he was going to take "Bait Me" to Coral Bay Marina. Whenever he needed service on his boat or yearly maintenance he'd take it there. The fact that it was on the bay side instead of the ocean gave it better protection. He knew they had dry storage for boats as large as 65 feet, but didn't think he'd need that at this time. Removing everything from the upper deck and tying it down good should keep it safe from the approaching storm.

"I'll catch you later," he told Taylor. "I want to take Jamie to his mother's and hopefully convince her to leave for a couple of days. Just have a bad feeling about this one."

Taylor nodded. "You go do what you have to do, and I'll see to my guests."

Once Colt had his boat secured he had someone drive him back to his truck and went home to pack a bag for Jamie. He called Sharon to let her know he was coming and to give her a heads up on the latest status.

An hour later, she opened the door to her apartment and her troubled eyes met his. "I have a shift tomorrow," she told him.

"See if you can get someone else to step in," he told her. "Failing that I think once you're through you should take Jamie and go to Miami. Stay with Grandma and Aunt Chrissy," he told them, his hand on Jamie's shoulder. "I'll call them and let them know you're coming."

Jamie glanced up at his mother. "I'm not afraid. Are you?"

"No but it's always best to be safe than sorry." She pulled him in for a hug, dropping a kiss on the top of his head. "You get to skip school and take a little trip with me. We'll both play hooky."

"What about you, Dad? Are you leaving?" His son sounded sixteen instead of eleven.

"No. I've got to take care of the boat, and our home. Need to board up if things escalate the way I expect they will."

He reached for his wallet in his back pocket. "You need some emergency cash?" He pulled out two one-hundred-dollar bills and handed them over. "Thanks for doing this."

"Not a problem. You take care too." She put the cash on the table. "And thanks."

"Bye, Daddy." Jamie hugged his middle. "I love you."

Colt stroked the top of his head. "Love you more. See you soon, buddy. Have fun in Miami."

"Wish you could come too."

"I'll see you in a couple of days. You had fun snorkeling today, didn't you? Tell your mom all about it."

He bent down and kissed Jamie's cheeks. "You take care of your mom, okay?"

"Okay." He kicked his shoes off and flopped on the couch. "Is Taylor staying too?"

"I hope not," he answered. "It won't be safe for her either."

"But she has the cafe and the cottages to look after." He shoved his hands in his pockets. "She should stay and look after you too."

Colt tried not to smile, but the idea had merit. He avoided the look his ex gave him, and headed for the door. "You two just take care of each other, and we will stay safe. I promise."

He drove right back to Paradise Cove Cottages and knocked on Taylor's door. Taylor answered it with tears in her eyes. "What's wrong?" he asked.

"Mom isn't here. I tried calling her, but she didn't answer."

He folded her in his arms, and felt her tears on his neck. "She'll be fine. You know your mom. She's probably kicking up her heels somewhere. What's her favorite place for happy hour?"

"She's always *here* for happy hour." Taylor frowned. "She was supposed to get a pedicure and come home."

"She's probably on her way back now," he said soothingly.

"I hope so, but I wanted her to catch a ride with John and Phil. They left already. Packed their bags once we got back and headed out of town." She let out a sigh. "Why won't she answer her phone?"

He held her shoulders and looked into her eyes. "I'll find your mom and bring her back, then you two should go spend a day or two with Kayla. She'll love that, and I'll feel better about it."

"What about our cottages? I need to board up. Miguel can't do it alone."

"I'll help Miguel with this place and he can help me with mine. We can get it all done tomorrow if the storm actually heads this way."

"No matter what, the weather will affect us at some level, even if it drops down to a tropical storm—but I'm not leaving. I've got the supplies loaded into waterproof bins and I cooked the food that might go bad. I'll divide it up for you, Miguel and his family, and give some to Mom to take with her to Kayla's."

"That's a good idea. You do that while I search for your mom."

She took hold of his arm as he was about to depart. "I forgot to ask. What did you do with your boat?"

"It's tied down at Coral Bay in a good spot. I need to get back there first thing in the morning and secure it better. Got a checklist of things to do at times like this. It'll be fine. Don't worry."

"I'm not worried about your boat. I'm worried about you, and mom. And the cottages."

"Then stop." He put a finger to her brow and then kissed the spot. "You'll get permanent worry lines right there, and I don't want that." He smiled. "Keep your cell phone close and call me if you hear from your mom. I'll do the same."

"Thanks, Colt." She closed the door behind him, and he cursed his luck. He had more on his mind than running after Taylor's mother, but she was a good-hearted woman who cared about everyone she came into contact with. If somebody needed her help? She'd be there in a heartbeat.

With any luck Anna had gone in search of a different happy hour since she had the day to herself. He knew just the right spot. Lorelei's.

The white clapboard building was the "hot spot" for viewing the sunsets, listening to live bands and sipping on your favorite beverage. When he arrived the lot was busy, and the bar was pretty much filled. Lots of people sitting around the outdoor tables, too. Enjoying the music and the view of the bay. Grabbing the last of the good weather while they could. People around here knew how quickly weather could change, and they were adaptable. Rolled with the punches. Bad one day meant fine the next.

Colt waved to some familiar faces, and then paused as Anna's laugh reached his ears. She sat at the inside bar, chatting up the bearded, younger man seated next to her. He watched her for a minute, more amused than angry. After all, she'd been working every day for the past year and a half, and deserved a good time too.

Anna was a vivacious and slim woman with a lot of fire. All three of her daughters had that same spark in one form or another.

"Hey, Anna." He put a hand on her shoulder.

Smiling, she turned around. "Wow. Colt. What are you doing here?" Her flashing brown eyes narrowed. "Are you meeting someone?" Her lips pressed tightly together in disapproval. "Where's Taylor?"

"She's at home looking for you." He quirked a brow. "She left messages on your cell phone. Lots of them."

"Oh, the battery died. I never plug it in." Anna shrugged and laughed, bumping shoulders with the man next to her, who eyed him with curiosity.

"Taylor's worried about you. Have you been tracking the storm?"

"No. I'm here to forget about it for an hour or two. Why don't you rush on back and take care of Taylor yourself?" She gave him a wicked smile.

"She wants you to go to Kayla's. I tried to convince her that she should leave too." He patted the bar counter. "I'll take care of your tab."

"Oh, no, you don't need to do that." She picked up her frothy drink, as if afraid that he might take it away. "Call her for me, and say that I'll be home in a few hours. I'll leave first thing in the morning. I promise."

"I'll give you the phone. You call."

"No. You know how convincing she can be. She'll want me to leave right now, and I'm not ready." Her eyes twinkled. "I know she'll be in excellent hands while I'm with Kayla. You will take care of her, won't you?"

He felt the trap she was setting for him as the cage came down with a loud snap. "Of course I will. I would never let any harm come to her."

"Good. Neither would I." She placed a hand on his arm, and her long nails raked gently over his skin. "You treat her right, Colt. My girls mean a lot to me."

"I'm sure they do. As they should." Colt glanced at the younger man seated next to Anna, and lifted an eyebrow. "Would you talk some sense into this woman? She knows the storm's coming, but here she sits." He gestured to the cool pink drink in front of her. "What are you drinking anyway?"

"A hurricane. Bill bought it for me. Yummy. Sweet though. Lots of rum and passion fruit and lime." She lifted the tall glass. "Here, try it."

"No, thank you." He shook his head. "Want me to tell Taylor what you're up to?"

"Why, I'm not up to anything." She giggled, and her knee bumped Bill's. "Not yet, anyway. Still, a woman hopes."

Bill chuckled and put his hand on Anna's thigh.

Colt backed up, his hands in the air. "I'm outta here. I'll call Taylor—but you promised to drive to Kayla's first thing in the morning." He looked at Bill, who looked like he'd won the lotto. "See that she does."

He raced back to his car, thinking it was a good thing his own mother and sister lived far enough away that he couldn't keep an eye on their shenanigans. There were certain things a son or a daughter didn't want to see.

Taylor picked up on the first ring. "Did you find her?"

"She's okay," Colt said. "She's having her happy hour at the Lorelei."

"Why didn't she call?"

"Dead phone battery. I think you should leave her be," he suggested. "She's sitting with a decent guy." He willed himself not to think where Bill's hand was going. "Anna seems... determined."

"Determined about what?" Taylor asked angrily. "To be foolish?"

"To have a good time. She deserves it too. Like you, she works all the time. You know that."

There was silence as fair-minded Taylor considered that. "I know, but why tonight?"

"I guess the opportunity presented itself and she took it." Anna was a bit of a free spirit, like her youngest daughter. "It's okay. She knows what she's doing."

"She darn well better. Hope she's got some condoms in her purse." Taylor spoke in a snappish tone and he could practically see fumes coming out of her pretty ears. "How embarrassing."

He laughed, glad it wasn't his mom. "Your mother is still young. And attractive."

"Don't you dare even think about dating her!"

"Me? Are you serious?" He laughed again. "She's hot but she has a much hotter daughter."

"Brittany's not around."

He frowned into the phone even though she couldn't see his face. "No, but you are." With that he hung up, feeling with this conversation less was better.

Colt checked in with Jamie, who told him they were on their way to Miami. Sharon got on the phone and said it was bumper-to-bumper and would take hours.

"I wish we had left last night," she told him, "but now they're saying it could be a Cat two and everyone's on the road. Oh crap!"

"What's wrong?" he asked, noting the change in her voice.

"There's an accident ahead. Now, we'll be stuck here for God knows how long."

"Dammit. Well, nothing you can do I guess, but wait it out. You need gas or something to eat? Pull over somewhere and take an hour's break. Maybe the traffic will move better after that."

"I can't," she said miserably. "It'll be worse then. Everyone's heading north it seems. You should too," she added.

"Got to take care of the boat first. Then board up the house. Don't worry about me. I'll hunker down someplace and keep safe."

"Okay. We'll call you when we get moving again."

"Good. Bye, Jamie. See you soon, son."

He had called from the car, and a few minutes later he pulled into the parking lot at Coral Bay. It would take him a few hours to ready his boat for a significant storm.

First on his list was to reduce the windage by removing the bimini canvas top, doubling up all the dock lines, and adding spring lines for storm surge. He stowed away all loose objects from above, and used duct tape to protect the exposed instruments on board and seal off the hatches. He made sure he had chafe protections on all the lines, beefed up the cleats, and had plenty of fenders so the boat wouldn't be damaged by the wharf.

Once he was satisfied that "Bait Me" was secured, he made the trip to the cottages to check on Taylor, and help out Miguel. The long day was just beginning.

CHAPTER FIFTEEN

Anna got home by six a.m. with dark circles under her eyes and her chin length hair wild and tousled. It was role-reversal, Taylor thought, not questioning her mom about the man she'd obviously slept with.

“Nice night?” she asked in a neutral tone.

“Very,” her mom answered without going into detail, although her smile spoke volumes. It occurred to Taylor that her mother had behaved like a naughty teen—no phone calls, sneaking in at dawn.

"I've just been talking to Kayla. She wants you, Juanita and the kids to go and stay with her."

"That's probably a good idea. I was thinking about going to Miami to see Brittany, but I couldn't face that long, long drive."

"Sean can't leave the hospital or his patients, so Kayla won't leave either. And it's away from the ocean, and she has hurricane impact windows, so it'll be good for all of you to hang out there."

"Yes, that is best." Anna gave an elaborate yawn.

"You should take a shower and head on over," Kayla suggested. "I have some food for you to take."

"Oh, honey, her home is only about twenty miles away. I think I'll just nap for awhile and go after lunch."

"No, you won't. The traffic going north is crazy now. Everyone's panicking since it might be a Hurricane Two. Haven't you been listening?"

"Hurricane Two? Oh dear! I didn't know. Sorry." She gave a mischievous smile and a shrug of her shoulders. "Guess I had better things to do."

"I don't want to know about them. Just go. Take your shower. You should leave as soon as you can. Pick up Juanita and Meri, they will be waiting for you. Miguel wants Raul to stay and help here. If we get it all done by tonight, Colt, myself and Miguel will join you at Kayla's."

"Oh, that would be a good idea." She sauntered to the bathroom. "I wonder what I should wear."

"Put on your best Hurricane clothes, and your party boots."

Anna stopped in her tracks. "What party boots?" She shook her head and laughed. "Are you giving your mother a hard time?"

"Maybe just a little." Taylor smiled. "But you know I love you. Now go get cleaned up and pack enough for a couple of days."

"Okay, dear. This is kind of exciting. We can have a hurricane party at Kayla's. She does have a lovely home."

Taylor rolled her eyes. Her mother lived in a different dimension. Clearly. Thinking of a hurricane as a form of amusement was just wrong. During her conversation with Kayla, they had discussed the repercussions in great depth, remembering the devastation that Hurricane Sandy had wrought to the New Jersey shore.

They hadn't seen it firsthand as they lived inland and were spared, but they'd never forget the television coverage. The faces of the victims as they looked upon what was left of their homes. The streets were flooded, leaving them cut off from everything. The boardwalk disappeared. Their whole way of life destroyed in an instant. It was heartbreaking, and anyone who lived through it would tell it so.

Miguel and Raul arrived while Anna was having breakfast. He accepted an offer of a cup of coffee, but refused to take the time to eat. After he downed his coffee, and Raul ate a warmed cinnamon roll, the two headed for the pool to secure the patio furniture and store the loose pottery.

About an hour later Colt showed up.

“Morning, Taylor. How’s your mom?”

"She made it back safe and sound."

Anna strolled out of the bedroom wearing a pair of canary yellow Capris and a flowered loose top. Her hair was freshly washed, and fell in soft curls around her flushed cheeks. "Hi Colt. How're things?"

"Things are good. Jamie and my ex are safe in Miami with my mother and sister. And my boat's snug as a bug in a rug." He grabbed a cup of coffee, leaned against the counter and gave her an appraising look. "You look all bushy-tailed this morning. Looking forward to the hurricane, are you?"

"Well it does add a certain excitement in the air, that's for sure. Long as no one gets hurt, and the property is not damaged, then I'd say it livened up things around here."

"Oh, Mom! Really? Do you know what it's like to go through something like this? Have you any idea?"

"No, and neither do you." Anna didn't take any offense, just grabbed a bottle of water from the fridge for the ride to Key Largo. "We were very fortunate not to have been hit by Sandy. Those poor, poor people. I swear it broke my heart seeing what they had to live through. I'm not callous. I just try to make the best of a bad situation. I'm worried as much as the rest of you."

Somehow Taylor doubted that. "Fine. I'm glad to see you have common sense. But please--let's wait until this storm is over before we start celebrating, shall we?"

"Yes, dear. Well, I'm off to pick up Juanita and Meri. I'll call you when we get to Kayla's." She kissed Taylor's cheek, then put a hand on Colt's arm. "Take care of my daughter, won't you?"

"It will be my pleasure." Colt winked at Taylor. "She's in good hands."

"I know that. And once you get all your work done, we hope to see you at Kayla's. If not, stay tucked in here and don't do anything I wouldn't do."

With that last comment and a saucy grin, she was off. Taylor was happy to see her go. She turned to Colt, with an embarrassed look. "She's really something, isn't she?"

He moved slowly to her, and put his arms around her waist, drawing her near. "She has her own way of coping. Her life hasn't been easy, and if this helps her keep her sanity, then who are we to judge? It's you I'm worried about. You take too much on. You should have left with her. Let Miguel and me, and Raul do what we need to do."

"This is my home. My responsibility. My livelihood. I need to be here."

"I won't argue. As long as you're here, I intend to keep you safe."

Her insides warmed at the thought. If she needed anybody by her side, it was Colt.

For several hours Taylor joined the men boarding up the cottages that faced the beach and would be most affected by the storm. They boarded up Birds of Paradise, but they couldn't protect all twelve units though they did their best. The cafe had a generator so the industrial refrigerator would keep most of their food from spoiling. How long they'd be without power was anyone's guess. But not losing it at all would take some kind of miracle.

Colt and Miguel left for a few hours to board up their own homes, then Colt returned alone. He brought half a dozen good size lanterns, and a radio with a package of batteries.

"Miguel's on his way to Kayla's." He didn't look at her as he spoke. He put the new batteries in the radio, then walked around the cabin, placing a lantern in every room. "Thought you and I might sit it out. Unless you want to join the others?"

She knew what he was asking, and her heart thundered in response.

"I'm staying. I couldn't leave."

"I hoped you'd feel the same way." He went to the wine rack and picked up a good bottle of red. Without asking, he opened it.

"You hungry?" he asked. "I haven't eaten since this morning."

Her mouth watered. "Neither have I." She felt a little tongue-tied, wondering how she could eat with Colt so close, so dear, so near.

"Let's finish up some of those leftovers. Then hunker down."

Her pulse raced. Not for the food, but the thought of hunkering down with Colt-- alone for a whole night with no one to answer to, no one to think about. There was no one she'd rather ride out a storm with.

Taylor poured two glasses of wine, and gave him one. "Sounds like a plan." She took a sip then put the glass down. She kissed him, her lips tasting like the full-bodied wine.

Colt seemed eager to get the food out of the way, and so was she. They pulled out containers from the fridge and nuked it in the microwave. They turned on the radio to listen to the news. They kept their spirits up, ignoring the sound of the wind howling around them, the cracks of lightning overhead, and the very real threat of danger they faced.

They polished off the wine, sitting on the sofa together. It had been a physically demanding day, and she snuggled into him, loving the warmth of him, the sexy smell of his aftershave.

"Are you worried?" she asked him, her head resting on his chest.

"Not really. We've prepared the best we can. Now it's all up to nature."

She lifted her head and gave him a weak smile, her hand on his chest. "I've never had so much to lose before."

He kissed her forehead. "Believe me, I understand. It's the same with me. I have everything sunk into that boat, and my home. They might not be much, but it's all I've got. Your resort and cafe is a whole 'nother story. It's an enormous responsibility and investment. And I know how much you love it."

"If anything happens..." tears welled in her eyes and she couldn't go on.

He lifted her chin, and kissed away her tears. "Paradise Cove has been around for at least twenty years, right? This place has weathered many storms, probably a whole lot worse than this."

Her mouth trembled. "You're right. Of course we'll be fine. I just couldn't bear it... you know?" Her voice broke and she buried her face in his neck.

* * *

Colt held her for a long, long time. He let her cry it out, knowing that she'd been so strong for so long, and that the floodgate had finally broken. Wet tears slid down his shirt melting something inside of him. Everything about this woman was precious, and he wanted to protect her, hold her, comfort her as he would a child. No, not like a child. He needed to be honest about his feelings. He wanted to comfort her--as a woman. A very desirable woman.

Oh, God, he hurt with wanting her. He kissed the soft side of her cheek, and put a hand in her hair, making a fist of the lush thick curls. She turned her head, offering him access to her slender neck. His lips tasted her skin and she shivered. But she didn't move away.

Colt gave her neck soft kisses and little nibbles, then followed the path down to her shoulder. He pushed the t-shirt aside, dropped heated kisses on her tender skin, eager to go lower. Much lower. Patience, he warned himself, don't rush this.

His lips returned to her neck and he nibbled her left ear. She moaned his name.

His hand tugged at her hair, gently pulling her head back—covering her mouth with his. Hot, needy, tongue plunging in, taking, seeking, engaging in a duel that had his pulse soaring, his body aching. He needed this woman. And, by God, he would have her tonight. Finally.

"Colt?"

"Hmm." He wouldn't remove his mouth from hers. If he did, he might never find it again. His free hand roamed over her breast. It was taut, firm, full in his hand. He let out a low growl, and flicked his thumb over her nipple.

Instead of pushing him away, she moved closer. Her hand lowered down his back and rested on the curve of his ass. He took that as a sign of encouragement and tilted his hips ever so slightly. His groin made contact with her center.

Taylor shuddered and opened her mouth wider, kissing him with more passion than he'd dared hope. She arched her back and pressed her breast into his hand.

"Colt?"

This time when she said his name, he had the presence of mind to listen.

"Hmm?"

"My bedroom is on the left."

He loved forward-thinking women.

He grabbed her hand and hurried her down the hall. She began to laugh. "Slow down. I'm not about to change my mind."

Colt grinned at her. "You're sure?"

"I've never been more sure of anything."

He pulled her into his arms and kissed her softly, gently, with all the tenderness in his soul. He wasn't sure how much there was, but what he had belonged to her.

"Did anyone tell you that you're a great kisser?" she murmured.

He decided not to answer, but to prove his skill instead. With his mouth still hot on hers, he walked her backwards to the double bed. A blue and white lightweight quilt, with two ruffled pillows, and a smaller heart-shaped one.

He tossed the heart on the floor, and whipped the cover off the bed. Then he laid her down and sat next to her. "Taylor...you are so beautiful. I want this to be special."

She put a finger on his lips and smiled sweetly. "Don't spoil it by talking. For once in my life, I just want to lose my head."

He chuckled. "I can help you with that."

He ripped off his shirt, and got to his feet, dropping his pants. He was commando and his manhood stood on high alert.

Taylor's eyes widened but she sat up and removed her t-shirt, then shimmied out of her shorts. She lay back down in a white lacy bra and matching panties, her hot gaze on him.

She reached and stroked him. His cock pulsed in her hand. He knelt over her and kissed her hungrily, knowing he had to have her soon. He had waited too long for her, and his patience was gone. He would take what she was offering, and give it back again and again.

He bent to suckle her nipple through the lacy material, and it budded and peaked inside his mouth. She squirmed under him and he knew she was impatient too. He unsnapped her bra and tossed it aside, filling his hands and mouth with her luscious breasts that reminded him of two perfect peaches. Being an expert on breasts, he'd already known the shape of them through the shirts she wore each day. The tiny budded nipples that exploded in his mouth were a delicious surprise. He could make her peaches into a steady diet for a long, long time.

At his nudging she widened her legs, allowing his painful arousal a place to call home. Through her underwear, he pushed against her, feeling her wetness, her answering need. She lifted her hips wanting him. Pushing the lace aside, he slipped a finger in and then another. She moaned and bit his shoulder.

She was breathing hard, pushing against him, and he couldn't take it anymore. He sat up and slid her undies down her long, slim legs, over her toes and to the floor. He stayed there for a second and took one toe in his mouth and sucked gently. She called his name. He waited, running his tongue along the bottom of her foot, over her ankle to her calf muscle, continuing to the soft skin behind her knee. Moving northward, his tongue lingered on the tender skin between her thighs. He felt her quiver, and his heart thundered in response. Damn, this woman turned him into mush.

He'd never wanted to please a woman the way he did with her. His own needs were forgotten as he watched her wither under him. Her body was flush and sweet, and for the moment it was his. He intended to enjoy every morsel and take his time doing it too.

He knew she was ready, almost over the edge, but still he waited, giving her soft kisses, his fingers doing their magic. She cried out, and his mouth followed his hand, but she pushed his head away. Moving quickly she grabbed a condom from the side drawer, expertly slipping it over the length of him.

"Where did you get that?" he asked in surprise.

"In Brittany's drawer. She shared a room with Mom and must have forgotten a fresh pack. Unless it's Mom's, but I don't want to think of that." She glanced up at him. "I want you to make love to me. Now."

His eyes held hers as he moved steadily toward her. She opened her legs with a welcoming smile. Clasping hands, he straddled her, then pushed hard. Once, twice, and was in.

Her legs wrapped around him and took him deep. Her hands held his head as she kissed him long and hard.

In his wildest fantasies, he had never imagined Taylor like this. He'd always thought she would be sweet and demure, warm and affectionate but instead she was like a hungry tigress.

He filled her completely, pounding inside of her until she whimpered and came. He didn't stop. He pulled out and kissed her tenderly between the legs, and then he built her up and did it all over again.

CHAPTER SIXTEEN

Throughout the long, blistery night they slept wrapped around each other, and it was near dawn when Taylor woke up to feel a hand curved around her breast, and one leg over hers. She peeked over at the face next to hers. Colt's blond hair was on her pillow. They were cramped in the double bed, and yet she had no desire to move.

She took a moment to study him as he continued to sleep. His breathing was steady, his lower lip slightly open. He had a full, sexy mouth that could do amazing things to her. She had experienced them all during the night. She loved his mouth. She glanced down at the hand covering her breast. That hand had touched her in places that would burn her memory for a long time to come. Speaking of coming, oh my! She had never known she was capable of more than one. And what a climax it was. It went on and on, like she couldn't shut down.

She smiled, thinking about it. Frozen? I don't think so! No sirree, buddy. She was like her sisters after all. Passionate in nature.

She glanced at him again and then bent over to kiss his lips.

His eyes popped open. "Taylor?"

"That's right. It's me." Hurt made her ask, "You forgot already?"

His lips curved in a smile. "Forget? Are you kidding me? I will never forget one thing about you. Or this night. Just wanted to know if you have any more?"

"More what?"

"Condoms. We used three last night."

She rummaged in the drawer. "Sure. It was a full pack."

"I just need to use your bathroom for a sec, then I'll be right back. You want some water or something? This could take us awhile."

"A while for what?"

"To work through the pack." Then whistling a happy tune, he strolled down the hall.

She watched his fine ass until it was out of sight, then giggling, she hid her face under the covers. She was thirty years old and had just discovered her sexuality.

And she damn well liked it.

Hours later, they sat at the kitchen table eating ham and scrambled eggs with whole wheat toast. They were on their second cup of coffee and listening to the news on the radio when they heard a knock on the door.

Colt opened the door to Miguel, and the older man glanced at Taylor, seeing her wearing nothing but a silk robe. She was seated at the table, spreading mango jam on a piece of toast.

She smiled. "Good morning, Miguel. Want a cup of coffee?"

"Uh. No." He glanced from her contented face to Colt's, then halted near the door. "The storm has been reduced to a category one. Should be hitting south of here possibly by midafternoon." He looked uncomfortable, his eyes shying away from the new lovers. "Kayla sent me. She wants you two to come and stay with them. She called last night and again this morning but never got through." He glanced at the floor. "It's safer and more comfortable there." He shrugged. "No boards. Her windows are hurricane proof."

Taylor glanced at Colt, stomach churning. She wanted longer with him, and didn't want to lose this fragile new connection. Once this storm disappeared, likely they'd return to friendship status, but she wasn't ready for that yet.

"What do you think, Colt?" Say no, she said silently, hoping he'd have the same strong reaction as her. This was too new, too wonderful and she wanted to extend this moment together. Was another night too much to ask?

"Up to you. It won't be pleasant staying here." His face was devoid of expression and she couldn't get a read on his true feelings. Once again, he was hiding from her. He shrugged, almost carelessly. "You might want your family around."

Really? He thought she'd prefer her family that she lived with day in and day out, instead of another night making passionate love? *I mean really?* She wanted to kick him, she felt so disappointed. How could he let her slip so easily out of his arms?

She jutted her chin out. "I'm not going without you," she said her eyes steady on his. "You want to go?"

"We're safe enough," he said, "but we could lose power. It will be stifling hot in no time, and the place will be like a cave, all boarded up."

"So what do you suggest?" Taylor asked, trying to hold in the hurt. She had to be a big girl. If the night and morning of incredible sex was enough for him, well, then that's all it would ever be.

"We should go," he said immediately. "Pack up enough for one night, and return tomorrow."

"I agree. That's a good decision," Miguel said. He nodded at her. "I'll wait in the truck."

"No, Miguel, go and tell the others we'll be there soon. I need to shower and dress and gather up a few things. We have board games. Monopoly. Checkers. I'll bring those too."

Miguel left and Taylor turned to Colt. She put a smile on her face when she asked, "You didn't want to stay?" Her voice almost cracked, but he didn't seem to notice. She clutched the back of the chair with knuckles that had gone white.

He glanced away from her. "Of course I did. But it was obvious that we'd slept together. Not that I care, but I figured you might."

"Should I?"

"I don't know how to answer that."

"Then don't." She left him standing there and went in to shower. Sadly, she washed away his scent, but she knew no matter how much she lathered, she'd be unable to scrub away the hurt. Was it over then? One night had satisfied him? How could that be? The way they'd made love--he seemed totally into her. And she was certainly hooked on him. After last night how could she not have strong, loving feelings? He'd touched her in ways that no man had ever done. But she had her pride and could never let him know.

Once she was dressed, she returned to pack up some food from the kitchen and collect the board games. Colt took his shower, then grabbed a few of the lanterns and the radio in case the storm knocked out the power at Kayla's waterfront home.

Within an hour they were reunited with her family. Kayla glanced at her and Colt, and smiled with satisfaction. "Did I drag you away from something?" she whispered, giving her a hug.

"Nothing important," she answered lightly. Afraid that Kayla would look too deep and see beyond her bright smile, she moved on to greet her mom, Juanita and to plant a big kiss on Meri, who squealed with delight.

Ignoring Colt, she chatted happily with Juanita and Raul, and leafed through a picture book with Meri, who tried to identify the farm animals. "Moo, the cow says." Taylor helped Meri pronounce the words, and didn't look up when Colt left the room. She hoped he got the message--loud and clear. She didn't need him. She didn't need anybody. She had everyone she loved right here.

* * *

While Taylor played with the baby, Colt joined Sean who was sitting in the great room watching the news station on his sixty inch TV. He was unshaven, wearing baggy running shorts and a Miami Heat t-shirt.

"What's the latest?" Colt asked, sitting in one of the two sofas.

"Hi Colt. Glad you both got some sense in your heads. You never know with these things. They can change on a dime. Right now the winds are at 70 miles an hour. It made landfall in the Bahamas yesterday as a cat two, and that weakened it some. Now it's picking up again."

"Damn." Colt ran his hand through his hair. "Those poor folks haven't yet recovered from Hurricane Joachim. That monster took out several of the smaller islands. People were evacuated, others stranded, and left without fresh water and food for days. Just doesn't seem right to be hit again so soon."

"I remember."

"So what happens at the hospital during all this? Just a watch and see?"

"Pretty much. Some patients may be moved, but basically the hospital has every emergency backup possible, so it's business as usual."

"And you? On call?"

"I visited my patients this morning, and hopefully they won't need me tonight." He stood up. "You want anything? Coffee? A beer?"

"I might take that beer. But I'll check and see if Taylor wants anything first." He glanced at Sean. A handsome man, early forties, successful cardiac surgeon--and someone who'd come back from unbearable pain. Colt didn't know how he could ever get up in the morning if something happened to Jamie.

"Not sure if I made the right decision by saying we should come here. There never seems to be a right answer with women."

Sean chuckled. "Ain't that the truth."

Colt entered the kitchen area and found Taylor sitting around the table teaching Raul how to play checkers. He took a seat beside the boy, wondering what his own son was doing right now. Would his mother or sister be playing games with him, or leave the boy with an iPad to amuse himself? Latter, probably. They never knew what to say to him, and the iPad was an easy solution. Jamie loved it, since he didn't have one. Win-win.

Kayla brought out sandwiches and a large bowl of sliced fruit and told everyone to help themselves. Colt stood--hoping to make amends for whatever he'd done to piss Taylor off-- and offered to get her a plate.

"I'm fine," she told him in a snappish tone of voice. One he'd rarely heard her use. "You help yourself. I'll get something later."

Stepping behind her, he put his hands on her shoulders and gave them a squeeze. "Did I do something wrong?" he asked quietly. "Should I apologize for something?"

She twisted her head and shot him a look. "Like what?"

"Like I don't know."

"Well, in that case, you didn't." She shrugged his hands off. "Don't worry about me."

"What does that mean?"

"Figure it out."

Raul looked from one to the other. "Are you guys fighting?" He pushed the checkerboard away. "I thought you liked each other. I want you to be friends."

"We are friends," Taylor said. "That's what we are."

"Good friends," Colt added, hoping for a smile from his favorite girl.

She didn't give him one. "Yes." She picked up Raul's hand. "Like you and me."

"Taylor..." Colt sweetened his voice, "would you like to step out for a moment. Could we talk?"

"Out? Like outside? It's a torrential downfall in case you didn't notice. And the winds must be about ninety miles an hour. You want to drown me or something?"

"I want to find out what the hell is going on in that head of yours. I came here to make you happy and all you've given me is grief!" He had raised his voice, and when he looked around he could see everyone was quiet. Her family was staring at them--shaking their heads and whispering together.

He'd blown it for sure. Up a creek without a damn paddle.

CHAPTER SEVENTEEN

Taylor watched Colt storm off into the living room and bit back tears. Kayla came over to her and sat down at the chair he'd vacated. "Want to talk, honey?"

"No. Not now. Still processing it." She kept her eyes averted. "After a great night, this morning he jumped on the opportunity to come here instead of remaining alone at the cabin with me." Her voice broke and she covered her mouth.

"Oh, sweetheart." Kayla put her hand over hers. "I'm sure you misunderstood his intentions."

"Maybe. I'm just not sure. I mean, I knew it wasn't going to last forever, but I wanted one last night."

Blinking back tears, she fled the room, and went to wash her face in the guest powder room. Her mother knocked on the door. "You okay, honey-bunch? You want me to have a word with Colt?"

"No. It's fine," she mumbled, unable to talk about it. Last thing she needed was a total meltdown. Maybe Kayla was right. Maybe he hadn't been eager to leave the cabin either. Made sense. How many men would pass up an opportunity for free sex?

"It's just something Colt and I have to work through," she added.

"Okay, dear. But if you want me to intercede, happy to do so."

"No. I'll be out in a minute." She left the bathroom and found Colt sitting alone next to the TV. Everyone else was in the kitchen having their sandwiches and giving them some space.

"I'm sorry," she said, sitting next to him.

"For what?" he asked, not looking at her. "Do you even know why you were mad?"

"Of course. Don't you?"

"No. What the hell did I do to set you off?"

"You wanted to come here, instead of spending another night with me alone."

"That's what you think?" He shifted so he could look at her.

"That's what I know. I gave you every opportunity back at the cabin to tell Miguel no. That we were staying. But you didn't..." her voice broke.

"Are you crazy? You'd think I'd choose this over making love to you right now? We still had half a box left."

She laughed, tears coming to her eyes. He took her into his arms and kissed her, swiping the pad of his thumb over her cheeks to dry them.

"You know that I'm crazy about you."

"Likewise." She put her head on his shoulder, knowing that everything now would be all right. The world outside might not agree, but in her heart she was happy. Jumping to the conclusion she did had been so silly. But she was vulnerable and inexperienced when it came to men. She'd never doubt him again.

Taylor went with Colt into the kitchen, hand in hand, and everyone gave them a warm smile, accepting whatever had gone down before. She refused to linger in embarrassment, and fixed a plate for herself and one for Colt. He grabbed them each a light beer and then they ate, hip to hip, at the counter. When they were through, Taylor brought out the Monopoly board.

Her mother moaned. "No. Please. It takes forever."

"Exactly. All the more reason to play it," Taylor answered. "Come on, everyone. This will occupy our time, and give us something to do together."

"I'm in," Miguel said. His wife nodded, and Raul jumped to the table too.

Colt patiently explained the game to the three of them, and Taylor could see the excitement in their eyes. She was so pleased that she had thought of it--if for no better reason than to take their mind off the approaching storm.

Juanita caught on quickly, rushing to buy real estate. Kayla was the banker, and Anna was the Queen of the Railroads, getting all four pieces. Taylor didn't mind going bankrupt first, as it allowed her to watch them all and cheer as Raul bought Boardwalk. She was constantly amazed--in a good way--by this delightful Cuban family. Seeing their joy in this old board game made her heart feel light, even though the sky was getting darker as the wind howled outside.

A gust rushed against the patio doors and they shuddered inward from the force of the wind. The windows were being pelted with heavy rain, and they could hear it beating on the roof and against the frame of the house. Lights flickered and Sean, who had lost all his money and was out of the game right after her, got the lanterns ready.

Raul looked up, his eyes wide, and Colt handed him the dice. For a little while longer they could concentrate on winning Boardwalk instead of the dangers of the storm.

"Did you know that this game originated in 1903?" Colt asked. "My father told me that it was created to show people that the accumulation of wealth should be rewarded." He took a slug from his water bottle, then wiped his mouth. He continued his history lesson as the kitchen window shook. "As you buy up property and put up your hotels and homes, you then charge rent and force people into bankruptcy. You win by having more than anyone else, by being powerful. This is a Monopoly, real world style."

"Why that's terrible," Taylor said. "I didn't think of it that way." She was intrigued by the fact his father had educated him with this piece of knowledge. What else had his father taught him?

"Like Cuba," Miguel said, rolling the dice. A four and a two. "The important people own everything. The economy is controlled by the government, not the people." He landed on his property and handed the dice to Anna.

"I own Boardwalk," Raul said proudly. "Does that make me rich and important?"

"What makes you rich and important, my son," Miguel said fondly, "is your love for your family, and your values.

If you work hard and lead a good life, you will be a wealthy and powerful man. Your wealth comes from your family. They are what matters."

Colt stood up suddenly, almost knocking the board over. "Taylor, will you take my place for a sec? I'm going to make a few calls. Want to check on Jamie. Carry on without me."

Taylor watched him leave, wondering what part of that conversation had driven him away. Wealth, or family? Although she felt closer to him than any man she ever knew, he was still a stranger. He hid part of himself away and didn't share it with anyone. If they were ever going to make it as a team, he would have to open up and expose his real self.

Juanita rolled doubles, but then landed in jail. She passed the dice to Kayla. She tossed a ten, and landed on Boardwalk, giving all of her money to Raul—but then she was out of the game. "Your turn, Tay," she said.

Loving a shell of a man would never cut it. Not with her. There were no secrets in her family. Nothing too sacred to share. Every one of them had the other's back, and would stand by them regardless of what they'd done, or had not. She rolled for a total of seven, squeaking by for Colt.

And she was an all or nothing girl. When she chose a partner, she would give everything of herself and demand the same thing back.

They went around the board one more time, and the game was between Anna and Raul—her mom's railroads didn't stand a chance.

Raul high-fived his dad. "I won!"

"In America, anything is possible," Juanita said.

Colt returned ten minutes later. "Jamie's good. Called the marina, but nobody picked up. Guess I shouldn't have expected them to," he said. Deep crevices lined his mouth, and worry fanned his brow.

"You worried about your boat?" she asked.

"Shouldn't be. She's protected, but still. Got a lot invested in her." He glanced toward the windows. "Sean's watching the storm tracker, and we're about to be hit the hardest, according to the chart. Let's move into the living room, away from the windows." After that things got crazy outside.

Not having been in this situation before, Taylor wasn't sure how well the cottages would hold up, and she knew her mother was concerned too. Taylor comforted Anna the best she could, but it was out of their control and at the hands of Mother Nature.

Meri was terrified by the noise and sobbed in her mother's arms--it was heart-breaking to watch. Raul tried to act manly, but he inched up close to his father. Miguel put his arm across Raul's shoulders. Kayla sat next to Sean on the couch, their hands entwined as their new home rattled around them. Two hours into the relentless pounding of the storm, Taylor couldn't take another minute of it, and went into one of the spare bedrooms. She lay down on the bed and closed her eyes--and prayed for everyone's safety, and for Paradise Cove.

A little while later, Colt entered and lay next to her. He took her in his arms, and she cuddled into him, her head on his chest. Being with him helped ease her worries. He seemed so solid and safe, and she knew he'd do anything to protect her. Not that she was worried about herself or her family, it was her resort and everyone else that she knew with families in the area, and businesses to protect.

"Colt?"

"Hmm?" He stroked her arm, and his tender touch soothed her.

"What do you think is happening out there? My cafe? Do you think it's still standing?"

"I'm pretty sure it is. A category one can be pretty damn scary, but it usually doesn't do that much damage. Makes a heck of a mess, and the landscaping will take a beating, but it shouldn't knock down your cabins or the cafe."

"I hope you're right."

"I usually am." He said it with a soft chuckle, and she put a hand on his chest, enjoying the warmth of him, and the fact they were in this together.

"You were right about a few things last night," she whispered, remembering how hot they'd been for each other. "I'm sorry I acted like a jerk this morning," she said, wondering what was going to happen to them now.

"What was I right about?" He stroked her cheek.

"Well, you are a really good kisser. And we were pretty darn great together. And I feel like we can still be friends. Sex doesn't have to ruin anything between us, right?"

"Right. I think it makes our friendship," he made a mockery of the word, "all the more special. I care about you a lot, Taylor. I'd happily give up other women for you."

"Why would you do that?" She raised herself on her elbow to look at him. "That would be silly. It's not like this changes anything between us. We just acted on impulse."

"Is that what it was?" he asked slowly, his hand slipping down to the curve of her ass.

"Kind of. It was impulsive, and I'm usually not like that. But I don't regret it. Not at all. I'm happy we did it."

"Which time?"

She sucked in a breath. "What do you mean?"

"Are you happy you did it the first time, the second, the third, or early this morning? Which time was impulsive?"

"Why are you asking me this?"

"Just curious. I'm feeling a little impulsive right now. If the family wasn't outside this room I might want to try for a fifth. Bet I could score a home run."

"Now you're the one being a jerk."

"Taylor. I'm serious about giving up other women. Just because I don't plan on getting married anytime soon, doesn't mean I can't date one steady girl, does it?"

She didn't answer. Being Colt's steady girl had never occurred to her. Neither had making love to him all night long. She had enjoyed the second part--a lot--but what would being his steady girl mean? How often would they be doing what they did? Two or three times a week? After all, he had his son the other nights, so weekends then. Hmmm. Possibly doable. Certainly exciting. She'd have to think more on that.

"Did you fall asleep or are you going to answer?" He sounded annoyed.

"I'm thinking." She closed her eyes, trying to imagine her life with Colt as a lover instead of a friend. She couldn't. She had so much going on with the cafe and the resort that the idea of making love as a steady diet sounded--well, exhilarating but equally exhausting. When would she ever get any rest? Or alone time? She'd be with customers and people all day long. She'd never be alone again.

Colt was still beside her, but no longer touching. She wasn't sure what to make of that, so she pretended to sleep.

What seemed a lifetime later, the awful noises and shuddering of the walls began to subside. The storm had done its worst and moved away.

Colt sat up. "It's over, Taylor. At least for now. I've seen a hurricane change direction and come back, but I don't expect this one will."

She lifted her face and looked at him. "Thank you for being here. I don't think I could have handled it, if not for you."

"Sure you could." He kissed her lips softly. "You're one of the strongest, bravest women I know." He kissed her again. Gentle, warm, friendly. He was wise enough to know that this was the time for comfort, not passion. "I hope my suggestion didn't frighten you off." He caressed her cheek with the palm of his hand. "I'll always be here for you. As long as you want me."

She gave him a small smile, her heart fluttering. "I want you."

He sat up in bed, and pulled her with him. "Let's go check on the others."

Everyone was gathered in the great room, Meri in her mother's lap, Raul glued to his father. When Colt and Taylor returned, their worried looks turned to smiles.

"You both okay?" Anna asked.

"We are now," Colt answered, holding Taylor's hand.

"*Si.* Storm is gone. Life is good," Miguel said, and nodded at Colt, accepting their relationship for whatever it was. "How about you and I go take a look around?"

"I'll get us some flashlights. Hold on a minute." Sean took off and returned with wet gear for the three of them and lanterns. "We won't be long," he said to the others. "Probably won't see much anyway."

"I'll make coffee, and open some wine," Kayla said, then her face brightened. "Sean, mind if I tell them?"

"Not if you feel ready." Sean moved forward to put a supporting hand around his wife's waist.

"Well, since we are all family here, I think it's time to let Miguel and Juanita in on our little secret." She glanced at Sean's face, then reached out for Juanita's hand. "I'm expecting again."

The announcement brought a round of cheers, hugs and good wishes. A bottle of champagne was opened when the men returned with further good news that they'd only lost one tree out front, and a few shingles from the garage roof.

The night became a celebration instead of a night of despair.

CHAPTER EIGHTEEN

Taylor slept in a room with her mother that night, but lying in her own twin bed all she could think of was the question Colt had asked. Did she want their relationship to explode into a full blown affair? Could she handle it if it did? On the other hand, now that they knew each other intimately, and liked each other so much, how could they not?

"What are you thinking about?" her mother asked, turning on the small lamp next to her bed.

"I'm sorry, did I keep you awake?"

"I probably wouldn't sleep anyway. Anxious about seeing our cottages in the morning."

"Me too, Mom. I have a lot on my mind. The cafe. The resort. Colt."

"Why don't you just admit you love him, and live happily ever after? Then we could all get some sleep."

Taylor laughed. "Wish it were that simple. Our feelings are not in dispute. But nothing has changed. Colt doesn't want a wife, and I'm not ready to be one."

"What is ready? When the time comes it just happens. Doesn't matter if you're ready or not. Now try and get some sleep. It's almost two in the morning and we will have a full day ahead of us tomorrow. Or today," she corrected herself. "Rest my dear. I love you."

"Love you too, Mom."

She must have fallen asleep because the next thing she knew the sun was shining through the window, and the smell of coffee had her taste buds watering. She sat up, and saw her mother was already gone.

She dressed quickly and joined the others in the kitchen. Bacon was frying, and Kayla was stirring scrambled eggs in a large frying pan. Raul was in charge of buttering the toast.

Taylor slipped up behind Colt and gave him a hug. "Good morning everyone. It's so great to see all these smiling faces."

"We have a lot of be thankful for," Anna said, handing Meri a slice of banana. "Brittany called, and she's fine. They didn't get anything where she lived except a lot of rain and heavy winds." Her mom glanced around the table. "Seems like we survived another storm together."

"Amen to that." Taylor poured herself a cup of coffee and hitched her butt on one of the stools next to the speckled granite island they'd recently installed. The kitchen had plenty of tall white cabinets and gleaming counters, and windows and light. But what made it so special were the people and the love they felt for each other. The rest was just material.

After a hearty breakfast, they all took their leave. Kayla stayed with Sean, and Miguel drove his family home, saying he'd get them settled first, then come around to check on the cottages. Anna had her own car, and was going to stay with Kayla and help her clean up, then would meet them back at Paradise Cove in a few hours.

Colt drove Taylor home, wanting to stay until Miguel arrived. She was glad for his company, knowing he must be worried about his boat and his own home too.

"Doesn't look too bad," he said as they first entered the grounds.

They stopped at her cafe which was still standing but her heart sank when she realized that the thatched roof was gone, the picnic tables destroyed, and a second tree had fallen, barely missing the cafe's tin roof.

"Didn't need that tree anyway," Colt said, wrapping his arm around her. He rested his chin on her head and held her close. "We'll put out heads together and figure out a different plan for this outside area. A roof that won't blow down and to get rid of a few more trees."

"Yes. I was the stubborn one and wanted this thatched roof, and Miguel told me it wouldn't last." She gave a short laugh. "Wrong again." She snuggled into him. "One thing I wasn't wrong about is you."

He kissed her gently. "I'm glad you came to your senses."

"Well, about some things." She still didn't know if she wanted to be a lover or a friend, but right now they had more important issues at hand.

They got back in the car and drove down to her cabin, and she let out a sigh of relief to find it untouched. "It looks perfect," she whispered. "My little home." She touched her heart. "Oh, I do love it here. This place." *You.*

"Come on." He raced to the front door. "Let's get some of these boards down, and let a little light in. Then we'll check the rest of the place out."

"Okay." She used her key and pushed the door open. It was dark and uninviting after being at Kayla's bright home overnight. "Looks like a bat's cave," she said, going into a cupboard and grabbing a hammer. "Let's knock those boards down." Gleefully, they ripped most of them off, then left the ones beyond their reach until Miguel could assist.

Together, they toured the property and assessed the damage. Other than a few shingles missing and some tiles from the roof, the cottages held up under the cat one force. The grounds were a mess, with a few trees down, but nothing that couldn't be fixed.

When they reached the pool she was able to see the beach. The palm trees had taken one hell of a beating, and the area was ravaged, but the high tide had been stopped by the mangroves. She hugged Colt, and broke down sobbing.

Colt put an arm around her and let her cry it out. When she peeked at him, she could see his eyes were wet too. Her emotions were so full right now, that she knew she couldn't trust them. Especially with Colt. She felt almost an embarrassing rush of love and gratitude, and a mixture of so many things that she needed to be alone to absorb them all.

She squeezed his hand and then let go. "I need to be alone right now. I'm going to take a short stroll down the beach and try to get my head on straight."

"Sure. I get it." He didn't look offended. "I've got to check on my own property too."

"Why don't you come back later? Tonight. Join us for dinner."

"I'll try. Can't promise anything until I see how my place held up. With any luck it fared as well as yours."

"Give me a call and let me know."

"I will." He turned and left, and Taylor saw Miguel standing not far away. He waved, and she walked over to greet him.

"How's your place? Okay?"

"It's fine. Glad to see all the cottages still standing." He took his cap off his head, and wiped perspiration from his brow. "This place is well built. Strong. Like you it can weather any storm." He glanced at Colt's retreating back. "You good?"

"Couldn't be better."

"Okay. I go to work now." And off he went.

Smiling, she realized how lucky she was to have such solid people around her. No matter what happened, or what decision she made, Colt would remain her friend and staunch supporter. And Miguel was worth his weight in gold. He always knew what needed to be done before she did herself.

Taylor picked her way over the mangroves and walked half a mile down the length of the beach. There wasn't much left of it. It had been washed away, but hopefully it would be presentable again for Kayla's wedding.

When she returned to her cabin, she called both sisters to let them know that the cottages had survived and that their Paradise Cove would soon be back in business.

Next, Taylor cancelled the few reservations they had up and coming. They'd already been in touch so the customers were happy to change their plans and come at a better time.

Anna returned, and got straight to work--taking out the pool's lawn furniture, and flowered pots. She helped Miguel with the light work, obviously enjoying the outdoors after being cooped inside. Taylor couldn't wait to join the two of them, and was heading out the door when Colt called.

She ran back into the cabin to answer. "Hey. How's things?" she asked, her heart racing just at the sound of his voice.

"I'm sorry, Tay, but I won't be able to make dinner. Yard's a mess, and I want to get the place straightened around before Jamie gets back. His mother is bringing him home now."

"No problem. Say "hi" to Jamie for me. Come by any day this week for happy hour. And breakfast when I reopen."

"You bet I will." He cleared his throat. "A lot happened this weekend, didn't it?"

"You can say that again." Taylor wasn't sure if he was having second thoughts. Perhaps he regretted his comments about being exclusive. Now that they were back on familiar ground, he might want to distance himself--or give her some space. She didn't know what to think, but one thing was for sure. Sex changed things. Their relationship would never be completely the same. Understandably, he was probably as confused as she was.

That day and the next flew by, and Taylor's emotions continued to sway like a tropical breeze. One minute she'd remember every detail of her night with Colt and cling to that memory, and then the next she'd try to hide from it--and bury it in work.

There was plenty of that. With her family back, and Miguel chomping at the bit, they all dug in to restore the resort to its pristine best. At the weeks' end, the grounds were greatly improved, but it would take time for some of the beautiful Palms to return to their former glory. Many branches had been clipped, and a few had only a branch or two remaining.

The following weeks flew by. Miguel hired a crew to assist him in clearing away the debris and restoring the beach in front of the resort. Colt and Jamie would join in every few days for happy hour, and he'd pop in once in awhile for a quick breakfast. Fast and friendly. He didn't seek her company alone, and she didn't know what to think about that. She never saw him with any other girl, but yet he'd backed away from her too. It was worse than it was before.

Pre-hurricane, they could lust after each other, but had plenty of good reasons to keep apart. The flirtation had been fun, and playful. Not for her anymore. She yearned, and yet she couldn't have, so she buried the confusion and the hurt deep inside.

Kayla's wedding was approaching fast, and the extra work involved helped her maintain focus. This was not the time for her to worry about what was or what might have been with buddy, Colt. This was her sister's time, family time, and the happiest day was just ahead.

All the arrangements were made, and the guests were flying in from all over. Their friends were staying at their place and Sean's guests were down the road at The Islander, a much larger resort with beautiful grounds, a full scale restaurant next to the pool and the beach, and a warm and friendly staff.

Taylor and her mom had insisted that Kayla stay away for the last two days. With Miguel's help, a beautiful atmosphere for the wedding had been created, and they wanted it to be a surprise.

CHAPTER NINETEEN

The day of the wedding, Taylor was up early, too excited to sleep. Her head was spinning with all the last minute details that had yet to be done. She slipped on an old tee and a pair of shorts and Sketchers, then headed down to the beach. All night she'd been dreaming about today, imagining the joy and wonder that would light up Kayla's face when she saw what had been done.

Rows of tiki torches were set up to enclose the wedding area just beyond the pool but before the mangroves and the beach. Six pillars with pink and white ribbons stood eighteen feet high—three on each side. Miguel and his crew had attached billowing sheer drapes from the pillars that floated like soft clouds over the rows of plastic white chairs. The palm trees were strung with fairy lights, and tables were set up amongst the trees for their guests to dine under the starry night and the twinkling lights.

Tears came to Taylor's eyes when she saw all this in the first light of day. She sat in the one of the chairs, too moved to go any further. What Miguel had done was nothing short of brilliant. He'd discussed it with her and her mom, but until yesterday it was only a drawing. It had taken a team of men to erect the pillars while Colt helped Miguel wind pink and white ribbons around each one. Anna, Taylor and their wedding guests had watched from the pool where they were having a champagne happy hour in honor of the wedding, and a big cheer had gone up when the sheers were attached. The breeze made the sheers flop around and the men had some trouble, but once it was complete, it was the most romantic thing Taylor had ever seen.

She couldn't imagine a more perfect wedding. Tears slid down her cheeks, and she swiped them away. Weddings made everyone emotional, and she was not exempt.

She stood up, feeling a little foolish. Here she was with so much to do, sitting and crying over this lovely setting. She and her mother had been responsible for the small path that separated the guest seating--a make shift aisle which Kayla and Sean would walk toward the arched altar to say their wedding vows.

Taylor's last minute chore was to lay out the pots of flowers along the path as they couldn't be done yesterday, getting in the way of the men constructing the pillars and sheers. While that was being done she'd made the pots herself, as her mother manned the office and Brittany drove their guests around. Cooking was her thing, not flower arrangements, but joyfully she had embraced the task.

She picked up a pot of pink hibiscus and placed it on the right side of the aisle, then went back for the second pot. There were thirty in all. Fifteen per side, and then a dozen smaller ones for the individual tables. It was hard and tedious work, but when she was done, Taylor stepped back to inspect her handiwork. She smiled with satisfaction.

"Hey, Taylor. Looking good," Colt called out to her.

Shading her eyes she watched him arrive. He'd been down at his boat, and his tanned chest was bare, a t-shirt slung over his broad muscular shoulder. He wore baggy cargo shorts that rode low on his hips, sun glasses, and a sexy smile.

"Hey, Colt." She waved her hand toward the potted plants. "Do you think I did the right thing by having one pot pink, then the next one white, or should I have made mixed pots?"

"Not mixed. It's perfect, just as it is." He gave her a quick once over and she wasn't sure if he was still talking plants.

"Thanks." She dropped her eyes, and seeing his half naked body made her mouth water. She wanted to touch him so badly, wanted his kisses so much. Why was he keeping his distance? Didn't he want her anymore?

His eyes when he looked at her told a different story.

They never discussed the proposition he'd made while comforting her in bed. She didn't know if he still wanted her as his one and only sex partner, or if he regretted the impulsive offer. Perhaps he was waiting for her to make the first move.

It was odd how he'd taken to walking around shirtless the past couple of weeks. She didn't think he was working on his tan. Did he hope to entice her with those great abs of his? Really? If he wanted to sleep with her, why wouldn't he just ask? One thing for sure. He was hanging around a lot lately. Helping Miguel with all the wedding stuff. Jamie was back in school, and tourist season wasn't in full swing, so Colt had free time on his hands.

"It looks so romantic, doesn't it?" *Thump, thump, thump.* Taylor put a hand on her chest in a futile effort to stifle the frenzied heartbeat. "I can't wait for Kayla to see it. She'll die."

"Well, I hope not. It *is* her wedding day," he said with a lazy grin, looking her up and down--which wasn't fair at all.

She was dripping wet, her white tee grimy with dirt and clinging to her breasts. She pulled it out to let the air in, and the moment she let go, it sucked right back in. Giving up, she used the back of her hand to swipe drops of moisture from her chin.

"Stop looking at me like that. I'm a mess." She turned away, toying with the flowers. If she looked at his abs again, she might combust.

"You're beautiful." He said it like it was the most natural thing in the world, then stuck his hands in his pockets. "You need any help around here before I go?"

"Nope. Got everything under control." She had nothing under control. Not anymore. And she was starting to like this edgy feeling inside of her.

She took a sip from the water bottle that had warmed under the mid-day sun. She offered it to him, but he shook his head. She glanced at his mouth, then away. "I've been thinking lately."

"Oh yeah? About what?" His eyes were glued to hers. She thought she saw a glint of hope, but maybe it was just the reflection of the sun.

"This. The wedding is going to be so beautiful. Beyond my expectations, that's for sure." She sucked in a breath. "I know I'm jumping ahead, but maybe after this, our resort can add destination weddings as another draw to entice people here."

His shoulders dropped a little. He glanced away. "I don't see why not. You have a great location. And who doesn't love a beach wedding?"

"Exactly." Taylor bobbed her head in agreement. "It's perfect for a small, inexpensive wedding--and of course the reception would be at my cafe."

"Sounds good. If anyone can make this happen it's you and your sisters."

"I haven't even mentioned it to them yet, but I'm sure they will jump all over the idea."

"Jump over what?" Brittany asked, coming up behind them. She was wearing her pink Paradise Cove t-shirt and a pair of white short-shorts.

"Destination wedding place." Colt answered, with a grin. "Taylor's thinking big."

"Great idea," Brit answered, "but I was hoping she meant you."

He laughed. "Why don't you work on her? I've got to deliver fish to the market, then get cleaned up for the wedding." He glanced at Taylor. "Want to take some fish off my hands?"

"No, thank you. We have all the food for tonight stuffed in the cafe's fridge."

"Don't look at me," Brittany said. "I only like fish on my plate." She playfully batted her eyes at him. "But I could always use a good man like you." She shot her sister a pointed look. "Especially if Taylor's still holding out."

"Thanks for the offer," Colt replied, darting a quick glance at Taylor. "But I'm afraid my heart's elsewhere."

Taylor's pulse speeded up. Damn, why wouldn't he just ask? "Later, dude."

"Yeah. Later." With a jaunty toss of his shirt over his shoulder, he swaggered off, knowing probably that both women's eyes were on him.

Brittany whipped around and glared at her. "Are you out of your ever-loving mind? What are you waiting for? He's smoking hot, and wants you. If you don't watch out someone else will come along and snatch him up."

"I'm not interested in a casual affair. That's why." Taylor dug her palms into her shorts' pockets. She knew it wasn't completely true. She was worried what would happen to her at the end. Because there would be an end.

"He's told me plenty of times that he isn't interested in a relationship. Marriage is off the table." She shrugged. "So why would I want to let him in my bed?"

"Well that kinda sucks, but you could ignore it, couldn't you? At least for a night. Give him a good work over, then Taylor, sweetie, you can go back to being a practicing nun."

"You say the nicest things."

Brittany grinned. "I'm just trying to help. I see the way you look at him. Your eyes go all soft, your cheeks turn rosy, and your skin gets prickly."

"That's a lovely image. I'll make sure I stay well clear of him from now on."

"No, you won't. It's adorable. I've never seen you ga-ga about a guy."

"Good thing if my skin breaks out with hives."

"Don't be silly. That's probably your body telling you that you need to get laid." She gave her a long speculative glance. "So you two have never done it? I thought maybe with the hurricane thing you might have. Mom hoped so too."

"The two of you seem to think the world runs on sex. And that a man equals happiness. It's not so. I'm perfectly happy..." she paused to think about it, "most of the time."

"So, no touchy feely, get down and dirty, fun at all?" Brittany gave her a disappointed look. Like she had failed miserably the test of sisterhood.

Taylor decided to give her a little hope. "Okay. We messed around some." She gave a careless shrug. "He'd like me for a steady lover." Her chin shot up. "But I said no."

"Oh, Taylor. From you, I'd expect no less." Brittany laughed and swatted her arm. "Me? I enjoy it too much. I don't want things down under to grow over from lack of use." She put a hand on her hip and gave her a pose. "On that note, I invited Jose. I'm hoping he'll drive down from Miami. I told him I'd make it worth his while."

"He's a lucky guy," Taylor said, meaning it. Everyone loved Brittany. Who could help it?

"That's what I keep telling him. But you know men. He's dark, dashing and delicious. And has an eye for the ladies. Who have an eye for him."

"Hmmm. Not sure if I like the sound of that."

Brittany shrugged. "I can handle it. And him." She turned around to see her mother weaving between the tables that were set up for the wedding reception, carrying two drinks in her hands.

"Hi, Mom." Brittany reached for the second glass. "What are you drinking?"

"A light fruity sangria punch. I just made a batch. Try it. Does it need more lime or wine?"

She tasted, and licked her lips. "Yummy. What do you think, Tay?" She handed over the plastic glass with flamingos and Paradise Cove etched on the sides.

Taylor sipped. "Good. Delicious. Offering a punch to our guests as they arrive was a terrific idea." They had seventy-five people attending the wedding. Several people from the hospital where Sean worked and a few old friends, including his family from California. Kayla's friends from Philadelphia were here, as well as three young women that Brittany had grown up with. Anna had invited a few couples that they'd all known for years that were delighted to come.

Taylor handed the still-full glass back to her mom. "I'm going to run off and take my shower. Kayla should be getting here to dress in the next hour." She hurried away, glad to get the shower first while there was still plenty of hot water. When she reached their cabin, she stopped short. Colt was sitting on the front step.

"Colt? I thought you had to drop your fish off to the restaurants before going home?" She walked slowly toward him.

"I wanted a minute with you alone." He stood up just inches from her, invading her space.

She could smell the scent of his body mingled with a light clean aftershave, and it made her mouth water. Oh, the things she'd like to do with this man. The things she *had* done with this man. If only she didn't have all these damn scruples. What was so wrong with being a friend with benefits? It worked for a lot of people. But she had a sinking feeling low in her gut that it wouldn't work for her.

She would wind up getting hurt. Her emotions would get deeply involved and she'd want a commitment, and to make him the father of her babies. All of them. Wasn't going to happen, and wishing it wouldn't make it so.

Taylor put a hand on his bare chest, holding him back. At least that's what she told herself. It wasn't to cop one quick feel.

"Have you been thinking about us? What I suggested?"

"Yes. A little." She looked down at the ground. Away from his eyes--his mouth--the temptation that was him. "We're friends." She tried for a light-hearted tone. "Can't mess with that."

He groaned. "Taylor. You're killing me."

She took a step back, her stomach in a knot. She wanted Colt, but not like this. "If you want instant gratification, you can always find it elsewhere," she told him, hoping for a denial. What would she do if he said okay? Well, then she'd have her answer, wouldn't she? With that mindset, she decided to press harder, eager to know where she stood. "You know the old saying--there's plenty more fish."

"Not the kind of fish I'm looking to catch. I want one worth fighting for. Anybody can get a flounder. But a spectacular beauty like a sailfish, now that's worth waiting for."

"Am I a sailfish?" she asked, actually liking the comparison.

"You sure are." He reached out a hand and scooped it behind her head, bringing her face down to his. "One kiss, then I've got to run."

She shouldn't have, but she let him kiss her. She tasted his salty lips, his sweet minty breath, and the wholesome scent of the sea. A whole mess of feeling swept through her--an awakening of desire, a need to fill the emptiness inside of her, a surge of longing to take what he offered, but caution pricked her consciousness, and she knew she'd say no.

She wished she could be like her sister, and live for the moment.

Yet he was still kissing her, and she hadn't stepped away.

CHAPTER TWENTY

"Taylor?" His lips caressed hers, slowly, tenderly exploring her full lush mouth, tasting her and feeling the heat grow between them with every breath. How long could she hold out? His patience was long, but his need was great.

"Hmm," she murmured, her beautiful breasts nestled next to his chest. She kissed him open-mouthed, wanting him as he did her. She might pretend she wasn't interested, but a man knew. She wanted him, and she wanted him good.

"You know that I care about you. Do you trust me?"

"Of course I do." She pushed back a little and looked at him with startled eyes. "Why do you ask? You think I'd be tonguing you if I didn't?"

"No. But I want us to be closer. I don't want other women. Just you." His eyes pleaded with hers. "Tonight my boat will be next door. I have champagne in the fridge. And roses for you. At least consider it. Okay?"

She chewed on that for a moment, a frown crinkling her brow. Then gently she pulled out of his arms. "You know I want to. But I can't. Having sex for fun sounds like a hellova an idea for most people, but I'm not made that way. I don't want anything from you, Colt. I'm not asking you to be different than what you are. You have your business and your son to take care of. I've got the cafe and the resort. Maybe one day things will be different, but it isn't now."

He admired that about her. She was hard-working, honest, and even-keeled. Good work ethics, like he had. But what did that have to do with sex? They could still enjoy each other. Didn't mean they needed to jump on the marriage train.

"I agree that we can't rush full steam ahead, but I'm just talking about you being my girl. We're both adults and we can have a little recreational sex if we want to."

"True, but still I don't think it's a good idea." She tossed her head back and straightened her shoulders. Her hazel eyes had that worried look she wore so often. "Sex always complicates things, and our lives are so complicated anyway, that I think we'd be making a really big mistake."

"Doesn't have to be. Not if we both go in with our eyes open." He gave her his sexiest, melting-the-pants-off-a-woman smile.

"Colt. Look at it from my point of view. Sex is different for a woman. What starts off casual doesn't stay that way. A woman's emotions always get involved. Men--they can do it 'til their dick falls off, and not have their hearts involved."

He laughed. "That's crazy. Men are just as much at risk as falling in love as women are."

"I don't believe it. Maybe Rhett Butler, but how many others?"

"Me, for one."

"All the more reason to stay clear of you." She shook her head. "Really. You and I would be a colossal mistake. I can't be a mother to your boy. I wouldn't even know how."

"Jamie already has a mother. Try another excuse."

"He's a good enough reason." She folded her arms around her middle. "He doesn't want to share you with me, or any other woman competing for your affection. Maybe you don't realize it, but he must still be hurting over the divorce. It hasn't been that long, and he's being bounced back and forth. It's tough on a child."

"How would you know?" She could be so infuriating at times. Why the hell wouldn't she just sleep with him and put them both at peace? They were walking around like two hormonal kids, all hot and bothered by each other. He wanted her. Period. And he wasn't the kind of guy who gave up easily.

"I just do." She tossed her head back and glared at him.

He took a deep breath and released it slowly. "I'm trying to get you to see sense. You want me. I want you. As far as Jamie's concerned, I know he'll be fine with it. He likes you. A lot."

"I adore Jamie too," she said softly. "But I know what this kind of upheaval can do to a kid. I've lost two fathers, neither from a divorce. Kids need both parents, and it's very hard when they lose one."

"Taylor, I know that must have been really tough. You girls didn't have an easy childhood, did you?"

"No, but we're doing fine now."

"I understand where you're coming from, but Jamie hasn't lost a parent. He still has both of us."

"Yes, but..."

He interrupted, wanting to get his point across. "If you and I hung out once in awhile, he wouldn't have to know. If it got serious, then we could tell him."

She shook her head, but her eyes misted up.

He stepped closer and cupped her chin. "Life is difficult enough without someone to hold once in awhile. I want to hold you in my arms, sleep with you." Before she could push him away, he kissed away her tears.

He felt her body shiver. "Stop trying to sell me on this idea. I said no. Why can't you just accept that?"

"Fine. No it is." Disappointment kicked him in the gut, and his groin was stinging like a jellyfish bite. He hated her stubbornness and common sense. Even more, he hated pressuring her, but he had been patient for the better part of a year. The night of the hurricane had changed everything. At least for him. He couldn't get her out of his head. Every night when he went to bed, he hurt for her.

"Thank you, Colt." Her expression softened. Her bottom lip trembled. "You'll see. It's better this way."

"If you say so." He turned away and took a step. Then halted. "Remember how we first met?"

"Uh-huh. Down at the docks. Brittany and I would go for long walks along the beach, and we'd see you half naked on your boat. Or fishing."

"And you'd always stop and say hello. Once you knew that I wasn't just a bum hanging around all day--that I actually made my living off the sea, you wanted to buy fresh fish from me."

"Which you wouldn't sell. You always made a silly excuse to give me one free."

"And you'd sit and talk for awhile, even flirted, if I remember right."

"Maybe I did. But I didn't know you were divorced and had a son. And at the time I didn't expect to open a restaurant. It's a big responsibility running two businesses."

"Always comes back to that, doesn't it?"

"Guess so."

"If that's what you want, I'll stop pestering you." He thrust his hands in his pockets, so as not to reach out for her. Touching her set everything inside of him on fire. If she didn't want that, he'd just have to find a way to live with it.

* * *

Taylor watched him go. Her shoulders slumped, and she let out a weary sigh. This was not easy. She knew she was hurting him, as well as herself. They did have strong feelings for each other. The only thing holding them back was her fear. Fear of loving him too much, and not having him for keeps. Everything else was just an excuse. That was the real issue at hand. She was afraid of the consequences if she chose to sleep with him regularly. She might lose her heart completely. How could she not?

He already owned a part of it. And since neither one of them wanted to commit to each other, she'd be better off to keep her legs shut.

Pushing all negative thoughts from her mind, she stepped into the single bathroom and turned the shower on, letting the steam rise as she tossed off her clothes. Tonight was going to be one of the happiest days of her life. Her best friend and beloved sister was getting married, and nothing was going to mar this special occasion. Certainly not worries about what or what might not be between her and Colt.

Stepping out of the shower, she wrapped a towel around herself and opened the door of the bathroom.

And there stood Kayla, peering into a full length mirror and struggling to zip up her wedding dress.

"Oh, my gosh," Taylor gasped, seeing her beautiful sister. She rushed over to give her a big wet hug. "Look at you! Stunning. Here, let me help you with that." She took hold of Kayla's shoulders and turned her around so she could zip up the back of the strapless gown. "Where's Mom?"

"She's getting dressed. They saw you talking with Colt, so they both grabbed the shower before you."

"Sneaky. I didn't see them pass."

"Maybe because you were kissing Colt," Kayla said with a laugh. "Oh, I do hope things work out with the two of you."

"They won't. I basically told him to forget about me."

"Why did you do that?"

"It's not important. Your wedding is all we need to think about right now."

"Oh, Taylor, I'm so excited and nervous." Kayla gave a shaky laugh. "Look. My fingers won't work." She pulled at the dress and patted her tummy. "Am I showing?"

"Just to the people in the know. The other guests will never suspect." Taylor spun Kayla around to face her again. "You are the picture of a radiant bride." She nodded at the mirror that captured their image. "Look at you. Pink cheeks, sparkling eyes, ruby red lips. And that dress! You look like a magazine cover. Only better. Sean is going to be climbing all over you."

"He better not! I just spent a fortune getting myself all primped for this today. Hair, nails, bikini wax." Kayla's sunny smile faded. She turned from side to side frowning at the mirror. "Is it too plain?"

The dress was simple but elegant. An ivory-colored mermaid dress with a sweetheart bodice, that clung to Kayla's lush curves and swept around her size nine feet. "Plain, my ass. Good thing we have more than one cardiac surgeon around tonight, because you're going to get everyone's heart pumping!"

"Oh, Taylor," Kayla laughed and kissed her cheek. "I do love you."

Their mother came out of the second bedroom. She wore a rose-colored fitted dress that fell to her ankles. It had sheer lacy sleeves, and was extremely modest compared to what she normally wore. Tonight she was playing the role of Mother of the Bride, and carrying it off beautifully.

"Kayla, my baby girl." Tears filled her eyes. "This is the happiest day of my life. You're getting married at last."

Taylor stifled a laugh. Kayla was thirty-two years old, not quite two years older than she was. And yet, their mother had worried that they'd all be old maids.

"Yes. I got lucky," Kayla said with a playful grin. "Went fishing last year and hooked myself a real catch."

"Don't get cheeky with me," her mom said with a twinkle in her eye. "You did do well, but so did he. Sean's a wonderful man and you've made him happy again. It does my heart good to see the love shining in his eyes for you."

"I know, Mom. It was hard seeing him hurting so badly."

"Yes, well, that's over now. You two are going to be very, very happy and give me lots of grandchildren." Anna kissed her daughter's cheek, then wiped the rose-colored lipstick stain left behind. "I know that this is the one." She touched her daughter's tummy. "A little Anna, maybe?"

Kayla grinned. "Maybe. With any luck." Taylor watched the exchange and felt a tug inside of her. Maybe she was wrong not to give Colt a chance.

"I better get my hair dried before it turns to frizz. I'll finish getting ready and then join you for a pre-wedding drink."

"Don't be too long," her mother warned, "or the first batch of sangria will be all gone."

Brittany popped her head out of the bedroom she once shared with her mother, and waved the empty glass in her hand. "I can second that. I need another one."

"Let's see your dress," Kayla said, clapping her hands in excitement.

Brittany pranced into the small living room, and swirled around. Both sisters had matching bridesmaid's dresses. They were a pale blue, with off-the-shoulder cap sleeves. The silky fabric danced around Brittany's toned calves, accentuating her tiny ankles and slender legs.

"Gorgeous." Kayla took her younger sister's hand. "You look amazing." She waved her free hand at Taylor. "Hurry up. I can't wait for a toast."

"Who's waiting?" Brittany asked, grabbing the pitcher from the fridge. "I'm going for seconds. You, Mom?"

"Oh, I better not," Anna replied with a longing look at her empty glass.

"Oh, when did that ever stop you!" Taylor refilled her mom's glass. "If you can't get tipsy at your daughter's wedding, when can you?"

"Just don't you two go falling in the pool," Kayla said with a loving smile. "Wouldn't be the first time I had to fish you out."

Taylor giggled. "I remember. Last New Year's Eve."

"Yes," Anna said, unabashed. "And what happened next? All the guests jumped in after me." She smiled at the memory. "I had a little romance of my own going on after that. Me and the pizza man."

Kayla nodded. "I remember. Whatever happened to him?"

"He needed a pacemaker, and I decided right then and there that I wasn't going to bury another husband. Keeping my eyes open for a younger man. Who knows? Maybe one of Sean's doctor friends."

Brittany shook her head and made a face. "Oh, Mother. Leave a few good men for the rest of us."

"I thought you had Jose coming," Taylor said.

"Not anymore. He sent me a text. Said he wasn't a big fan of weddings, but would make it up to me when I get back home." She rolled her eyes. "Whatever."

Anna looked disappointed. "I'm sorry, honey. I knew you were looking forward to him being here. And I wanted to meet him too."

"It's okay. I'm not really surprised."

"Well, tonight should be interesting." Anna smiled. "We should all keep our eyes open. Although I don't think Taylor's really in the market. Not after that hot kiss I saw outside our door. Right, hon?"

"That should never have happened, and I told him so." She squirmed a little, seeing the disapproval on all their faces. "I'm being cautious, Mom. That's all. Got a lot of things going on right here. Plus, we are both up to our eyeballs in debt."

"Well, maybe a rich man could solve a few of those problems. If you're not a hundred percent sure about your cute fisherman, tonight might be a good night to scout out further prospects."

Taylor made a face. "Mom. On that note, I'm really going in now to dress." She walked off. "Prospects, my ass. What is this? 1920?"

"Some things don't change," Anna said. "My mother always told me it's just as easy to love a rich man as a poor one. The rich guy just has a lot more benefits."

Taylor shut the door behind her, not wishing to challenge her mother on that line of thinking. Colton Travis was a good, honest, hard-working man who loved his son and wanted to provide a decent life for him. Those qualities meant more than a big bank balance.

Besides, he was harder on himself, than any one of them could ever be.

CHAPTER TWENTY-ONE

The ceremony took place at six-thirty, in time for the guests to watch the sunset fade into the ocean. The view was a gorgeous backdrop for the couple at the altar. Anna, Taylor and Brittany stood waiting for Sean to escort Kayla down the make-shift aisle. Facing them stood Sean's father—the best man, and Robert, his brother-in-law--and Ken, his best friend from med school. They all looked magnificent in their white tuxes, and smiling suntanned faces.

When the bride and groom appeared, Taylor felt a lump in her throat and her eyes grew misty. Kayla looked breathtaking, and sweet, wonderful Sean so very much in love. With her arm in his they stopped to smile and greet their guests--and to give each other adoring glances during the short walk to the altar.

Taylor's heart filled to overflowing--love for her sister and the immense joy to be sharing this happiest of all days--yet there was a sadness too, remembering both fathers who had loved them all, and could not be here.

It reminded her how fragile life was, and how fleeting it could also be. Sean had lost his beloved daughter when she was ten-years-old. His heart must be hurting right now--and yet, nothing could dim his bright smile, and the loving looks he gave his bride.

Brittany sniffed, and Taylor took her hand and gave it a squeeze. She envied her sister's ability to live in the moment and fully embrace every day. She'd tried it the night of the storm and enjoyed each pleasurable second—until she'd allowed her common sense to intrude.

Taylor glanced over at Colt as Reverend Martha Lewis, an attractive dark lady from the Bahamas, asked the guests to please be seated. He winked at her and she felt her cheeks flush. Her stomach jumped in anticipation of what might be--if she had the courage to let it.

She gave him a small smile before turning away, her insides in turmoil. Could they make love often, and not fall in love? Was it possible? She shot him another quick look, and he gave her that panty-melting double-dimple grin of his. Did he know she was actually trying to talk herself into it? Most likely. Yet, it went against everything she believed.

"We're gathered here today to celebrate the love of Kayla Holmes and Sean Flannigan and to be witnesses and supporters of the commitment they share with one another." The reverend waited a moment then said solemnly, "Kayla and Sean asked me if we could take a moment to remember their loved ones who couldn't be here today, and to let them know how much they are loved and greatly missed. Missed, but not forgotten on this day of celebration."

Taylor noticed the way Kayla reached for Sean's hand and a silent communication passed between them.

In her lilting voice, Reverend Lewis continued, "Marriage gives permanence and structure to a couple's love. It's telling the person you love that you're not going anywhere and that's a powerful commitment for two people to make to one another. A good marriage must be built on the foundation of this commitment." She glanced at the couple and said gently, "It's being never too old to hold hands, and to remember to say, "I love you" at least once a day. It's never going to bed angry, and standing together to face the world. Remembering to speak words of appreciation and show gratitude in thoughtful ways. Having the capacity to forgive and to forget. To give each other an atmosphere in which to grow, and a common search for the good and the beautiful. It is not only marrying the right partner, but *being* the right partner. The road that has brought Kayla and Sean here today hasn't been easy. It's been filled with challenges that they weren't necessarily prepared for. But together they've taken each one on and have used those experiences to strengthen, not weaken their love."

The reverend then read from the bible, and commenced the vows. Taylor sneaked a peek at Colt again. He scrubbed up pretty darn nice, she had to admit. He wore a light blue suit which brought out the blue of his eyes, a white shirt and some kind of fish looking tie. His long blond hair was neatly combed off his handsome tanned face. He sat quietly, one knee over the other, hands clasped around his knees--looking relaxed and elegant. Different from the laid-back, bare-chested, flip-flop guy she knew slinging around pails of smelly fish.

Catching her eyes on him, he held her gaze for a long moment, and she was the first to look away. Her sister and new husband were saying their vows and Taylor listened intently. It was as if the two of them were a million miles away--alone in the universe. Just the two of them, against the world, floating on a cloud of happiness. The setting could not have been more beautiful, but the love shining in Kayla's eyes and mirrored in Sean's took one's breath away.

God knew they deserved it.

The ceremony was coming to an end. "Kayla and Sean, you have professed your love by exchanging vows, and symbolized your commitment by the exchange of rings. You have expressed the end of your individual lives by the pouring of the unity sand. With all of this, there is just one more question I need you to answer and then we're off to the reception to celebrate." She gave them a warm smile and her eyes swept over the happy guests.

Raising her voice, she asked, "Kayla, do you take Sean to be your husband--to live together in the covenant of marriage? Do you promise to love him, comfort him, honor and keep him, in sickness and in health, and forsaking all others, be faithful to him as long as you both shall live?"

Kayla grinned and nodded, her eyes on Sean's. "I do."

"And you, Sean," Reverend Lewis slowly repeated the same question.

Sean cupped Kayla's chin and looked adoringly into her eyes. "You bet I do."

Reverend Lewis smiled. "By the power vested in me I now pronounce you husband and wife. Sean, you may kiss your bride."

And he did. Swooping her into his arms, he made it known that Kayla was his for keeps.

"It's my great honor and privilege to be the first to present to you Mr. and Mrs. Flannigan."

Everyone applauded and began snapping pictures as the couple returned down the flowered path, throwing smiles and kisses at their families and guests.

The bridesmaids and the grooms followed, and then the guests. The party had begun. Flutes of champagne were being served on the beach and also around the pool. Before she was half-way there, Colt snagged Taylor by the arm.

"May I join you?"

"Of course you may." She laughed, feeling giddy with joy. The wedding had been even more beautiful than she'd ever imagined. Her sister deserved this happiness and more. "Wasn't it wonderful?"

"Yes. Kayla made a beautiful bride." His eyes raked over her. "And you look stunning tonight."

"And you! Super hot!" She pulled his tie. "Love the tie. What is it? A whale?"

"No," he said in a scolding tone. "It is not a whale. As if. I have some class you know. It's a Blue Marlin tie." He stroked it proudly. "Bought it special to go with this suit. Don't think I've worn a tie since my own wedding which seems like a hundred years ago."

The reminder of his wedding deflated her. He had sworn to love another woman, and they had a son. When they said their vows, they must have loved each other very much. What had caused their love to die?

He looked at her and his eyes narrowed. "What's wrong?"

"Nothing. Everything." She took a step back. "I hate that you were married before." She bit her bottom lip, wondering why now the idea hit her so hard.

"Why? We were young, and it was good for awhile. I wouldn't have Jamie if it weren't for my ex-wife."

"I know. It's just that you've already had these things. A wedding. A wife. A son. I have all that to look forward to."

"You expect me to apologize for that?"

"No, of course not! I have no idea why it bothers me. It's just...how do you let something like that go?"

"Sometimes you have no choice. People fall out of love for different reasons. They grow apart, or aren't the person you expected them to be. People make mistakes."

She shook her head, taking another step back. "That's just wrong."

"No one gets married expecting it to end. A wedding is not a marriage. It's just a hope and a promise that may or may not last. Trust me, I know."

"I don't want to believe that." The giddiness she'd experienced watching her sister exchange her vows dissipated, leaving her stomach in a knot. "I'll see you at dinner."

She rushed ahead to catch up with Kayla, and put on a cheerful face. "Hey, married lady. How does it feel?"

"Like I'm dreaming and don't ever want to wake up."

Taylor wrapped her in a hug. "It was the most beautiful wedding ever. Congratulations." She pulled Sean in for a hug and kiss too. "You two are so perfect for each other. I'm so glad you found one another."

Sean kissed her cheek. "Me too. Finding my way here couldn't have been an accident. I think I was directed here for a reason." He glanced at his wife as he said, "Divine intervention. I was drifting along on my boat--no particular destination in mind. Then I stumbled upon these shores, and met the most wonderful girl in the world."

"Sean." Tears filled Taylor's eyes. "No wonder she loves you."

"You will meet the right one too." He glanced back at Colt. "Trouble in Paradise?"

"Oh, just the usual. He wants a bed partner, but not a wife."

Sean laughed and rubbed his clean jaw. "That's a problem I understand."

Kayla nodded. "It's a tricky situation, Sean. Taylor has to decide what's best for her." She looked into Taylor's face. "You don't want sex without love."

Sean hugged his wife. "Well, I vote you put the poor guy out of his misery. Colt has real feelings for her."

"Your vote doesn't count," Taylor told him. She lifted her chin. "Right now I need some champagne. And you still need to introduce me to some of your friends." She tossed her long hair off her shoulders, and glanced around the pool at the guests clamoring for a drink. "I haven't had a chance to meet them all." She put a hand on her hip. "I better, before Mom does."

He laughed. "Too late. She's already chatting up John. He's the only one single. Divorced. Forty-five. You interested? I can introduce you right now."

"Naw, that's okay. Later." Taylor's eyes were drawn to Colt at the bar. He was having a scotch and soda and talking to a friend of Kayla's. A young woman she'd worked at the hotel with in Philadelphia.

She was pretty, Taylor decided. With a mane of red hair and green sparkling eyes. Shorter too. Probably five feet five or six. She could easily wear high heels around Colt. And he wore that heart-melting smile, that he normally reserved for her.

Well, let him! If a pretty face could turn his attention elsewhere, then so be it. Obviously, she'd been feeling emotional and romantic tonight because of the wedding, but that was all the more reason to stay clear of his temptations.

CHAPTER TWENTY-TWO

Colt could feel Taylor's eyes on him, and was miffed enough to turn his back on her. How often did he have to prove his feelings for her, only to be shut down? He didn't want anyone else, but if she didn't feel the same way, well, he wasn't going to remain celibate forever.

Now what was Jennifer saying? Something about grabbing a table together. "Sure. I don't see why not." He took a sip from his scotch, and turned his head to catch a glimpse of Taylor storming toward the bar. By the way her shoulders were set, her back like a rod, and the icy glare she gave him, she was not happy. That made two of them.

"So, how do you like the Keys?" he asked Jennifer, who was looking up at him with the adoring expression he'd hoped to see on Taylor's face. "You ever been here before?"

"Yes, about ten years ago. Right after high school graduation. A few of my friends and I took a road trip. We stopped in Myrtle Beach for a few days, then visited Disney World in Orlando for a crazy time. Finally got to Key West and stayed for a week. It was awesome." She stretched her back, giving him an eyeful of her busty chest. He preferred just a handful himself. Like Taylor's.

Damn! Why the hell did he have to compare every woman to her? He'd bet his left nut that if he invited Jennifer down to his boat tonight, she'd be all over it. Wouldn't give a good goddamn if he'd been married before or not. What had that been about anyway? They weren't kids. They had pasts. It was the future he was interested in.

He turned his attention back to the luscious lady beside him. "Sounds like you girls had a blast."

"We did. So how about you? Lived here long?" She sipped from her champagne, her eyes never leaving his face.

"We moved to Florida when I was sixteen. I grew up in New York."

"I thought I detected a northern accent." She smiled. "Where abouts?"

"Long Island for the most part. Dad had an apartment in the city, which he used mainly for work."

"Sounds pretty nice."

"I guess. Things happened. My parents got a divorce, and Mom took my sister and me to Miami."

"Are they still there?" she asked.

"Yes. They have their own real estate company. Wanted me to join them, but that kind of life wasn't for me. Came to the Keys."

"So." She gave him an accessing look. "The charter business is good?"

"If you mean profitable, probably not." He grinned. "But I like it here. During the season, "Bait Me" is pretty much booked every day. In the summer, I make a living by fishing."

"I'd love to go out on your boat sometime. I'm staying another five days." She finished her champagne, and held out her glass for a waiter to refill.

The waiter was Miguel. He nodded at Colt. "Another scotch, Colt?"

"Not yet, thanks, Miguel. But I'll have some of those oysters that Juanita is carrying around--when she has a moment."

"I'll let her know. She's filling up another tray."

Jennifer spoke up. "Did I see a tray of crab cakes?"

"Yes, ma'am. We'll get that out too."

"Thanks, buddy," Colt said, watching Miguel hurry off.

"So, I was asking you if I could get out on your boat sometime?" Jennifer tilted her head and gave him a flirtatious smile.

"Sure. We could probably arrange that." Leaning against the railing, he glanced around the pool. He spotted Taylor speaking with her mother and an older guy with graying hair. Kinda had that smooth George Clooney look. He'd bet his other nut that the guy was a doctor down at Mount Sinai. Brilliant, successful, everything he wasn't. Probably thought his shit didn't stink.

Colt turned his back once more, concentrating on the fading sun over the ocean. Jennifer leaned over the railing as well. "It sure is pretty. I can see why Kayla loves it here. I'm more of a city girl, I guess, but I could get used to this."

"It gets in your blood. When I want to do something special, I can always fly away for a few days, but I don't get that urge very often."

"What do you get the urge to do?" She asked it quietly, but the meaning was clear from the look in her eye, and they way she shifted so her breasts brushed up against his arm.

"Well, I don't have a whole lot of urges either. I have a ten-year-old boy that lives with me, and between him and my business, well there isn't much free time."

The sparkle in her eye dimmed and he was almost sorry he'd mentioned Jamie. But Jamie was the most important thing in his life. Getting laid was a distant second. "Oh. You're married?" She glanced down at his ring finger which hadn't seen a ring on it for the past year.

"Not any more. Divorced."

"Oh!" She grinned. "I went through one of those. Not much fun, is it?"

"No. Pretty crappy, matter-of-fact. Not such a picnic for Jamie either, getting shuffled back and forth. His mom lives in an apartment just south of here. She's a nurse at the Lower Keys Medical Center. Got a boyfriend down there. A resident doctor. Which is quite a few steps up from someone who catches fish for a living."

She laughed and tossed her hair over her shoulder. "I see."

"Well, just telling it the way it is." He shifted toward the other guests again. Taylor was laughing with the George Clooney look-a-like.

"If you're happy, it doesn't matter what you do. Bottom line, that's all that counts."

"I am happy. Sure beats working in an office or cutting into people all day."

She snorted with laughter. "You are too funny. Come on, let's grab another drink and a table before they're all gone."

He gave Taylor another look, but she seemed to have forgotten him already. "Sure. Sounds good."

* * *

Taylor turned just in time to see Jennifer and Colt refilling their drinks at the bar. She watched them leave the pool area and take the stairs to the beach. They headed over to the reception area, found a nice view table, then he pulled out a chair for Jennifer and sat down. They didn't have any formal seating arrangements, but she had thought he'd be eating with her.

She bit her lip, fuming inside. Her eyes smarted, and she wanted to smack something. Like his too-handsome face. She could see him leaning in Jennifer's direction and their shoulders bumped as they laughed over something he'd said. If she hadn't acted like an idiot over the fact he'd been married once, she might be sitting with him now. He'd be whispering nice things in her ear, smiling at her.

Sean had been married and had a child too, but that hadn't stopped Kayla from loving him. Yet it was more than that. She wanted to believe in happily-ever-afters, but deep inside she knew it was a lie. Life didn't come with guarantees. And she wasn't the sort to gamble. That's why she continued to push Colt away. Not because he'd been married before, or had an eye for the ladies. She believed him when he said he didn't want anyone but her. The real problem was, as much as she cared for him, she was afraid to risk her heart.

She was the problem. Not him. And it wasn't fair to keep him dangling. He deserved companionship, a loving woman to share a part of his life with. If he found it tonight--even for a few hours--she should be happy for him. After all, he'd offered it to her plenty of times and she kept turning him down. Always wanting to play it safe. Avoiding heartache at any cost.

Glancing at them again, she had to admit that Colt seemed more than content to be where he was. And more than likely he would get what he wanted tonight. Not with her, but with someone else. Brittany had warned her that she might send him into another woman's arms, but she hadn't expected it to happen so soon. Not tonight.

This was her sister's wedding, dammit! Nobody had the right to mess with that. Nobody. Not some hot-to-trot dame from Philadelphia who would be going back to her real world soon. And not Colton Travis either.

He should respect her enough to wait for another evening. Another woman. Someone she didn't know. Not a guest of theirs--a long time friend of Kayla's. Not in front of her. It was wrong, wrong, wrong.

She wanted to be with him again. To share his hot kisses and feel his hands and mouth everywhere. He had been the best lover she'd ever known. She remembered every detail of their night together, and relived it day after day, all alone in her bed. And yet she'd sent him away. This was her doing, and she just had to suck it up. Timing in life was everything, and this wasn't their time. How many times had she told herself, and him, that?

Dr. John Sinclair came up to her and put his hand on her back. "Your mother would like to get a table. Will you be joining us?"

She turned with a forced smile. "I will indeed." She pranced along beside him and her mom, who kept up a lively chatter with the handsome doctor.

Taylor would have chosen a table on the far side, away from Colt and Jennifer, but John took the decision out of her hands. He pulled a chair out for her mother, and Anna sat down like the Queen herself. She had one of those little Chinese decorated fans that they sell in junk shops and she fanned herself prettily, giving John fond looks behind lowered lashes. It was almost embarrassing to watch.

Although this was the last table she would have chosen because of it's proximity to two people she preferred to ignore, it did have the nicest water view. Now that the sun had set, the sky was a mauve and pink shade, and the ocean glimmered with the help from the tiki torches. On any night this would be extremely romantic, but she was sitting with a guy who was a little too full of himself and *her mother*.

Only two tables away Colt sat with a pretty young woman, who unlike herself, drooled over him. She kept touching his arm, inching her chair closer and closer, like she wanted to end up in his lap. It was all too obvious that Colt, *her* Colt would not be lacking for female companionship tonight. And she didn't like it. Not one bit.

She shot him a look, and catching it, he lifted an eyebrow. Dammit, if it didn't make him sexier than he already was. He gave her a slight nod and a half smile, which she determined to mean--see, I got lucky. Thanks for the tip.

She grimaced, and wiped her sweaty hands on the napkin. "So, John. Are you in the same field as Sean? A cardio surgeon?"

He smiled. "You mean cardiac surgeon. No, I'm not. I'm a lung guy. A pulmonologist. I do get to see too many of Sean's patient's though. After cardiac surgery they are highly susceptible to catching pneumonia. If they return to the hospital after they've been released from his care, more often than not, it's to see me."

"Why, that's terrible. Isn't it, Mom? To get deathly ill again when their immune system is down, well, that just sucks."

"I'll tell you what sucks," Anna said. "I'm out of wine. John, dear, would you mind waving over that waiter?" While he was distracted, her mother leaned close and whispered, "What are you doing? Why are you with us, instead of saving your boyfriend from that barracuda over there?"

"She's not a barracuda. And besides, even if she is, it's obvious that he doesn't mind. She'll be leaving at the end of the week, so it'll be one night of hot sex and it's Hasta La Vista, baby!" Taylor shrugged. "So let him have a good time. What do I care?"

"A lot more than you let on. I've seen you sending him looks all night. Your face is beet red right now, and your skin is all prickly. That means something."

"Yeah. That I'm allergic to him. I get this every time he's near. And my breathing gets bad too. Maybe I need a lung doctor." She glanced at John, then back to her mother. Leaning over she whispered in her ear. "You like him?"

She nodded and blushed like a girl. "And you?" she asked.

"Not like that."

Her mother beamed and Taylor excused herself and got up from the table. She sashayed over to Colt's table and put her hands on his shoulders. She smiled at Jennifer. "Everything all right, here? Is Colt being attentive? He's one of our favorite people here at the Cove."

"I'm sure he is," Jennifer said with a big smile for him. "He's been awesome. He was telling me about his son, and I told him I'd love to meet him. We were trying to figure out a time when we could all go snorkeling together."

"Really?" Taylor dropped her hands and moved to Colt's side. "Aren't you a little busy for a snorkeling trip? You're booked with Sean's father and brother-in-law tomorrow. And we've pretty much got you working all week."

"Jennifer said she could take a few extra days and stay over." His eyes locked with Taylor's, and he put his hands in the air. "I've been telling Jennifer that this is a crazy week with the wedding guests, but that I'd do my best to fit her in."

Taylor felt heat radiating from her. Like her skin was on fire. Especially when he turned to his new best friend with a smile, and put his arm casually around the back of her chair. "Right?"

"Right." Jennifer bumped his shoulder. "You might see me snorkeling tomorrow over by the pier. Hear it's a great place to see plenty of fish."

Taylor gnashed her teeth. She'd never had a hissy fit, but could feel one coming on. "There is certainly a lot of fish in the sea. I've been telling Colt that. He's divorced, you know."

"So he said." Jennifer gazed up at her. "He also has a son living at home."

"Well...yes..." Taylor sputtered, furious to see amusement in Colt's eyes. "But Jamie spends weekends with his mother."

Jennifer smiled. "Then he's free every weekend."

Taylor spun on her heels and marched off, desperate to get away before she made more of a fool of herself.

CHAPTER TWENTY-THREE

Colt had watched the interchange between the two women, and probably should have put a stop to it, but he'd wanted to hear what Taylor had to say. And damn, he wanted to pump his fist in the air. If that woman wasn't crazy about him, then he didn't know jack shit.

She'd been spitting mad, and he loved her for it. Not love, exactly, but admired her, that's for sure. He admired everything about her. Her stubbornness, her integrity, her passion in all she did, and even the damn fact that she stuck to her principals knowing she possibly faced a personal loss.

Not that she was gonna lose him. He had no intention of sleeping with Jennifer no matter how hard she begged. But Taylor didn't know that, she actually thought he was getting lucky tonight. Well, after seeing that streak of jealousy, he had hope again. All was not lost. And all was fair in love and war.

Whoever said that, sure knew what he was talking about. Because the game was on. He had the rest of the night to woo Taylor back into his arms...and hopefully his bed. No, he didn't feel bad about it. They were good together. Very good. If she could just accept that fact and stop fighting it with every breath, both of them would be a whole lot happier. He wanted to make her happy...in so many ways.

Sex was a primal need as much as hunger and thirst. He'd love to convince her of that, one tasty nibble at a time.

"What are you smiling about?" Jennifer asked, giving him a pointed look. "What the hell was that? Are you two hooking up or something?"

"I'm sorry. That took me by surprise too." He gave her a lazy grin, and removed his arm from the back of her chair. "Not sure what to call it, but we *are* something."

"And that means what, exactly?"

"I wish I knew. We're definitely friends, but I would like us to be more. She's got a problem with that."

"I see." Jennifer tossed down the last of her champagne. "I see I'm wasting my time. You need to figure things out between you, and I'm just getting in the way. It's been a pleasure getting to know you, Colt--but I think I'll join my other friends at their table."

He nodded. "I'm sorry. You're a terrific girl and if I wasn't such a complete idiot, I'd be all over you."

"You can't always choose where your heart is." She stood up, and touched his shoulder. "Good luck. You might need it with that one."

He chuckled. "So true. She's a spitball, that's for sure."

Colt didn't want to watch Taylor enjoying herself at the table with the doctor and her mother, so he shifted his chair to watch the moon over the horizon. It was half full, a beautiful backdrop in the magnificent sky. The music had started and people were getting up to dance. He'd wait it out a bit, and if Taylor didn't come to him, he'd make the move himself. Jennifer was gone. What in the world was Taylor waiting for?

Out of the corner of his eye, he saw Taylor get up and move around the tables, stopping to talk to people. His heart raced. This was all an act. A ruse for her to casually come over to him, as if it was nothing more than a courtesy. He'd let her play it anyway she wanted. He'd take what he could get, and give more back in return.

She was two tables away, smiling and laughing with a couple of men. Dammit to hell. He tapped his fingers on the table, crossed and uncrossed his legs. Sat up straighter, then pushed his chair back. He couldn't sit still another minute.

He pushed himself up and strode over to her. Sliding an arm around her tiny waist, he pulled her toward him. "Let's dance."

"But I was talking...

"You still are." He smiled. "Dance with me."

"I don't want to." She tilted her chin in the air and he laughed.

"Are you pouting?" He couldn't get the grin off his face. "You look about twelve. A beautiful sexy twelve. But still too young for me to want to do this."

He tugged her again and she came up hard against him. He walked her backwards onto the grassy area set up for dancing. She tried to push away, but his grasp on her waist didn't relax. "You are going to dance with me."

"No. I'm not."

"Yes, you are. I might have you do more than that, if you're not careful."

"And what the hell is that supposed to mean?"

His eyes flickered across her mouth, down to her chest, and back up again. "I might want a lot more than just a dance."

He could feel her heart pound, and he tightened his grip, moving her slowly between the other dancing couples. They were the only two doing a slow dance to a fast number, but he liked it that way.

"What did you have in mind?" She sounded breathless.

"You know exactly what I have in mind, and after your little hissy fit with Jennifer, I'm pretty damn sure you want it as much as I do."

"That's where you're wrong."

"For once in your damn life, will you please shut up and kiss me?"

"No!" she sputtered. His mouth came down on hers hard, making her incapable of speech. His leg was moving between hers and if she didn't cling to him, she would have tripped.

He gentled the kiss, but didn't let her mouth go. It was sweet, tasting of champagne and strawberries, and for now she wasn't fighting him. He was tired of fighting too. He just wanted...everything.

* * *

Taylor sighed with pleasure. They were kissing on the starry-lit grassy dance area, in front of guests, her family, beneath the moon and the stars. It felt so right, so good, so magical. His arms held her like a safe anchor where she could dip and twirl and be more than herself, and he'd be there to keep her from harm.

Maybe it was too much champagne, but she let herself relax in his arms, and allowed him to guide her though the moves. He was a wonderful dancer--another surprise. It was as if a more sophisticated Colton Travis had come out to play. Dressed in his new suit, he was self-assured, polished, exciting in ways that the hunky shirtless, self-deprecating guy she knew was not. Although that Colt got under her skin too.

She looked at his face in the moonlight, and her breath caught. The sharp angles of his face, his full mouth, blue eyes and fair hair made her weak-kneed with want. He looked so impossibly handsome. Swoon worthy, but of course, she was not a swooning kind of girl.

No sirree! She pulled herself upright, and took a step back evaluating what to do next. Put an end to this nonsense, or for once in her practical life allow the emotions swirling inside of her to guide her.

"What are you thinking?" he asked with caution. "I prefer when you don't think."

She laughed. "I bet you do." Her eyes roamed over his face. "You look incredible. Like The Gatsby. That's what I was thinking."

"Hmm. Okay, you can think some more."

"Really? I have permission?"

"If you're going to get cheeky about it, then no." He pulled her up close again. "Just think about us, and how good I can make you feel."

"That's the worst thing I should think about." Her steps faltered. "I want to think about the moon and the stars, and the beautiful wedding--and the fact that my sister is so very happy, and so dearly loved."

"Okay. I'm good with that." His hand was warm on her back, sliding up and down, making her feel very...very unpractical.

"Now you're telling me what I can think."

He smiled, not taking offense. "No. I'm just happy you're having good thoughts."

"I guess that's okay then." She snuggled up to him. "Could we maybe go for a walk on the beach? I'd like to kick these heels off. They're starting to pinch."

"Let's go." He took her hand and they left the music behind and strolled down toward the sand. Just before the mangroves, he bent down to remove her shoes, and then before she knew what he was doing, he picked her up in his arms and carried her across to the other side.

"Are you crazy?" she asked, laughing and clinging to him.

"Not yet," he replied, sliding her down his body, and taking possession of her mouth. "But I'm going to be."

"Crazy good, or crazy bad?"

"How about wickedly wonderful?" he said, dimples flashing.

"You are different tonight."

"In a good way?"

"Uh-huh. I think so."

"Fine. Anyway you want me, you've got me."

Then they were kissing again. The walk on the beach didn't seem as important as his mouth on hers. The warmth of his body made her feel achingly hot. So hot. So needy.

Her tongue delved inside his mouth, eager to taste and explore and know the essence of him. She knew a lot about Colton Travis, but not like this. He was different. Exciting. Confident in ways she'd never known him to be before.

She knew where all this kissing would lead, but for once, one night, she wanted to forget her fears, and just go for it. If there was the slightest chance to have the same happiness as Kayla, she had to take a risk. She had to try.

Instead of being ruled by common sense, she wanted to feel emotions that she'd never felt before. Not with Jack, or with her New York live-in boyfriend--not with anyone.

Colt wanted the same thing she did. Passion. Passion in Paradise, and she intended to give it to him before she convinced herself otherwise. She didn't want to stop! She didn't want to think! She wanted to toss the dice and make love to this beautiful man, and deal with it later if the gamble didn't pay off.

"Come on!" She tugged at his arm.

"Where are we going?" He swung her shoes in his hands as he followed her along.

"Your boat. It's waiting, isn't it?"

"My boat's been waiting a long, long time." He shot her a look. "You're sure about this?"

"As sure as I'll ever be. And you should know better than to ask. Don't let my head get involved, and we should have a very nice time."

He laughed. "I don't want to make love to your head. It's your body, your gorgeous sexy body that's been driving me crazy. The things I want to do with you..."

She wavered for half a sec. Visions of what he had done, and would do again darn near scared her. The intensity of their love making was nothing to trifle with. She knew after tonight she might never recover.

"Yes." She released a long, shaky breath. "Colt. I want it too."

"I've waited a long time to hear that."

"Then let's go." She hiked her long dress up to her thighs and gave him a teasing look. "Race you there." She was off and running and heard his footsteps right behind. She was racing toward something unknown. A new day when she could stop worrying so much about the future that she missed out on the present. Accept the here and now, and find happiness in the moment.

CHAPTER TWENTY-FOUR

They reached his Hatteras, puffing and sucking in wind. "You okay?" he asked.

"Yeah." Laughing, she lifted her heavy hair from her damp neck and fanned her face. "I'm such a tomboy," she confessed. "Just can't help myself."

He glanced at her flushed face, heaving chest, and the perspiration shining on her skin. Drops of moisture slowly slid down her neck and into her bra, and his tongue longed to follow. He pulled her into his arms. "Tomboy or not, you're the hottest girl I've ever met. Even if you are feisty."

"I'm not feisty." She lifted her chin and frowned. "Maybe just a little bit." She gave him a quick kiss. "So, are we going to stand here all night, or are you going to invite me on board?"

"Come on." Grabbing her hand Colt helped her aboard, then unlocked the cabin door.

When he left the boat earlier this evening, he'd put some low lighting on in the event that Taylor would change her mind after their kiss on her porch step. He kept it dim, going for a romantic mood.

"This looks nice." She glanced around the salon, at the white leather corner settee, the table top with an ice bucket and a chilled bottle of champagne. A bowl of strawberries sat next to the two fluted glasses. "You really did prepare for me."

"I had high hopes."

She turned around and slid up to him. She put her hands around his neck. "I have high hopes too," she whispered, and kissed his neck. His hands slid around to her bottom, and he pulled her in close. He gave her a hungry kiss, she answered back. After a minute or two, she pulled away.

"Your boat suits you. Kind of elegant, you know?"

“Elegant?” He ran a hand over his chin. "Never thought I'd hear that word applied to me."

"Surprised me too," she admitted, her brown eyes flashing. "I've never seen you like you were tonight."

"Because I was dressed? With a tie?”

“It was more than a suit.” She crossed her arms and leaned back against the counter. "It was how you held yourself, your demeanor. And the way you came on to me."

"I always come on to you."

"No. Not like you did on the dance floor. You weren't taking no for an answer, and I liked that."

"No problem. I'll assert my will from now on."

She laughed. "Don't get me wrong—I'm fond of the half-naked fisherman with great abs, but I caught a glimpse of the real you—a man who knows his worth. You looked like someone just as much at home in a yacht as you'd be conducting million dollar deals from a penthouse suite."

The comparison stung. He knew she meant it as a compliment, but it hit too close to home. "I'm the same guy. Different suit."

"You've never told me about your family. Your upbringing. I would like to know more about you, Colt."

He grabbed the bottle of champagne. "Let's have a toast and then you can get to know me a whole lot better—in bed."

She blinked and dropped her hands to her sides. The mood was detouring downhill as she asked, "Do you mind me asking you questions?"

There would be no going forward if he didn't answer at all, so he opted for honesty. "Not really, but I would rather do something besides talk about my past." He put the bottle down and reached for her hand.

"Fair enough." She let him tug her forward. "Maybe I can dig out some secrets after post-coital sex."

He dragged her face close so he could kiss her mouth and shut her up. "Stop talking." His lips moved against hers, and he cocked his head to take the kiss deeper. He heard her soft sigh and felt her body surrender.

His hands slid around her back, riding low, feeling the soft curves of her behind. "You want that champagne, or would you like to see my boudoir?"

She giggled and kissed his neck. "I've had enough to drink. Take me to bed before I change my mind."

Colt quickly led the way to the master suite. Hoping for a miracle, he'd put clean sheets on the bed and filled a small fruit jar with some roses for the bedside table. She smiled when she saw them.

"You told me you had champagne and roses. How did you know I'd come? I wasn't sure myself."

"I didn't." He kissed her fingers. "But I hoped you might want me, too."

"I do." Her eyes were warm with appreciation. "This is so sweet and thoughtful."

"Like you are."

Her mouth trembled, and her skin turned pink. Damn but he loved that about her. Hell, he didn't want her any more perfect than she already was.

"Can I help you off with that dress?" His hands were on her back zipper, and when she whispered, "Yes," he slid it all the way down. He bent and lifted her feet, one at a time, then flung the dress over a chair.

She stood before him in a pushup bra and matching silk underwear and he grabbed the back of the chair, his body on fire. "God, Taylor. You are so beautiful."

Holding his gaze, she undid the back of her bra and let it fall. His heart thumped.

"Hurry," she whispered.

Not needing further encouragement, he unbuttoned his shirt and flung it aside. When he undid his belt buckle she jumped into bed, her eyes glowing in the dark. "Hot damn, Colt. But you're beautiful too."

He dropped his pants, and peeled down his boxer shorts. He was already hard and swollen, and he heard the sweet sound of her gasp. He fumbled for a condom from the top drawer next to the bed and slid it on. He ripped the sheet off of her and lay down, taking her into his arms.

They kissed for a long, long time, until her kisses became more heated, and she started moving against him. He suckled her breasts, teasing the nipples into perky rosebuds. She let out a whimper of pleasure, and he kept that up until she squirmed, placing a leg over his.

"Don't tease me any longer, Colt. I can't stand another minute."

He slid his hand into her panties and found that she was hot and wet. In a quick movement he had her underwear off, and was on his knees, straddling her. He gave her deep throated kisses that had them both groaning and arching toward one another. Their bodies were slick with sweat and heavy with desire.

A second later she took him in her hand and guided him home.

He continued to kiss her even while he was buried inside. His tongue made love with hers, matching the motion of his hips as he thrust deep, then receded, going back again and again and again.

He built her up slowly, caressing her breasts, nibbling on her neck and shoulder. Then he flipped them so she was the one on top. He let her set the rhythm, keeping his hands on her hips to guide her and slow her down when needed.

* * *

She collapsed on top of him, panting, her head resting on his chest. He caressed her hair and kissed the top of her head. His hand stroked her back, and she could feel the rise and fall of his chest, as they both tried to recapture their breath.

She didn't think she could ever move again. He had sucked every ounce of strength that she had. "I'm just going to lie here forever," she whispered. "Is that okay?"

She felt the ripples of his laughter. "Help yourself. I'm not going anywhere. Jamie's with his mom, and I've got all night."

"You don't understand. I mean forever. I feel like a sponge. Boneless."

"I feel a bone," he said, stroking her ribs. "And another one. Can I kiss it?"

"As long as you don't have to move."

He flipped her over before she knew what was happening, and he was back on top. Kneeling beside her. She looked into his smiling blue eyes. "I'm not done with you yet," he said and dropped his head to nuzzle her stomach.

"I can't move," she said, giggling as it tickled.

"Just stay still. I'll do all the work."

"You've got to be joking. We're good. More than good. We're depleted. Aren't we?"

"Not even close. That was only a warm-up."

"Seriously. How can you have such stamina?"

He gave a wicked grin. "I haven't done half the things I plan to do to you. Lay back and enjoy it."

"Pretty sure of yourself, aren't you?"

"When it comes to pleasing you, I am."

"Oh, Colt. That's so sweet."

Then his head went lower, and she convulsed when his mouth found her sweet spot. She stopped talking. She stopped moving. She stopped breathing. Colt was right about everything--he did know what she liked, more than she'd known herself.

CHAPTER TWENTY-FIVE

Taylor must have fallen asleep because when she woke up, she was still wrapped in Colt's arms. The sky was dark and the stars were out. How long she'd slept she had no idea. Colt snored softly beside her. He looked so endearing, all rumpled, and sexually sated.

As he damn well should! She'd never known anyone so inventive. She'd always thought sex was two dimensional. On top or on the bottom. But Colt had thrown that theory out the window--finding numerous new positions in which to enjoy her better.

Not that she was complaining. Heck no! She'd never felt so well loved, *so appreciated and desirable.* He'd made her feel like something special, and his appetite had been insatiable. Taylor had never thought of herself as the type of woman that a man couldn't get enough of. But Colt had been like a man starving--afraid that this might be his last meal.

Hearing a soft snore and a whimper, she felt a tug inside of her. Knowing she shouldn't, she brushed the back of her fingers against his cheek. She didn't want to wake or arouse him—he needed his sleep. He had to take

Sean's family out fishing in a few hours. She only wanted to touch him a little more before she left.

It was true that women, most anyway, couldn't have casual sex without their feelings getting involved. Her heart felt like it was bursting out of her chest. She didn't expect him to feel the same way. He'd wanted to get laid and he'd been laid good. She didn't regret it. Matter-of-fact, she wanted to do it again.

Call her foolish, but maybe there might be a slight chance for them after all.

The sheet was only barely covering him so she took another minute to feast her eyes. She already knew what his chest looked like since he paraded around half naked most of the time. She could practically name every rib he possessed, possibly every ripple in those delectable abs too. Her eyes were not used to feasting on the slim hips, the muscular legs, the tantalizing sight of...

Oh My! Was he hard again?

She felt her skin get prickly and knew she was getting turned on again. Sliding slowly, ever so carefully she crept to the edge of the bed. She had one leg out when she felt a hand grab her.

"Where are you going?"

"Home. I don't want anyone to know."

"They know. We were sucking face on the dance floor last night. And trust me, they don't care."

Her cheeks flamed. "I remember that, and you're probably right, but I care. We shouldn't have done that--not at the wedding. It was Kayla's big night, and we kind of made a spectacle of ourselves."

"I'm sure she's very happy for us. Your mom too." He ran a finger down her arm. "Get back in here. Before I tie you up."

"What? You wouldn't dare!"

"I might have to. Besides, that's something new I haven't tried." He grinned. "Got a rope down here somewhere. You want me to blindfold you too?" He gave her a teasing smile, but she grabbed a pillow and tossed it at him.

"You're incorrigible."

He moved quickly, pulling her down on top of him. She felt the naked length of him, his arousal prodding her tummy. She tried to ignore it, but her body quickened with desire. She put a hand down and stroked him.

"Just one more hour."

Again he took her, and pleasured her like no other man. When it was over, she clung to him and wept.

"Why are you crying?" he asked softly, brushing her hair off her damp cheeks.

"Because."

"Because why? Did I do something wrong? Are you having second thoughts?"

"No, and no. You did everything right. So much so, that I'm not sure how I'm going to do without you."

"You don't have to. I've been telling you that all along."

"It's just so damn complicated." She sniffed and turned her head away.

"Doesn't have to be. Don't over think it." He gently stroked her back. "We enjoy each other and have strong feelings for one another. Isn't that enough?"

"I guess it is." She sighed. "I hope it's enough. I want it to be."

"We're good then?" he asked, putting his weight on his elbows and looking down at her.

"We're good." She sniffed back more tears and blinked rapidly. "I'm going to freshen up in your bathroom then take off before anyone else is up." She gave him a quick kiss. "You're really something, Colt. Your wife was a fool."

"Different priorities." He winked. "But I have to thank her, because if she hadn't left, I'd never be here with you."

She smiled and climbed out of bed. She teetered off to the bathroom, used the facilities and took a two-minute shower. Having washed the scent of sex off her body, she felt more confident and in control.

She picked up her dress off the floor, where he'd sent it flying last night. What if one of the guests caught her sneaking back to her cabin in her bridesmaid dress? How humiliating that would be!

"You're gonna put that on?"

"What choice do I have?" She put on her underwear then stepped into the silky gown. "I had a great time last night. Thank you."

He laughed. "You're very welcome. It was my pleasure," he said, watching her.

"Not all of it," she said, with a cheeky grin. "I had pleasure too."

"Can you slip away tonight? I know you're busy with your guests and everyone, but I'd like to see you if possible."

"I'll try, but no guarantees." She turned around for one last quick kiss. "It was great. The best. Ever."

"If you let me, I'll make every night special."

Her heart sang and filled with hope. "I might like that." She was half way out of the bedroom when a thought occurred to her. "Colt. I have a great idea. Why don't you invite your mom and sister to join us at the cafe? I'd love to meet them, and it's a perfect opportunity with everyone in town."

When he didn't answer, she gave him a puzzled look. "What's the problem?" She sighed. "I'm not trying to be pushy or overstep my grounds. We slept together, we're not getting married or anything. If you don't want me to meet them. Fine. Forget it."

"It's not that." He raised his eyes to hers. "We're just not close. Not like you and your family. I doubt they'd come."

"You could ask, couldn't you?" She tried not to let her disappointment show, but she wasn't good at hiding her feelings.

"Uh. Sure. I could ask. But don't get your hopes up. I haven't seen them in over a year."

"Do they even know you're divorced?"

"Of course, I told them. They like my ex, probably better than me--and love my son."

"You never mention your family, or anything about your life before Paradise Cove. What's the big frickin' secret?"

"No secret. Just nothing to tell."

"Hell, Colt! If I'm ever to get to know you better, I should have the right to ask."

"Taylor, if I thought my past was important I'd tell you my whole life story, but it isn't. You know me, and whatever happened years ago doesn't make me any less or any better of a man."

"Invite your mom and sister, Colt. I'd like to meet them." She turned and walked away.

* * *

Taylor tiptoed into the cabin, hoping to sneak into her bedroom. Unfortunately she encountered Brittany coming out of the bathroom.

"You're just coming in?" she asked, knowing the answer to the dumb question. "So how was he?"

"As if I'd kiss and tell." Taylor grinned and shrugged. "We had fun, if that's what you want to know."

"They why are you sneaking back here in the middle of the night? Why aren't you still wrapped around that gorgeous body of his?"

"Because it's five in the morning and I didn't want the guests to see me in my bridesmaid dress coming home. Besides. Nothing has changed. We enjoyed ourselves, but it's not like we're going to fall madly in love and have a dozen kids. It's not like that."

"How do you know? You guys are crazy about each other, and you never know what the future will bring."

"Well, the future might be brighter, but for now we'll take it one day at a time."

"That's not so bad, is it?"

"No, of course not. I know life doesn't come with guarantees, but I like having some control over it. With

Colt...I'm just not sure. I keep feeling as though I'm the one who will get hurt, and he'll walk away unscathed."

"Really? I think he's the romantic at heart, and you might be the cynic."

"How can you say that? I'm just cautious, that's all."

"Then cautiously go into this affair with your eyes open and your heart willing." She smiled. "He's a great guy."

"I think so too, but he's being really guarded about his past. He has a mother and sister in Miami who have never visited him in the past year. He let's his son visit, but doesn't himself. And he won't talk about his upbringing. It's like a big, dark secret."

"That's funny. I thought he was an open book." Brittany frowned. "Guess everyone has a skeleton in their closet." She followed Taylor into her bedroom and sat on the bed while she undressed. "Is his father still alive?"

"No. But he won't talk about his family at all." Taylor slipped on a robe and sat down on the bed next to her sister. "I suggested that he invite his mom and sister here for dinner tomorrow since we have so many out of town guests. But he made excuses, and obviously didn't want to do it. It just seems weird."

"Maybe he thinks that's moving a step too fast. Like you're getting engaged or something."

"I thought that at first too, and clarified it right away." She shook her head. "It's more that that."

Brittany gave her a hug. "Want me to ask?"

"No, Brit. I know you mean well, but if Colt and I are going to be sleeping together, then he needs to open up to me. Or it's a no go."

"Okay." She stood up. "Good luck with that."

Taylor got dressed and went to her cafe. With all the guests staying at their resort, she expected half a dozen tables for an early breakfast, and that she'd be busy for most of the morning. Her worries over Colt could wait.

Besides the usual breakfast dishes, and fresh croissants and muffins, she had a few specialties in mind that would use up some of last night's appetizers. She got busy doing the prep work, and was enjoying her second cup of coffee when Juanita came in.

"Good morning," she called out, putting her small handbag under the counter. "You are here early. What smells so good?"

"I have smoked salmon frittatas warming in the oven, and a tray of ham/egg and cheese rollups in pastry. We also have crab Benedict."

"My, my, my! I do love working for you."

Taylor grinned. "We aren't opening for another half hour. What should we have for breakfast?"

The two of them sat down with coffee and a rollup each, then turned on the outside neon light and unlocked the front door. Open for business.

CHAPTER TWENTY-SIX

Colt was taking Sean's father and brother-in-law out on the boat at ten which gave him a few hours to shower, shape up and figure a way out of this mess. He hadn't slept a wink after Taylor left, knowing he'd better come up with a damn good excuse as to why his Miami relations couldn't attend tonight's dinner, or Taylor would cut him off at the knees. Worse--she might never sleep with him again, and he sure in hell didn't want that to happen.

What had got into her all off a sudden? She'd never shown any curiosity about his family, or his past before. He knew sleeping with her was different than hooking up with one of the girls in town or a passerby once in awhile. Taylor was special--their relationship unique. Going to bed with her had altered their situation a little. It gave her some privileges and deepened their connection. Didn't give her the right to pry into things that were none of her business though.

On the other hand, it might be something as simple as her sister's wedding that elicited this response. He knew how important family was to her--not only her own, but people like the Hernandez family when they'd landed at their door. Her family had not only sheltered them, but given them clothing, food, comfort and love. They'd welcomed the Cuban immigrants into their lives and cared about them like blood relations.

He didn't feel that kind of love for his own family. He should he supposed. It wasn't his mom's fault, or his sister's that they had been spoiled rotten with worldly goods, and then it had all been taken away. They were not bad people. They worked hard. They were honest, or at least fair when it came to real estate deals and keeping their clients happy.

He didn't have anything against them--he had nothing in common. They were like two peas in a pod--he was the odd man out. Truth was--they embarrassed him. Their identical fake looks--long blonde hair, inflated boobs, false eyelashes, veneered white teeth. They were like walking, talking Barbie dolls. He cringed at the idea of having them here, mingling with his only true friends. Their fancy apartment on Miami Beach, a new Mercedes every two years, their ritzy glamorous life was everything he abhorred. A cutting reminder of his father, a man he'd once loved and was so proud of, who'd been nothing but a fraud. A despicable human being who had made a mockery of the art world he'd claimed to love.

He never spoke of his father--to anyone. Not to his sister and certainly not with his mom. His dad had been dead to them the minute they knew he was nothing but a scam artist.

It had taken Colt a little longer than that. He'd hurt deeply for a long, long time. Shame and anger and frustration burned a hole inside of him. He'd wished his father hadn't died. He'd wanted him alive so he could ask him why--why a man with so much natural talent would allow it to go to waste, and to copy other masters instead of becoming one himself? For years he'd been consumed by questions, dying inside to know.

But he never would. He'd go to his own grave still wondering why his father would bury the best in himself, hide it from the world and choose to imitate--and lie to his friends, his family and the entire art world.

He hated his father with a passion. A passion that might have been spent on so many worthwhile endeavors had his upbringing been different.

Whatever. He wouldn't make any apologies for the life he led, and he had better things to do than spend another minute regretting or reflecting on his past. If Taylor couldn't accept that, well he'd be no worse off than he'd been before. A woman like her deserved an equal partner, a man with ambition, someone eager to light the world on fire. The only damn thing that lit his fire was her.

* * *

Colt spent an enjoyable day on the water with Sean's father and brother-in-law, trolling for dolphin and mahi-mahi. For the first hour they didn't catch anything of regulation size, but they moved to another location and within minutes Robert had caught his first dolphin--a good fifteen pounder. The lines got busy for the next twenty-thirty minutes and the two men were reeling them in faster than they could count.

Suddenly Colt saw something flash out of the water. It jumped high, but he only caught a glimpse of the underbelly. He saw the length of it, and knew they had something big. "Big one. Portside," he shouted down to the men. Then Jonathon saw it too. A Blue Marlin was following their boat.

Seconds later the marlin pounced, crashing the right rigger lure and making a huge explosion as it hit the bait. It was still a hundred yards out when the marlin jumped completely out of the water, its tail kicking. Jonathon, Sean's ophthalmologist father, was a seasoned angler and kept the reel tight. Colt shouted down to Robert, telling him to reel the other lures in.

Colt had his hands full moving the boat forward in lurching motions, helping Jonathon to keep his line from going slack. The marlin put up a good fight, changing directions and doing acrobatic leaps out of the water. Unfortunately, after forty minutes of a heroic battle between a middle-aged man and a feisty fish, the marlin lived to see another day.

Still, undaunted by their efforts, the men celebrated with a couple of cold beers, and they returned to the marina in high spirits. Colt had managed to snap a few good photos of the three to four hundred pound catch before it snapped the lure and dived below. With their ice chest full of dolphins, and a tale to tell their wives, both were happy men.

After they were moored, Colt helped the men off with their prized fish and took more pictures which they could show with pride.

"How about we ask Taylor to fry these babies up for dinner?" Jonathon suggested. "We sure can't take them home with us."

"I'm sure she'll be happy to do that," Colt said. "You want to run down and ask her while I clean up the fish?"

"Sounds good to me." He watched the men leave, and knew he was being a chicken shit. He could easily have taken the fish to Taylor himself. But that would require his talking to her, and he wasn't ready to face her just yet.

Once the fish were cleaned and gutted, he washed up and headed toward the beach and the resort. He saw a couple out in kayaks, and two young boys skimming the waves on a boogie board. Then he spotted Sean's buddy Ken from med school sitting with Jennifer on the edge of the shore. She was in a light blue bikini and a big straw hat. Her head was tilted back, and she was laughing at something Ken had said.

He waved at them and kept on walking.

Ken was recently divorced. He had two kids around the same age as Jamie. Ken lived in Boston and Jen in Philadelphia, but he was glad the two of them had found each other this weekend--might do them both a world of good.

He made his way past the mangroves to where the wedding had taken place. He eyed the exact spot he'd danced with Taylor and kissed her last night. He had shouted his intentions to the world by seducing her into leaving with him, and wasn't ashamed of it either.

Perhaps he did owe her something, but what exactly? They were consenting adults who liked each other a lot. They could damn well make love if they wanted to, and it was nobody's business but theirs. And yet, he knew that wasn't quite true. Her family treated him like one of their own. They respected him and expected him to do the right thing.

What did that mean? He squinted in the sun, and saw Anna and a few of the women sitting under a big umbrella table at the pool. She waved him over, and he thought about pretending he didn't see them, but she deserved better.

"Hey, ladies," he said, flashing them his best smile. "Isn't it too hot out here for you?" It was three in the afternoon, and must have been darn near a hundred degrees. "You're all going to wilt in this heat."

"We've been in the air conditioning all day, and Jane and Maggie wanted a walk on the beach. So here we are. Enjoying a pitcher of strawberry and lime mojitos too. Want one?" Anna asked.

"Don't mind if I do." Thankfully, he sank into a chair and let her pour one into a tumbler for him. "Cheers, ladies." He raised his glass and chug-a-lugged, expecting it to be light and sweet. Instead, he sputtered his mouthful, and grabbed a napkin on the table. "Crap. What are you women drinking? This is awfully damn potent for this time of the day."

Anna laughed. "It's an early happy hour."

He raised a brow, then directed his attention on the guests. "So did you speak with your husbands?" he asked the two women.

Maggie waved her drink in the air. "Oh, my! They are excited. Jonathon wouldn't shut up about that big fish they nearly caught." She shook her head and the silver in her hair glinted in the sun. "Too bad they couldn't reel it in. Still, they had the best time ever," she said, her hazel eyes twinkling.

"Robert too. He's not much of a fisherman, but he loved every minute." Jane said with a friendly smile. She had a brown ponytail that bounced when she spoke, and intelligence radiated from her light blue eyes "They're talking about wanting to go out again. Maybe we could all go."

"Sure. I'd loved to take the four of you out. I think I'm free on Wednesday, if you'll still be here."

"We were going to return that day, but perhaps we can stay another night." Maggie laughed and refilled her glass. "We're having so much fun, I hate to leave."

"At least you don't have to go back to the cold." Colt knew they lived in California. "Your weather should be very pleasant right about now."

"True, but then I've got to get back to my real life. Running committees, bridge and golf." She sighed. "This is a holiday." She laughed again, and he figured she'd probably had enough to drink.

"You ladies take it easy on this punch. Especially in this heat."

"Oh, don't be a worrywart," Anna said. Then she leaned over and nudged him. "So we're all wondering what happened when you and Taylor disappeared last night. Know you'd had a spat early on. Everything all cleared up between you?"

He felt a rash of heat crawl up his neck. "Yup. We're good." He slid a finger down the condensation from his glass and kept his eyes on the drink. "Is she still down at the cafe?" he asked, eager to change the subject.

"She should be closing right about now. Go see her, why don't you?" Anna winked at the two ladies. "Wasn't last night wonderful?" She sighed and put a hand to her heart. "I swear it was the most beautiful wedding ever. I sure hope to see more of them here in Paradise Cove."

"I'm sure there will be." He added quickly, "Taylor's already talking about selling this as a destination wedding venue." Perspiration dripped from his brow. His entire body felt bathed in sweat.

"Of course. But I wasn't talking about that. I was thinking about Taylor. She's not getting any younger you know."

Jane sent him a sympathetic look. "Why don't you talk to Jonathon and Robert and see if we can all stay another day?"

Colt stood up and polished off the rest of his drink. He shot Jane a grateful glance. "I'll do that." Time for him to leave.

Perhaps he'd been wrong to flaunt his intentions to everyone last night. It had been obvious that he intended to sleep with Taylor, and had seduced her right then and there. She had family that cared about her. Friends too. They had a right to wonder what his intentions were today.

Problem was--he had no answer. His intentions were muddied for sure.

In a way, he felt caught up in a trap. Marriage right now was not on the table, but he had strong feelings for Taylor just the same. He didn't want any more pressure that's for sure. Taylor had already laid it on him this morning.

He only had two options:, call his mother or piss off Taylor. Neither held any appeal.

CHAPTER TWENTY-SEVEN

Colt found Taylor sitting in the newly restored A-frame structure that was now the outdoor area. It was made from solid wood but had open windows to let the breeze blow though. Definitely hurricane proof. She was seated with Jonathon and Robert discussing various ways she could do the fish.

"Hi guys," Colt said, taking a seat at the table. "Just talked to the women a few minutes ago. They're all down at the pool getting soused on mojitos. Your mom pours a mean drink," he said to Taylor.

She nodded, her eyes guarded.

"They wanted to know if you could all leave Thursday instead of Wednesday so I could take the four of you out on the boat. Wednesday's my only free day."

"Works for me," Robert said, sipping on a chilled beer. "Okay with you, Jon?"

"Sounds good. Need to change our flight though." The younger man used his iPhone and got right on it.

Jonathon stood, and stretched out his back. "Anyway you want to prepare the fish is good by us," he told Taylor. "We don't know much about cooking it, but we sure enjoy eating it." He grinned. "There'll be a big tip in it for you."

Taylor stood too. "You don't need to tip me. You're part of the wedding party." She put her hands in her pockets and rocked on her toes. "Please. Don't even think of it."

"You're running a business, and from what I hear you just got started. Then along came the hurricane which nearly wiped you out a few weeks back. So I want to pay for our meals. And I refuse to take no for an answer."

Taylor glanced at Colt for help.

"Don't look at me." He grinned. "Take the money. You need it, and you deserve it."

"That's settled then." The men polished off their beers, then left through the back door. Colt and Taylor were alone.

She didn't waste any time. "Did you call your mother? Or your sister?" she asked, hands on her hips.

The question annoyed him, but he stood his ground, refusing to be bullied by this feisty woman or her mother. "No, and no."

He saw the way her face fell and her gaze dropped to the floor, and felt a tug of guilt. He took a step closer and lifted her chin.

"I'm sorry, Taylor, but I can't. I don't want to hurt or disappoint you, but you're asking me to do something that I'm uncomfortable with. One day I'll explain everything. I promise. But for now, just trust me. There are things in my past that I'm not proud of, that I still can't talk about."

"Why, Colt? Why?" Her voice was bitter, and there were angry tears in her eyes.

"It doesn't matter. It was such a long time ago and it has no bearing on the here and now. My family is a closed subject." He ran a hand through his hair in frustration. "Don't make a big thing out of it. You're driving a wedge between us for nothing."

"I don't think it's nothing. It's important to me." Her eyes beseeched him, but he didn't flinch. He was making a stand, come hell or high water.

She glared at him for several seconds, then when he didn't budge she sensed defeat. "Whatever it is, I'll try to understand. It won't change my feelings for you. I just want you to be able to talk to me about anything and everything. After what we shared last night...what we did together...I feel as if I have that right."

"You can expect me to be faithful to you as long as we're seeing each other, but I don't owe you my life story." He didn't want to argue with Taylor. Not now. The intimacy between them had brought a lot out in the open. Her feelings were raw, but so were his.

"You have one hell of a nerve," she said, turning away in anger.

His cell phone rang sparing an answer. "I have to take this. It's Jamie." He stepped aside. "What's up, bud?"

"You have to come and get me!" The boy cried. "Now. Please, Dad?"

"Why?" Alarm shot through him. He could hear the panic in his son's voice. "What's wrong?" Colt tossed Taylor a look, his jaw clenched. "Is your mother all right?"

Jamie cried harder. "She's fine, but Daddy, she wants to take me away."

"Away where?" He paced up and down, trying to make sense of this call. Where did Sharon want to take him? And why would it upset his son so much?

"What did she say to you?" he asked more slowly. He needed to be calm. Jamie was blubbering and not making sense.

"Mom said she's getting married. At Christmas." He sobbed and hiccupped. "To Dennis." Another sob ripped out of him. "He's going to be working in Chicago, and they are going to live there. I want to stay here." He cried harder. "With you."

"You are not going anywhere. Your mother can't take you out of state. Not without my permission, and I'm not giving it." He shot another glance at Taylor, and her face was no longer angry, but concerned. She reached out a hand and touched his arm.

"Are you home?" Colt asked. "At your mom's?"

"Yes. I'm in the bedroom," he said choking on the words. "Come get me, please?"

"I'll be right there. Half an hour, maybe forty minutes tops. Hang tight, kiddo. I'm coming, and you're not going anywhere." He ended the call and turned to Taylor. "Sharon's getting married and wants to take Jamie to Chicago."

"She can't do that, can she?"

"I hope to hell not. But if she couldn't, why would she tell Jamie this?" His voice rose. "I can't believe she told him without discussing it with me. She has to know I won't allow it." His hands curled into fists. "She can be a real bitch, but she's usually fair when it comes to Jamie."

"Oh, God, Colt. I'm so sorry," she moved forward to put her arms around him. She pressed her cheek against his chest.

"It's not going to happen. Our home is here. I don't care if she wants to marry this guy and move away, but she's not taking my son with her. Over my dead body will that happen." He dragged a hand across his face, and sucked in a couple of deep breaths. "I have to go, Tay. I'm going to pick him up, then I'm calling my attorney. I'll fight this, don't worry. We're not losing Jamie."

Taylor slipped away from him. She nodded, tears in her eyes. "Go get your son, Colt. Do what you have to do. And I'm sorry about today. I should never have doubted you, or made such a frickin' big deal out of nothing. You're a good father and a good man, and that's all I need to know about you."

He didn't answer her because he was already on the run. He dialed his attorney's number as he hit the Overseas Highway and was chatting with Bernie Lewis a few minutes later.

"Look, this is the way it is," Bernie said. "A Florida court will agree to one parent relocating if both parents sign a written agreement. Since that's not the case here, your ex-wife would have to prove that the move would be in your son's best interest."

"Well, how can she prove that? Being with his father is in his best interest." His hands shook on the steering wheel, and he could see the whites of his knuckles. "I love him, and we have a good life together." His voice broke, and he cleared his throat. "I can provide for him. Better than some interloper."

"Let's not jump ahead of ourselves, Colt. First--your ex-spouse must serve you a signed petition. That's step one. The petition needs to include the address, telephone number, and description of the new residence. She'll have to state a date of the intended move or proposed relocation, and a reason for the move."

"This is the first I've heard of it. She hasn't given me anything, not even a hint of this."

"When you pick up your son, she might surprise you with it. So be prepared."

"Nothing will surprise me anymore." He swore. "Look, if she marries this big city doctor, how will that affect my chances? I'm guessing the job in Chicago is a step up." Colt cleared his throat again. Felt like he had a frog stuck half way down his windpipe. He could hardly breathe. "Dennis is his name. And together they can certainly provide Jamie a wealthier upbringing, but that doesn't make up for a father's love."

Tears were rolling down Colt's cheeks, and he swiped them away. Everything he detested, every single thing he stood against was rising up and threatening to take his only son away. How could this be happening? He'd fought so hard not to let the pursuit of money play an important role in his life.

And now this.

"Don't give up hope," Bernie said, trying to be the voice of reason. "This is only the beginning. A child custody order will not be modified unless a parent can show that the move serves the child's best interests. I don't see how this does."

"A bigger home. Better schools. A two-parent family. I can see why a judge would be influenced by this."

"Whatever you have to do, make sure to prove to the courts that your son's happiness and wellbeing depends on his living with you. That's about the best advice I can give you."

"Thanks, Bernie. I'll darn well try."

Thirty minutes later he pulled up in front of the apartment building that his wife lived in, and he paid for. He buzzed her apartment number, and she let him in. She answered on the first knock.

"He's in his bedroom. Won't come out." Her face had paled and tears streamed down her cheeks. "I'm sorry. I was talking to Dennis on the phone and I didn't know Jamie was listening."

"Jesus, Sharon. How could you let that happen? And why in hell didn't you discuss this with me? You know I won't let him go. You can't ask me that."

"Daddy?" Jamie peeked out of the bedroom door then ran down the hallway.

In spite of how heavy the boy was, Colt swung him easily in his arms. Jamie wrapped his legs around his back, making gut wrenching sobs.

"There, there, son. Everything will be all right." Over the boy's shoulder, his eyes connected with his ex-wife's.

She patted Jamie's back in an effort to soothe him too. Colt was furious but he could see that Sharon was equally distraught. She loved her son. And she loved Dennis. She wanted both.

"Jamie, honey. I'm so sorry. I love you, and I didn't want you to find out this way."

"Go away," the boy shouted. "I'm staying with my dad."

Colt felt his heart surge with love and pride. No way in hell would he let Jamie go. The boy was the best of him.

Sharon had a hand to her mouth, and her eyes overflowed with tears. Her shoulders shook and she clutched at her son, who roughly pushed her away. This couldn't be easy for her either. She had to know that he wouldn't give up Jamie without a damn good fight.

Colt walked over to the sofa and put his son down. He put a protective arm around his shoulder, and held him tight. His ex stood a few feet away, shivering and crying.

He didn't give a fuck. She was not taking Jamie from him. Not now. Not ever.

"Sit down," he told her coldly.

She grabbed some fresh tissues off the counter, then sat as directed. They faced each other from a space of six feet, a square coffee table separating them. "Colt, I know you are both upset right now, but we have to be rational, and try to figure out a happy solution for all of us." She swiped tears from the corners of her eyes. "I love Jamie as much as you. He's my son, and a son needs his mother."

"He's not going to Chicago." His voice did not waver. He felt cold inside and out. Like an ice pick had split open his heart. "You can't take him from me." He wanted to be reasonable, so he tried to soften his voice and hold back his fury. "Marry Dennis. Be happy. Have a wonderful life. You can see Jamie anytime you want. But he will live with me."

"He's my son. I'm his mother. He needs to be with me." She bit back a sob, and wiped her eyes again. "Dennis cares about him too. He will be good to Jamie. You don't have to worry about that."

"I'm not." He moved away from Jamie, his gut in a knot. "I'm not worried, because it's damn well not going to happen." He jumped out of his seat and paced the room. "I'm warning you, Sharon. Don't pursue this. If you do you'll regret it."

"Are you threatening me?"

"I'm not threatening you. You're threatening me. I'm taking my son and going home." He reached out a hand. "Come, Jamie. Let's go."

The boy's eyes were wild as he looked from one parent to another. "Stop fighting. Please stop fighting. Why can't we all get along and be a family? We don't need Dennis. You and Dad should stay together and we can all live together like we used to." His eyes swam with tears. "Please marry each other. I don't want to lose either one of you."

Colt's knees went weak as he grabbed for his son. He held Jamie in a tight grip, afraid that if he loosened it, he'd slip away and be gone.

CHAPTER TWENTY-EIGHT

Things happened quickly after that. The front door opened, and Dennis strode through. "What the hell?"

He rushed to Sharon's side, and put an arm around her shoulder. "You okay?"

"No." Her mouth trembled and she gasped. "No. Nothing is all right. Jamie doesn't want to leave his dad, and Colt's threatening me."

"I didn't threaten you," Colt said in an exasperated voice. "It's just not going to happen."

Jamie lifted his head. "I'm not going anywhere, and you...you...you're not wanted here," he said to Dennis, tears streaming down his cheeks.

"I'm sorry, Jamie, but your mother has agreed to marry me." Dennis reached into his pocket and pulled out a couple of tissues. "Wipe your nose, and go to your bedroom. We'll settle this between us."

"Stay right where you are, son." Colt stood up and confronted the man standing next to his ex-wife. "You have some nerve."

"This doesn't concern you." Dismissing him, Dennis turned to Sharon. "It's okay. Everything will work out fine. The lawyers can handle the details."

Colt's shoulders straightened and his chest hurt. "You want to take my son to Chicago, and this doesn't concern me?" He took two steps and breathed down the shorter man's face. "Son-of-a-bitch."

"Tell him, Daddy. I don't want to go away and live with him. I'm staying here with you."

Dennis looked at Jamie. "Your dad is leaving now. He will be hearing from my lawyer."

"You need a lawyer to do your battles? Not man enough to do it yourself?"

"You weren't man enough to keep your wife," Dennis said with a smug smile.

"That's enough!" Sharon cried.

"This is the guy you want to marry?" Colt asked, shaking his head. "Thought you had better sense."

"Jamie, go to your room," Dennis said roughly. He reached out a hand and grabbed the boy's arm.

"Let go of my son," Colt hissed, pushing himself between them.

"Step back," Dennis said. "I'm asking you to leave right now."

"You afraid of me?" Colt asked, getting in his face.

In answer, Dennis drew back and then took a swing at him. Colt ducked, but the shorter man's knuckles grazed his chin.

That was all the incentive needed. Colt didn't like bullies. Especially when they thought their money could do the talking.

"That lawyer?" Colt said. "Here's something else to tell him." And then Colt let him have it right between the eyes. His nose spurted blood, and Sharon screamed.

Colt grabbed his son. "Let's get out of here. I can't stand the sight of blood."

"Why you..." Dennis lunged for him, spurting blood over the cream-colored carpet.

Colt had an arm at Jamie's back herding him toward the door. He glanced at his ex-wife who was holding a dish towel under Dennis's nose. "I'm sorry," he said, surprised that he actually meant it. "Send me the bill for the cleaning."

Then he left.

That evening he sat home with his son, eating pizza and popcorn and watching old Rocky movies. Jamie thought his dad was a real live hero breaking Dennis's nose, and bragged that he could probably outbox Rocky. Colt stopped the movie long enough to explain that getting into a fistfight was not a gentlemanly way to settle an argument. Still, even as he spoke the words, it didn't take away the satisfaction he got reliving the vivid images of Dennis holding his nose, blood flying everywhere. If that made him a bad father, so be it. He'd fight to keep his son, and anyone who got in his way.

He excused himself long enough to call Taylor to tell her not to expect him at the cafe, and updated her on how things stood.

"You hit him?" she squeaked. "I can't imagine you getting physical with someone. You're the mellowest man I know."

"Don't let that fool you. When it comes to protecting my own, I can fight as well as any man. I can't lose Jamie." His voice cracked. "How can I convince a judge that he's better off with me when they could provide him with so much more?"

"Oh, Colt. That shouldn't matter. You have a good job. You're honest, loving, a wonderful father who gives his son everything he needs to be safe and happy. Jamie doesn't need a fancy upbringing. Who has the most money can't possibly influence a judge."

He hoped that was true, but knew things about the way the world worked, probably better than most people. "Well, we will have to see how it plays out."

There was a loud knock on his door. "I'll have to call you back," he said to Taylor. "Someone's at the door."

"Better check before you open it," Taylor warned. "Could be Dennis coming back for more."

"You might be right." The doctor had looked plenty angry when Colt left with Jamie in tow. He hung up. “Hey, Jamie? Go to your room.”

"Why, Dad?” His son’s wide eyes matched the alarm in his tone. “Who's banging on our door?"

"Don't know. But I don't want anything to happen to you. Go now and lock your door. Might be your mom and Dennis wanting to take you from me."

"I won't go," Jamie said. He stepped inside his bedroom, leaving the door ajar so he could see through.

He put his hand on the knob as another bang sounded. "Police. Open up."

Colt had been afraid of this. He opened the door and stepped back.

"You Colt Travis?" the young officer asked.

"That's me. What can I do for you, Officers?"

"We're serving you with papers. You're to appear in court on September 20th. Charged with simple battery."

"What if I said it was self-defense? The guy wanted to take my kid away from me. He also landed the first punch."

"Tell that to the judge," the older guy looked him in the eye. "We can't help you with that."

Colt swore under his breath. "He's marrying my ex and wants to take my kid to Chicago. And he's charging me with a crime?"

"Misdemeanor." The cop's eyes showed a little sympathy. "You might want to get an attorney. The sentence can be as high as a year in jail."

"Shit." He ran a hand over his face, and looked at the two cops. "Sorry, but I can't do time. I'd lose my son."

"Daddy?" The boy stood there, bedroom door open, his eyes filled with fear.

"You okay, son?" The portly older cop asked.

Jamie came forward, tears running down his cheeks. He ran into his father's arms. "Yes, but they can't make me leave. This is my home. With my daddy. And you can't put him in jail. He didn't do anything wrong. He was just protecting me."

"I understand, kid. It's not our call." The older cop shook his head. "We're just doing our job. Good luck to you both." With that said, the two men left, and closed the door behind them.

"Dad? They can't make you go to jail, can they? You didn't do anything!" he shouted. "It wasn't your fault. Dennis hit you first."

"I know, and I'm sure the judge will see it that way too. I'm not going away or leaving you. That I promise. Now come on. Stop crying. We have another Rocky to watch, and boy, can that guy pack a punch. Doesn't whimper when he gets one either."

Jamie wiped his eyes. "I'll tell the judge everything. Maybe they'll lock up Dennis instead of you. Then we can stay together--as a family."

"I don't want either of us to get locked up. I'm just not letting you go, that's all."

"Good, Daddy. I'm staying right here. With you."

* * *

Taylor didn't hear from Colt again that night and she couldn't help but worry. When the dinner for her guests was over and everyone had left, she decided to drive over to his place and give him some needed comfort. It was after eleven when she showed up, but the light was on and she could hear the sound of the TV.

She knocked softly and at first she thought he wasn't going to answer. She knocked again, and the door opened an inch.

"Oh, it's you."

"Colt? Are you all right?"

"Not exactly." He closed the door behind him and stepped outside. "Jamie's finally asleep. He's pretty upset. The cops paid us a little visit. The good doctor is charging me with battery. Carries a one year don't-get-out-of-jail-free card."

"What do you mean?" she asked, alarmed.

"The worst they can do is throw me in jail for up to a year. But Dennis hit me first, and was man-handling Jamie. So I don't think he stands a chance with this bogus charge."

"Holy crap, Colt. You can't do *a day* in jail. That will give them an excuse to take Jamie."

"You think I haven't thought of that?" His eyes were blurry when he faced her, and she could see he'd had a drink or two. Or was it the tears swimming inside that blurred his vision?

"We will think of something. Anything. We can't let this happen."

"I've been wracking my brains too. Trying to figure out a sure way that I can hold on to my kid. He's the most precious thing in my life. I can't lose him." His voice broke and his shoulders shook with anguish. "I couldn't survive that."

Tears filled her eyes at this rare display of raw emotion. "What can we do?"

"Marry me, Taylor." His answer came swift. Sure. As if he'd already thought of marriage as a viable solution. Her breath stuck in her throat. "If you were my wife, they'd probably let me keep my son." His eyes pleaded with her as he reached for her chilled fingers. "You and I together have a fighting chance."

She breathed deep, her heart breaking open. "How could you ask me that?" He would marry her for his son. But he wouldn't marry her for her.

Why that should hurt so much, she had no idea. But it was like he'd driven a dagger into her heart and twisted.

"Taylor, I know you don't love me, but we're good together. We could be great, the three of us. Think about it." Colt tried to pull her close, but she moved away. "I do love you, you know," he said softly, his eyes moist. "If you won't marry me and I lose Jamie, then I'll have no choice but to sell everything and move to Chicago."

"You'd do that?" She didn't think her heart could hurt any more than it already did, but the thought of his leaving and never seeing him again sliced right through her. She flinched and raised a hand to her chest, in protective mode.

He released a heavy sigh. "This isn't easy, Taylor. I can't bear the thought of leaving here and living in a place like Chicago." His strong jaw clenched. "Or losing you."

She didn't say anything. She had no words of comfort for him. Or for herself. The pain was too intense, the thoughts running through her head were too hard to grasp.

"Say something," he pleaded. "I know I sprung this on you and you're probably still in shock, but we'd make a really good team. We care deeply about each other. I've been crazy about you for a long, long time."

She shook her head and took another step back. *Colt would leave? Just walk away and out of her life? How could that be love?*

He cleared his throat. "Taylor. Stop looking at me like that." She noticed a tick in his cheek, flicking in and out. "You look like a wounded deer with no place to turn."

She had to get away from him before she lost it. But her knees were shaking and her feet seemed rooted to the spot.

As if sensing her indecision he stepped toward her, his hands open. "I'm here, honey. I don't want to leave you. Not ever." His eyes searched hers. "It's not the most romantic proposal in the world, but it is sincere. Paradise Cove is our home. I want to make a home with you, and Jamie."

She stood stiffly, her arms wrapped around her waist. She couldn't, wouldn't reach out for him. If she clung to him now, she might never let him leave. And leave he would if he lost his son. Jamie needed his dad—she would never step in the way.

She had never felt so alone, so powerless, and so wanting.

His gaze lowered. "I'm making a botch of this, aren't I?"

Taylor straightened her shoulders and lifted her chin, calling on all her internal strength. She knew he was desperate and her heart ached for him. She would gladly have done anything in the world for him, anything but this.

Marriage was sacred to her. A vow between two people that was unbreakable. She wanted to marry one day. For love. Not for necessity, or pity, or to be a pawn in some horrible game.

"I will support you in your fight for custody." She kept her voice calm, wanting to be fair to him, even if his asking had been the cruelest blow to her heart that she'd ever known. The only thing that justified it was his love for his son. For that, she forgave him. "I can be a character witness or whatever you need to help the court rule in your favor. But I can't be your wife."

"Why, Taylor? I know you care for me."

"I do. But when I marry it will be for love. I want someone to love *me*." She looked him in the face. "Not because of his son, or because he needs me when life kicks him to the ground. I want love for me to be his strength, his driving force." She sucked in a breath, holding on by a string. "I deserve that."

"Of course you do, and I might be the biggest ass in the world for putting you through this. But I would want to marry you and only you, no matter what." He rubbed his jaw and swore. "You might not believe that right now, but it's true. I swear."

Her head shot up. How could he say those words to her? Had he no conscience? Would he do anything to keep Jamie, even pretend he wanted this?

Her stomach churned, and she swallowed a lump in her throat.

"The answer is no." With that she turned and walked away.

CHAPTER TWENTY-NINE

Taylor drove home, frozen. She parked in front of the cabin and ran through the mangroves to the sandy beach. The moon drifted in and out of the clouds, creating a shadow to hide in as sharp pain brought her to her knees.

For the first time since 9/11 when her father didn't come home, Taylor allowed her emotions to the surface. For so many years, she'd kept a small part of herself closed off—but now her emotions bubbled over and threatened to drown her. Sobs buried some place deep inside of her swelled and churned and rose like a tsunami, choking her until she could hardly breathe through the hot, salty tears.

She grieved for Colt, and what might have been. Taylor fell back in the sand, staring up at the night sky as the sobs came. Her chest ached from holding them in. She could barely breathe, and she gasped at the night air, wishing she could turn off her feelings so the pain would lessen. Eyes swollen, throat tight, she'd never let anyone inside because she'd been protective of her emotions, but Colt, he'd gotten past her defenses. The jagged edge of pain lasered through her and she honestly doubted she'd survive.

She loved Colt. She hadn't known that before, but his hard-pressed proposal had made her realize how much she wanted the proposal to be real. If things had been different, and he'd asked her before she knew about his son moving to Chicago, then they might be celebrating right now, planning their own wedding.

Instead, she felt like a raw piece of meat that had been carved up and discarded.

His love for his son was absolute, and by the way, he sure liked her a lot. They'd make a good team?

She got to her knees, letting the tears fall hot to the sand. She relived each harsh word, each kiss, each moment of shared pleasure and accidental hurt until her sobs subsided. Taylor walked the beach until the midnight black sky turned into grayish pink and orange streaks of dawn. Only then did she feel numb enough inside to return home. Taylor entered the cabin she shared with her mom, going directly to the shower to hide the evidence of her loss of control, reburying her love for Colt. Nobody had to know—not even her mom or sisters.

She evaded direct confrontation for three days, keeping busy with the cafe—when her mom asked where Colt was, Taylor told the truth. The custodial battle over Jamie consumed him right now.

Taylor set two loaves of banana bread on the rack to cool as Juanita finished the dishes for the day. Instead of leaving, Juanita took Taylor's arm and sat her down with a cool glass of iced tea. "Taylor, why doesn't Colt come around anymore?"

Taylor accepted the tea but avoided the compassion in Juanita's maternal brown eyes. "He's busy with Jamie. Lawyer stuff."

Juanita sat opposite Taylor and waited for Taylor to look up. "I see how heavy your heart is." She covered her own with her hand. "Why have you pushed Colt away," she asked softly, "when that man loves you so very much?"

"Juanita, you don't understand." Taylor had found a compartment to put her feelings for Colt inside, but the hurt was too raw to stay buried. "Colt doesn't really love me. He's just so desperate to keep his son that he's lost his head." She sniffed and her eyes misted up.

"What does that mean?"

She'd kept his horrible proposal to herself. "He's not thinking clearly." She'd witnessed the regret on his face before she'd left his house and hadn't heard a word since.

"Taylor, my girl, you are the sweetest, kindest, young woman—so explain to me, *por favor*, why you have turned your back on your friend, the man you love, when he is in trouble." Juanita's tanned brow furrowed with concern. "He's in pain. Why have you not gone to him?"

Taylor stabbed at the lemons in her iced tea. "It's complicated, Juanita. I don't want to talk about it."

"Oh, *mi hija*, you can't carry on like this. You've lost weight. Your eyes look sad and you have dark bruises under them, like you're not sleeping."

Taylor swallowed a lump in her throat, and took a sip from her drink. Her hand was shaking when she put the glass back down. She lifted her eyes and saw Juanita's loving face.

"What is it? You can tell me."

"He asked me to marry him," she whispered, her pride stinging as she heard the words aloud. "Not because he loves me or wants to be married to me, but to help him keep Jamie." She focused on the wooden table top, the wave of pain rising as her own love cried out to be heard. "How could he do that to me?" Taylor gasped, then a heart rendering sob escaped her mouth. "He knows how I feel about marriage!"

Understanding dawned and Juanita left her seat to hug Taylor tight. "Men can be idiots at times. It seems like this was one of them." She kissed Taylor's damp cheek and handed her a napkin. "He does love you, Taylor. And he loves his son, as he should. Colt doesn't want to lose either one of you. Think how this must be tearing him apart." Juanita let that sink it, then added, "He needs you. You are a strong and loving woman."

"I want to help, but not that way." Taylor rubbed at her eyes and sniffed. "I'm *not* strong enough to see his pain and not agree to marry him. But then I'd never know if he loved me, or did it to save his son."

Juanita reached across the table and lifted Taylor's chin with gentle fingers and met her eye to eye. "Don't let your head rule your heart. Love should be your guide."

"I'll try, Juanita." Taylor sat back, sorting through pride and love. He'd taken her ideal of marriage and turned it upside down. She understood why he'd done it, but she hadn't heard one word from him since he'd opened his mouth. “But the ball is back in his court now. If he loves me, he'll have to prove it."

"Ball in his court? But it was in yours?” Juanita scrunched her nose as she imagined that. "Well, I hope he picks up that ball soon and carries it and his love back to you."

Taylor laughed softly. An apology would be a nice start.

Juanita got up, signifying the end of the painful conversation. "You still want to babysit Meri tonight? I don’t mind taking her to Raul's ballgame. She's so easy. She'd probably fall asleep."

"No, you and Miguel go. I'm looking forward to my date night with my favorite girl. I'm going to bake a special quiche. She loves the one with Swiss cheese and tiny bits of ham, with strawberries on top."

"She loves everything you make." Juanita took the two glasses into the kitchen to be rinsed. "I'll see you in an hour? The game starts at four, but Raul has everything he needs in his locker at school. Doesn't matter if we're a little late."

"I'm leaving right after you—drop her off at the cabin anytime."

Juanita gave her a quick hug before she left but thankfully didn’t say another word about Colt. It was so hard to keep from calling him but in order to hold her life together, she had to stay away.

When Taylor walked into the cabin, her mother was making banana daiquiris for happy hour. She had a platter of sliced fresh fruit with an assortment of fancy cheeses and crackers, and another tray with bite-sized quiche

Lorraine's that Taylor had made in the cafe's kitchen an hour ago.

"Looking good, Mom." She kissed her on the cheek. "So how did the day go with our little baby girl?"

"It was a pleasure as always. And she's looking forward to spending time with you. Miguel has her now while I set up for our party."

"Who's all coming tonight?" Taylor poured herself a small glass of the daiquiri, and tasted it. "Yummy." She licked her lips. "Bet Meri would like this, without the rum of course."

"I thought of that and put some in the fridge for her." Anna poured herself a good-sized glass and toasted her daughter. "To living the good life."

"We are very lucky to be here, aren't we?" Taylor said, thinking about Colt moving away to Chicago. She knew he would hate it, but he'd sacrifice himself just the same.

"Yes. I wish Allen had lived long enough to realize his dream."

"I wish he was here too. I miss him." Taylor hitched her butt on a kitchen stool and sipped her drink. She felt tired suddenly, and older than her years. Older than her mom even, who'd survived such terrible heartache. Although happily married twice, she had not been lucky in love. "Allen was a wonderful man."

"Indeed, he was."

"So what's going on with you and Dr. Sinclair? Can't help but notice a twinkle in your eyes, and an extra spring in your step." Taylor arched a brow. "It wouldn't be the handsome doctor by any chance, now would it?"

"Well, now that you mention it, yes!" Anna put her glass to her cheek. "He said he'd stop by for happy hour, if he can get away. If not, he's picking me up at eight for a late dinner." She blushed like a young girl. "He's a cocky son-of-a-bitch, but I like a man with attitude."

"As long as he treats you right, I'm all for it." She hoped her mom never stopped giving love a chance. And at this rate, it seemed likely.

"Thank you, dear." Her mom put a hand on her shoulder. "I'm so sorry about Colt, honey. I know you're hurting even though you never talk about it. What is he going to do if he doesn't get custody?"

"Move to Chicago to be close to his son."

Her mother was silent for several seconds. "He wouldn't do that, would he?" Her eyes got misty and she sniffed. "What about you?"

"What about me?" Taylor shrugged as if it didn't matter. "It's his son that's important. We are fond of each other, but he'll forget me soon enough."

"Oh, honey." Anna put her glass down long enough to give her a hug.

"It's okay. I'll survive. Got lots to do right here. Sure don't need to be chasing after a man in Chicago."

"What if he asks you to go with him?"

"He won't, Mom." The days of keeping her heartache to herself were over. It was a relief to share it now, and get it out in the open.

Her eyes were dry as she said, "Colt asked me to marry him," she held up a halting hand before her mom got too excited, "so we'd be a family. It was a desperate plea to save his son." She swallowed. "Of course I turned him down, and haven't spoken to him since."

"Oh, Taylor," Anna said sadly. "No wonder the man never comes around anymore. Do you know what you did, honey? Have you any idea of how devastated he must be?"

"What about me?" Taylor asked, angry. "He only asked me to marry him because of Jamie. He never once told me he loved me before this." Although she'd felt his emotion when they'd made love, and in so many other ways.

"What does your heart say?" Anna walked to where Taylor sat, and gently pushed aside a loose curl from her cheek.

"My heart's telling me to be patient." Which was true. She added, "To wait for the right man to come along. Someone who loves me the way Sean loves Kayla, and both dads loved you!" Tears filled her eyes as she recalled the immediate regret in Colt's gaze. "I want that kind of love, Mom. And I will damn well wait for it."

Her mom wrapped her in a hug. "And so you should. I might not have had that love for long, but in both cases, it was worth the heartache in the end." Anna gave her shoulder a squeeze and then released Taylor to pick up the tray of warm appetizers. The show must go on, Taylor thought to herself.

"Could you help me down to the pool with this? Our guests will be wondering what's taking so long." They had six cabins occupied and more guests arriving in a few days.

"Of course." She carried the pitcher of drinks down to the pool, then returned for the cheese platter. After greeting all the guests, she hurried back to the cottage to shower and change into shorts and a t-shirt for her play date with Meri. They had a small space set up for her with Play-Doh, wooden blocks and soft toys, and a magical doll house. A little girl's dreams come true.

There would be plenty of time later for her to grow up and realize that dreams didn't last and happiness was as fragile as an over-full balloon one tap away from bursting.

CHAPTER THIRTY

Colt had a miserable week. Although miserable might be a mild description of the hell he'd been put through. First his wife tells him she's taking his son away, then he gets a court order to defend a charge of battery--as if the guy didn't deserve a good punch in the nose.

Worse, he had made a real mess of things with Taylor. His stupid proposal, or whatever the hell it was, had wounded her deeply. On hindsight--and he'd had a lot of time to mull it over and dwell on it in his spare time--he'd realized that she'd been right. Marriage was something really special--not to be entered lightly or for the wrong reasons. And his had been all wrong. True, he'd done it nobly enough--wanting to keep his son from moving away and to create a home for him, a home with two parents who cared about him. Taylor had been instrumental in that part of the plan.

Unfortunately, she didn't realize how much he wanted that idyllic picture he'd painted. Wanted her. Because fool that he was, he'd never told her. Fact was, he hadn't realized it himself. Not until he pissed her off good and she stormed out. And never came back. Didn't call to ask how he was, how things were working out with Jamie. Nothing.

Every minute of every day he'd relived those last awful moments. If he'd done something different, might there have been a better outcome? Had he gotten down on his knees and proposed properly, or swept her into his arms and proven his love once again? Every kiss had been heartfelt. Every touch he'd ever laid on her. Every smile, and hug, and caress had come with love.

What were words anyway? Had he not shown her in dozens of ways how much he cared about her and her family? He loved them all, but he only wanted to marry her. Damn woman. He hadn't wanted to get married again so soon. Heck, his divorce was not much more than a year ago. He'd been quite happy bedding every single girl in town. Visitors too.

It had been good for a while, but then she'd caught his eye with her long-limbed gait and dancing eyes--the warmth of her smile, the music of her laughter. Suddenly everyone else had paled in comparison. They had been cheap substitutes for a woman he couldn't have, and didn't deserve.

Bedding Taylor had been a big mistake. He knew that she wasn't the kind of girl he could take to bed and not commit to. For many reasons--one being that he respected her so much, and her family. And two, she wasn't the love 'em and leave 'em kind. She was a gal that would get so deep under his skin, he'd never get her out.

Hell--he didn't want her out. He wanted her to own his heart, to be so much a part of him that he couldn't live or breathe without her.

No one had ever mattered this much before. How foolish he'd been to hide himself from her, and not explain about his past. As if she'd care about the son-of-a-bitch he'd had for a father. She wouldn't judge him for that. And she'd understand why material things held no allure for him. Sure he could become a private boat captain and be at the beck and call of some filthy rich billionaire, but he'd hate every damn minute of it. Taking the money would slowly rot away at his soul.

Luckily, he'd been busy for most of the week taking her guests out on his boat. He'd avoided seeing her by parking his car in the marina lot, and not taking his normal route through the resort. He'd needed to work out a few things in his head, and to have all the answers when he saw her next.

Well, he still didn't have all the answers, but he knew one thing. He wasn't going to take no for an answer. She was going to marry him, whether she liked it or not.

He chuckled and ran a hand over his chin. Now, that would go down well. Matter-of-fact he couldn't wait to tell her so and see the fire in her eyes, and the haughty look she'd give him.

Tears sprang to his eyes. Damn he missed her. And he needed to tell her.

An hour later, he was spruced up and drove over to Paradise Cove. He made his way to the pool, knowing that happy hour would be a good place to start the comeback trail. She wouldn't put up a fight and kick him out--not in front of their guests.

"Hey, Anna." Colt swept a hand around Anna's waist. "I don't see Taylor. Is she coming back?"

"Why, hello, Colt. We haven't seen you here for awhile. Thought maybe you'd lost your way."

"No, ma'am." He grinned. "I found it at last. Now I need to make my intentions clear. Where is she?"

"At the cabin. With Meri. Miguel and Juanita have gone to the baseball game at the school. Taylor's taking care of the baby."

"Ah. Two of my favorite people." He winked at her. "I'll just head over. Wish me luck."

"Luck." She watched him leave, and he knew that he'd made one important women in his life happy. Now for the other.

He knocked on the door, but knowing it was unlocked he opened up and entered.

Taylor was sitting on the floor with Meri in her lap, playing with a couple of plastic dolls. The sight of her and the baby sent a low thrill riding through him. He wanted to see her with more babies of her own. She was so beautiful, inside and out, and would make a great mother too.

"What are you doing here?" she asked.

Meri jumped out of her lap and came running into his arms. "Hug, hug," she said, as he swung her up high, then cradled her against his chest.

He walked slowly over to the woman he loved, who wore a scowl instead of a smile. He plopped down beside her, and settled Meri between them. "I came to see you. We have things to discuss."

"What kind of things?" Her beautiful eyes narrowed. "I thought I'd made myself perfectly clear."

"Uh. Yes, you did." He flashed a smile, which wasn't returned. "But in my haste, I didn't."

"It doesn't matter anymore. I understand what you have to do." She refused to look at him, but played with the toy doll in her hand. "I'm sorry, Colt. I know leaving here will be hard for you."

"I'm not leaving. Matter-of-fact, on my way over here my lawyer called." He grinned and bent over to kiss Meri. She had climbed back into his lap and was patting his cheeks with her plump small hands.

"What did he say?" Suddenly Taylor looked at him with interest.

"He said..." he held the baby's hands in his, so he could focus on Taylor. "He said Sharon has agreed to let me keep Jamie, and she'd work out a plan where she could have him for the summer and holidays." He kissed Meri's little fingers. "She loves her son as much as I do, and knows he'll be happier here with me."

"Oh, my gosh. That's wonderful, Colt. I'm so happy for you."

"Yes. And I don't have to go to jail either. She got Dennis to drop the charges."

"Wow. That's really great news." She stood up, and brushed Play-Doh from her shirt. "Want a drink to celebrate?"

"Not yet." He put the baby down and stood as well. He moved toward her. "I have more news for you."

"What's that?" She stepped behind the kitchen counter to put some distance between them. But nothing was going to keep them apart. Not anymore.

He stepped around the counter, and put his hands on her waist. "We're getting married."

"What the hell do you mean?" Her head shot up, and her eyes flashed with anger.

"Don't swear around the child," he said then bent his head and kissed her.

"What are you doing?" She pushed at his shoulders, but he didn't break away, only tightened his grip and pulled her in so his legs could straddle hers.

"I mean that it's time to admit defeat. You and I have been fighting this for darn near a year now, and I'm done fighting. I want you. Forever. I love you and you love me. We are good together."

"No." She shook her head, her hair flying about her face. "We're not."

"Yes, we are." He cradled her head and looked deeply into her eyes. His heart thumped and swelled. He loved her so much and could only see pain and confusion in her beautiful dark eyes. "I'm sorry, sweetheart. So sorry for hurting you. For making you doubt me. This proposal is for real. I want you to be my wife. I want to wake up every day with you. I want to fall asleep with you in my arms. I love you and have never loved anyone more. I want to make babies with you."

"I...uh...don't know what to say." Her eyes filled with tears, and he kissed them away. Then he dropped to his knees before her.

He looked up and reached for her hand. "Will you marry me, Taylor, and make my life whole again? I'm nothing without you. Say yes. Please say yes."

Meri had crawled over to him. She hugged him from behind, but his eyes were only on Taylor.

Finally, the magnificent woman he adored smiled back at him and laughed. Then she bent down to kiss him. Her hands clasped behind his head and Colt could feel her tears on his cheeks. Her mouth was warm and sweet, and clung to his for so long he grew worried.

He broke away, needing her answer. "Taylor, will you be my wife? Don't make me wait any longer. I've waited my whole life for you."

"Then the answer is yes. I love you, Colt Travis, and will be very proud to be your wife." She cocked her head to look him in the eyes. "What about Jamie? Is he on board with this?"

"Jamie doesn't know yet. But he will be pleased, since he already adores you."

"I adore him too. You know why I turned down your proposal, right? Not because of Jamie, but because I didn't think your love was real."

"It's real, baby. And I'll spend my life proving it every single day."

Her eyes lit up. "One question. Can we have the reception here? At my cafe?"

He laughed and kissed her again. "You can have the reception anywhere you want, but I thought it might be nice to take you to Europe for a honeymoon. There are a lot of places I want you to see, and a lot of stories I need to tell."

"Then we have the rest of our lives to hear them, don't we?"

"I guess we do. I haven't always been a fisherman you know."

"Well, whatever you were, and the man you are now--one thing I know for sure. From your first dazzling smile, I was hooked on you."

He grinned, and kissed her nose. "Lucky me. You are the finest catch of all."

THE END

A NOTE FROM THE AUTHOR

Thank you for reading HOOKED ON YOU. If you enjoyed this book, I'd appreciate it if you'd help others find it so they can enjoy it too.

• Lend it: This e-book is lending-enabled, so feel free to share it with your friends.

• Recommend it: Please help other readers find this book by recommending it to friends, readers' groups, and discussion boards.

• Review it: Let other potential readers know what you liked or didn't like about.

If you'd like to sign up for Patrice Wilton's newsletter to receive new release information, please visit www.patricewilton.com

You can follow Patrice Wilton on Facebook or on Twitter. @patricewilton

Book updates can be found at www.patricewilton.com.
I would love to hear from you at patricewilt@yahoo.com.

Made in the USA
Columbia, SC
09 August 2019